THE ADOPTED SON

THE ADOPTED SON

A NOVEL BY

CLAUDE RENAUD

PUBLISHER: Hunter Publications
EMAIL: huntpubs1@gmail.com

NATIONAL LIBRARY OF AUSTRALIA
CATALOGUING-IN-PUBLICATION DATA

AUTHOR	Renaud Claude
TITLE	The Adopted Son
ISBN	978-0-6487808-2-3
SUBJECTS	Novel
DEWEY NO	A823

Author's note: an earlier version of this book was published in 2013 under the title 'The Son: Out of Vietnam – Love, Death and Survival after the Vietnam War', and the pseudonym Marc Santailler. The present version has been slightly revised and edited but the story and the characters remain unchanged.

For those who didn't make it

CHINA
MYANMAR
NORTH VIETNAM
Hanoi
LAOS
HAINAN
17th Parallel
THAILAND
Bangkok
CAMBODIA
SOUTH
South
China
Sea
VIETNAM
Phnom Penh
Saigon
Gulf of Thailand
Plain of Reeds
Main outflow of boat-people
post 1975
Songkhla
Pulau Bidong
MALAYSIA
Kuala Lumpur
SOUTH EAST ASIA DURING
THE VIETNAM WAR
SUMATRA
SINGAPORE
BORNEO

CONTENTS

Prologue 9

Part I   Aftermath of a war 13

Part II   Need to know 105

Part III   A reckoning 189

Epilogue 237

Appendix 243

Prologue

Between Sadec and Mytho, as you head back towards Saigon (or Ho Chi Minh City as it's now called), along the old Highway 4 in the Mekong delta region of southern Vietnam, lies the Plain of Reeds. This is a desolate, inhospitable stretch of country which juts down from the Cambodian border in the shape of an inverted triangle, and the road cuts across its lower extremity for about forty kilometres. Long used as a refuge by bandits and rebels of all kinds, during the Vietnam War it was a stronghold of the southern communist guerrillas known as the Viet Cong.

Harper drove carefully, his eyes straining in the weak headlights of his rented car to detect the worst potholes before his front wheels actually hit them. The road was too rough to allow for much speed, and in any case the advice at the last check point had been very clear: drive slowly, no more than thirty kilometres an hour, with your ceiling light on. That's the signal that you're local traffic, and they're more likely to let you through. As an extra precaution Harper had swapped his cigarette lighter for a greasy cap, tucked his fair hair as much as possible under it, turned his shirt collar up. You couldn't rely on the Viet Cong being colour blind.

A rough-looking lot these local government militia, barely distinguishable from the VC in their black pyjamas, guarding a bridge and a minuscule hamlet through the hours of darkness. They probably had some deal going with the VC, and it was a toss-up which was more dangerous: to stay there the night or take his chances on the road. But they knew the area, and they'd calculated the risks. By daylight the road was safe enough. It was only at night that the Viet Cong came out to assert their control, and until about eight or eight thirty you had a good chance of getting through. After that the risk of being shot at increased with each passing hour. After ten you had to be suicidal to try it. It was now twenty to nine.

A torch waved him down ahead, a string of armed men along the road. VC or good guys? Harper's heart beat faster, until he saw the GI-style helmets. An army patrol, six or seven slim figures in khaki, led a diminutive sergeant. Harper slowed to a stop.

'Why you on this road?' the sergeant asked in halting English, pistol on hip, his head in its tin pot huge on his wiry body. 'Too much danger.'

'I've had a breakdown,' Harper answered in Vietnamese. *'Xe tôi bị hư', phải xửa, mất nhiều thì giờ.'* The sergeant stared. How do you say radiator hose in Vietnamese? 'I have to be back in Saigon tonight.' In the background, occasional thumps in the darkness, grenades or mortar rounds, a flare or two and the rattle of small arms. A local firefight, or someone just showing he's awake?

'Dangerous!' the sergeant repeated. 'You shouldn't be out so late.'

'How's the road ahead?'

'Alright so far. Don't waste time. You've still got twenty clicks before you're clear.'

'OK, thanks.' Harper passed over his remaining cigarettes. The sergeant grinned briefly.

'Good luck.'

Harper drove on, thinking of the girl waiting for him in Saigon. Hien, looking like a school-girl in her white *áo dài*. She couldn't stay beyond eleven, her parents would have a fit if she stayed the night. Even if they were virtually engaged. Like all young men facing marriage, Harper still had twinges of doubt. How would it work out, taking an Asian bride of nineteen back to his family in Australia? How would she face up to the demands of the job, the moves, the constant shunting from pillar to post? She'd fared well enough with his colleagues in the embassy, her English was good and improving fast, she had brains as well as beauty: this was no shop-worn bar-girl, everyone could see that at a glance, but a girl of good character from a well-known family, and she had the strength and the toughness to adapt.

And how would he fare, as a faithful loving husband? Think of the girls you're leaving behind. His mind did a quick review of the more recent ones. No regrets there. You couldn't live like a playboy forever. She was the nearest to permanent bliss he would ever find.

What was it she wanted to tell him, that she'd refused to say on the phone? Guess, she had said that morning. If you guess right we can do it again tonight. Harper had a vision of her face, her impish face split by a grin of glee as she wriggled naked on top of him, biting his nose, her rump sliding like silk under his hands. Yes, he had said, and yes, he said again, you and me together, we'll make it work.

Another waving torch, another patrol. Same routine. Danger, what are you doing here at this hour? More thumps and flashes in the night. Some poor bastard must be copping it. Harper was relaxed, unafraid. Perhaps he should have waited until the next day, but how could he foresee the burst hose, the stops to fix it with wire and sweat rag until by sheer luck he'd found a good mechanic at the last place? Luckily it now seemed to be holding, and what was the point of living if you couldn't take a risk from time to time? There'd be time enough for caution when he was old and spent and had only memories to live on.

'About five clicks. *Chừng năm cây.*'

Ten more minutes. Two, three kilometres ahead, the lights of another hamlet glimmering through the trees, Thiên Lương, the end of the bad stretch. After that, the main road from My Tho to Saigon, total safety, an hour and a bit to get home and hold Hien in his arms.

The tracer bullets cutting across the road twenty metres ahead of the car registered in his mind before he heard the sound of fire from the trees. AK 47, he thought automatically. Shit! Favourite weapon of the Viet Cong. Stop or crash through? Keep going, that was the only hope. He tightened his grip on the wheel, slid down into the seat, put his foot down hard. Keep grinning Hien. I'll be home tonight.

The next burst caught the car side on. Harper heard the hammer blows against the body, the burst tyre, fought to hold the wheel as the car slewed across the road. The shattered window, the splash of light in his shattered brain were the last things he knew as the car plunged over the embankment and into darkness.

PART I

AFTERMATH OF A WAR

Chapter One

My name is Paul Quinn. I'm Australian.

Many years ago, when I was a young man and considered by some capable of almost anything (except treason), I was recruited into a secretive government organization in Canberra that used diplomatic cover. My first posting was Saigon, near the end of the Vietnam War. It didn't last long. The war ended sooner than anyone expected, and we all had to leave in a hurry. But during that time two things happened which were to have a major impact on my life later on, and on the lives of several other people.

First, soon after my arrival, I met a girl at a party. A Vietnamese girl, or young woman. The party was at the house of my predecessor, another young man, named David Harper. He worked in the political section of the embassy, where among other things he was in charge of press affairs (always a useful cover for an intelligence officer), while I did some language training in-country before taking over from him at the end of his tour. In those days the organization was still small and junior officers were often sent out on their own.

The girl was very attractive, with that mix of willowy grace, strength and intelligence which I found so captivating in Vietnamese women, and I would have liked to know her better. But she was there with her fiancé, a gangling young man from the Faculty of Sciences, and I didn't insist. There were lots of attractive girls in Saigon. I soon had other things to worry about.

Two weeks later David was killed. He had gone down to Can Thơ, a large town on the Mekong, to meet a new contact with links to the Viet Cong leadership, and on the way back his car was shot up by – it was presumed – a Viet Cong sniper. Naturally I was pulled off my course at once to replace him. My first duty after informing headquarters was to go down to the delta to bring his body back to Saigon. Put some iron in your soul, my ambassador said, and teach you not to do anything so stupid.

The embassy was in shock. Diplomats' lives were not without risk, but they rarely ended so brutally. Nobody could work out why Harper was on that road after dark. There was no need for him to rush back to Saigon that night, and he'd been around long enough not to take foolish risks like that.

David had died in late February. In mid-March the North Vietnamese launched their last offensive of the war, in the Central Highlands, six weeks later, after a series of lightning successes on their part and dismal failures by the South Vietnamese, they were on the outskirts of Saigon, massing for the final assault. The embassy withdrew in stages, the last wave leaving on the twenty-fifth of April, Anzac Day, 1975, five days before the end of the war.[1]

Fifteen years of war had killed 58,000 Americans, over 500 Australians, and probably millions of Vietnamese of both sides, if you included the civilians as well, and now it was over. An uneasy peace fell on the south, as the communists imposed their harsh and unforgiving rule. The era of the boat people was about to begin.

By then I'd forgotten all about that girl, and our brief meeting.

She remembered.

Twenty years later, in early 1995, many things had changed in my life. I had long since left government service to try my luck in business, and I lived in Sydney, where I ran a small personnel agency. I was forty-five, divorced, and I lived alone.

One afternoon in the late Australian summer of that year a Mrs Hao Tran phoned me at work. I'd never heard of her, but it turned out she was the girl I had met long ago at that party of David's in Saigon. Tran was her married name. She lived in England now, she said, and she was in Australia on a visit. She asked if she could come to see me, as she needed my advice about a problem she had.

When I asked what kind of problem, she said it was personal, and too complicated to explain on the phone, but it had something to do with David. She was quick to add that they'd never been close, and yet the problem related to him. When I pressed she pleaded.

------

[1] A brief history of the Vietnam War is included in the Appendix.

'Please, Mr Quinn. Apart from you I don't know anyone in Australia who might be able to help me. You were his friend...'

She told me she was staying in Marrickville, about forty minutes by train from our office in North Sydney, and I agreed to see her that afternoon. It was a Friday, just after four, with work about done for the day. We were on the sixth floor of an old office block, not far from the station.

'Thank you very much, Mr Quinn. You don't know how much I appreciate this.'

She sounded as if she meant it. I wondered what I was letting myself in for.

Chapter Two

Mrs Tran was a slender, very pretty woman in a dark two-piece suit, somewhere I thought in her mid to late thirties. I didn't recognise her of course. Twenty years is a long time. But I was struck by how attractive she was. I was used to seeing pretty women in my office – we dealt mainly with secretarial applicants – but she was a honey.

She was tall for a Vietnamese, almost as tall as me in her heels, with the long legs of a swimmer or a ballet dancer, and she had beautiful eyes, dark and intelligent in a pale oval face of almost classical purity. Long black hair pulled back and gathered at the back of her head, light make-up, almost no jewellery. When we shook hands I smelt the delicate scent of jasmine. I also noted dark shadows under those eyes, an air of strain and tiredness. Her problem must be keeping her awake at night.

We sat in my office. Vivien Berridge, my assistant, offered us some mint tea, and while waiting for it I asked my visitor some questions. She said she lived in Leeds, where she and her husband had settled after being accepted in Britain as refugees in 1980. This was her first visit to Australia. In Marrickville she was staying with relatives, cousins of her husband, who owned a small Asian supermarket there. (Marrickville is a suburb not far from the airport, which housed part of Sydney's Vietnamese community.) She had been there over a month.

'Is your husband with you?' I asked.

'No. I'm a widow, Mr Quinn. He died over a year ago.'

She spoke excellent English, with just a trace of an accent: more a question of rhythm, a way of detaching her words which gave them a faint metallic edge.

'In fact that's one reason why I'm here.'

Vivien brought the tea, and left soon after, having stayed long enough to get a good look at my visitor. She was a kind, grandmotherly woman of sixty-two who had herself lost her husband some years earlier, and we got on well together. I foresaw questions on the Monday morning.

Meanwhile I went on with my own questioning.

'I don't expect you to remember me,' Mrs Tran said. 'There were lots of people at that party. I was there with my sister.' I could recall the party, more or less, but of a sister I had no memory. Yet something tugged at my mind. 'I remembered you because you spoke such good Vietnamese.'

I couldn't help smiling. *You spee Yetnamee so goo*, the girls used to croon in the bars of Saigon, in gross exaggeration. I'd already done three months of Vietnamese before leaving Australia, but it takes much longer to master the language.

'You wouldn't say that now. It's so rusty I doubt I could string two words together. How did you find me, by the way? How did you know I was in Sydney?'

'I rang your former office in Canberra.'

'Foreign Affairs and Trade?' I said, naming the Commonwealth department which provided cover to my old employer.

'Yes. Your Foreign Office. I thought you might still be working there. But someone told me you were here.'

'I'm surprised they remembered me. It's more than ten years since I left. Who did you speak to?'

'A Mr Bentick, I think,' she said. 'He asked to be remembered to you.'

'Roger Bentinck. I know him. He's an old friend.'

That explained it. Bentinck was another of my former colleagues in the organization, who had stayed on and was now a senior officer there. Someone in the Department must have put two and two together and switched the call through to him. We still kept in touch, although I hadn't seen him for over a year.

Time to get down to business. She sat upright in her chair, patiently putting up with my questioning, like an applicant being interviewed. From the start we'd been formal with names, but there was a deeper reserve about her, almost a wariness. Her handshake had been cool and firm but quickly withdrawn. Maybe this was just a standard defence for such an attractive woman. When I drank my tea the scent of jasmine lingered on my hand.

'So,' I said. 'You have a problem, you said. Something to do with David. Don't worry. I'll be happy to help if I can.'

'Thank you.' She took a deep breath. 'It's about my son. My adopted son rather. Eric. He's here in Australia, and I'm afraid he's getting into trouble.'

'What kind of trouble?'

'I think he's fallen into dangerous company. I'll explain. It's a bit complicated. He's actually my nephew. His mother was my sister, and his father was David.'

'I didn't know David had a son.' I said.

'David never knew him.'

She began to tell me her story. Because, as I soon realised, it was hers as much as her nephew's.

Chapter Three

When David Harper met Hien, in late 1974, she was eighteen, the younger of the two sisters. Their father, Hoang van Lam, owned a newspaper in Saigon, and was a deputy in the National Assembly, a member of the opposition. David used to visit him at home from time to time to discuss politics. It was a case of love at first sight. She was pretty, intelligent, vivacious, he was handsome, single, spoke fluent Vietnamese. Their parents tried to warn her against mixing too freely with a young foreigner, but she was an independent girl and soon they were seeing a lot of each other. By the end of that year they'd decided to get married, at the end of David's posting, due in mid-1975.

'You may remember her, Mr Quinn. She was working in the embassy by then, in the Aid section. David had helped her get the job.'

'Vaguely. I wasn't in the embassy very long. She worked in another building.' I had a faint picture now, of a strikingly pretty girl in a white *áo dài,* the traditional dress that women often wore in those days.

'She said you were very kind to her at the end.'

'If you mean that I tried to help her come to Australia, we all did that, for the local staff. But it was no use. Canberra wouldn't hear of it.'

That was something else I would never forget.

The Americans, after investing enormous resources into the war, had turned away from it later on, leaving the South to fight on alone against the stronger North. But they had rallied in the end and tried to save as many South Vietnamese as they could before the final collapse. American helicopters laden with civilians lifting off from Saigon rooftops told only part of the story. Over a hundred and sixty thousand Vietnamese civilians were airlifted from Saigon during the final month, more than fifty thousand in the last week alone, to be resettled in the US.

Australia at the time had been less generous.

As America's faithful ally Australia had also sent troops to Vietnam, and like the Americans it too had turned against the war later on. But it had gone further still. The war had been very unpopular with the left, and as the victorious North Vietnamese advanced on Saigon the Labor government in Canberra made it clear it would not welcome anyone from the south. Many of the people who came to the embassy seeking help had no prior association with Australia and were simply knocking on any door they could find in their haste to get away before the communists came. Others had been good friends of the embassy over the years, the kind of contacts and supporters that diplomatic missions need and cultivate to do their job properly.

Canberra was adamant, despite all the embassy's entreaties. Even the local embassy staff had to be left behind in the end, as we took off in a half-empty plane, taking with us instead eleven cats that belonged to some UN official! Australia I knew had more than made up for it since, with the numbers of refugees it had taken in later on, but I still remembered how bitter we had felt at the time. It had been too much like a betrayal.

'She said that you tried to give her some money.'

'It was the only thing I could do. She wouldn't take it. I thought she was angry with me. I told her to try the Americans.'

'She was proud, Mr Quinn. But she never blamed you.'

The scene was clearer now, the girl in my office, the dismay and incomprehension on her face when I told her the final decision. She couldn't understand that the ambassador had no authority, had been expressly forbidden by Canberra to accept anyone without specific approval in each case – only to have it refused at the last minute, when it was too late for most of them to try any other route.

'What happened to her in the end? Did she manage to get out?'

'Not then, no…She's dead, Mr Quinn. She died when we got out by boat in 1980.'

I was silent for a moment. David's girl, lost in such a stupid, cruel, totally avoidable way.

'I'm terribly sorry,' I said at last.

'It's not your fault. Please don't think I'm reproaching you for it.'

'If I'd known she was pregnant…'

'No one knew, apart from me. She hadn't even told David yet. Besides, what could you have done, short of marrying her?'

I shook my head. 'Tell me about the boy.'

He was born in September of that year. By then life had become difficult for the Hoang family, as the communists bore down on anyone connected to the old order. Considering their situation, the birth went well. David had had fair hair but the baby's was dark, which helped hide his origin.

He was named Huu, in Vietnamese, *Hòang Minh Hữu*, but Hien called him Eric. That was David's middle name. She decided at once that she would take him to Australia one day. Easier said than done. The exodus of boat people was only just beginning, it was dangerous and expensive, Eric was five by the time they managed to get on a boat. There were four of them: Hien, and Eric, and Mrs Tran as I still thought of her, and Khiem, her husband. She had married by then, the young man from the party, now a lecturer in mathematics at the Faculty of Sciences.

It wasn't their first attempt, but this time they got away – until a storm hit the overcrowded boat, and the engine broke down. By the time a British freighter hauled them in Hien and some others were dead. The survivors reached Singapore.

'Hawkins Road camp?' I asked.

'Yes. You know it?'

'I've been there.'

She sat quietly for a moment, her eyes withdrawn. Then she sipped her tea and went on.

From Singapore they were resettled in Britain. They wanted to come to Australia, as Hien had planned, but Singapore only allowed boat-people ashore if they'd been accepted first by a third country. For those picked up at sea by a foreign ship that usually meant the ship's country of origin.

Eventually they settled in Leeds, where Khiem found a teaching post at the university. Naturally they took the child with them, in due course adopted him and gave him their name - Eric Tran. That was her husband's name, Tran van Khiem.

'You had no other children?'

'No.' Once more she sipped her tea, before going on.

Over the next fourteen years life was easier for the Tran family. They were both well-educated – he had studied in the US, she had done a degree in Saigon, a *licence* in French and English. She requalified, got a job, they put Eric through school: a normal uneventful life. Eric knew they weren't his parents, and they didn't pretend to be. With his mixed looks it would have been difficult. And he still had memories of his mother.

'Two Vietnamese with a Eurasian child!' she said with an ironic smile. 'I'm sure most people thought he was really mine, that I'd married an American or been a bar-girl before I met Khiem. But we loved him and looked after him, that's what mattered. It was after Khiem's death that the difficulties started.'

Eric was nearly eighteen by then, in his second-last year of school, and seemed happy. During all these years she and Khiem had been careful not to tell him much about his father – only that he was a white man who had died before he was born. They didn't know anything about David's family, and were worried that if Eric went looking for them later on the family might reject him.

But now Eric began to ask questions. It was as if his adoptive father's death had unsettled him, caused him to question his identity. He asked mostly about his father. Hao Tran was reluctant to say much, but he persisted, until it became almost an obsession. Finally she told him what she could, including how David had died. That proved a mistake.

'You'll see why.'

Eric immediately became very interested in Australia. He began to talk about coming out, getting a visa, he started collecting all the information he could, posters, tourist brochures, immigration details. He read how Australia had accepted many Indochinese refugees. She tried to talk him out of it at first, afraid that he had a rosy picture of life here, but he persisted, saying that when he turned eighteen he would get a visa, and in the end she gave in on that too, and promised to help. First she made him finish his schooling, which had suffered. Earlier he had been near the top of his class. Eric sat through his final exams, with patchy results.

That was in June the previous year, at the end of the English school year. Eric turned eighteen the following autumn, and with no difficulty obtained a one-year working visa. By then the whole family had British nationality. He came out in October.

At this point Mrs Tran and I both seemed to notice that the building had gone quiet, apart from the occasional hum of the lift. The sound of evening traffic came up to us muffled through the closed windows. I drank some tea, switched on some lights, came back to my seat. Neither of us mentioned the time.

At first Eric went to Melbourne. It seemed he had a friend at school from there. He found some part-time work, but didn't like it much. Soon he moved to Sydney. Some Vietnamese he'd met in Melbourne had given him an address in Cabramatta, where he could find work and somewhere to stay. He came up in early December and went straight there. Cabramatta, more than twenty kilometres south-west of Sydney, was where most of the Vietnamese refugees had settled.

'Why didn't he go to Marrickville, to stay with your cousins?' I asked.

'They're not my cousins. They're my husband's, and there's no close relationship. They're not blood relatives of Eric. Besides –'

She had written to them in advance, asking them to keep an eye on Eric if he came their way, but he hadn't gone to see them until some time after his arrival in Sydney, and they'd felt slighted.

'Vietnamese can be sensitive about things like that, Mr Quinn. When Eric did go to see them, they didn't like the look of him. They wrote to me afterwards, to say that he'd called, but they were very critical. He had long hair, he was roughly dressed, he even had a ring in his ear. And he'd brought two or three friends along, and they didn't like the look of those at all. *Bụi đời*, they called them. You know that expression?'

'Yes. *Dust of life*. I remember. Riff-raff.'

'That's right. They used words like *du côn*, thugs, hooligans.'

What worried her was that his visit to them coincided with a change in Eric's letters to her. At first he'd only written about places he'd seen, things he was doing. But now he started telling her about some of the young Vietnamese he was meeting. He talked of a group, some kind of anti-communist organization, and she didn't like the sound of it.

'I didn't know much about Vietnamese in Australia. I still don't. But it sounded too much like – well, *bụi đời*, the kind of foot-loose young refugees you hear about, who can't settle down and turn into gangs. And all that militant talk, of demonstrations, fighting the communists, of reconquering the south. He was very scathing about his cousins, too. Now that I've met them I can see why they didn't get on – they're northerners originally, and very prim and proper, and the people Eric is with are mostly southerners, and they're young and brash and not respectful of their elders. That in itself was a concern.'

She wrote back warning Eric against getting mixed up in expatriate Vietnamese politics. He replied that he knew what he was doing, she shouldn't judge his friends by what the cousins said about them. If the war had been lost it was because of people like them, small-time profiteers who thought only of themselves and didn't care about their country.

That too was disturbing.

Then, in late January – just before *Tết*, Vietnamese New Year – something nastier happened. The cousins' shop in Marrickville was broken into, with considerable damage. The cousins wrote immediately to Mrs Tran, and while they didn't accuse Eric directly, they blamed his friends, who were questioned by the police. There was no evidence that any of them were involved, but some of them had been in trouble before. The whole episode had become very unpleasant, with the cousins asking for compensation, and doing their best to make her feel responsible. That was when she decided to come out.

'And you went to stay with them. That can't have been very pleasant either.'

'I didn't have much choice. I don't know anyone else in Australia, my own relatives are in the United States, and – well, I felt I owed it to them, as well as to Eric, at least to come out and find out what had happened.'

Her arrival hadn't helped much. The cousins by then were so set against Eric that they wouldn't let him into the house at first, when he called round to see her. She had to go for a walk in the street to talk to him. Eric indignantly denied having anything to do with the break-in. He said they were maligning his friends, just because they didn't like the look of them.

She believed him. About his friends she wasn't so sure, when she went to see him in Cabramatta. Some of them did fit the cousins' description – brash, untidy, boastful, with long hair, tattoos, the lot! And the language to go with it.

'I know Vietnamese can be a pretty earthy language, but it was all a bit much! And the house was full of silly posters and anti-communist slogans. Down with the Viet Cong, reconquer the south, fight for a free Vietnam, that sort of thing. But they didn't look like criminals, just brash and boastful and uncertain of themselves. They were friendly enough when Eric told them who I was.'

Eric also took her to the restaurant where he worked, in the centre of Cabramatta. It was large and looked well-run. The owner wasn't there but Eric appeared to fit well into the place. That wasn't what worried her.

What did worry her was all that rabid anti-communist talk.

'We've always been anti-communist, Mr Quinn. Anything else would be unthinkable for people like us. After what they did, after what we've been through. And we never tried to hide it from Eric – on the contrary, we wanted him to know what we left behind, why we felt the need to leave Vietnam. So he could understand why his mother had died. So he wouldn't blame her, or us, for taking that risk.'

'But we didn't hate the communists. I don't hate them, not for the war, they suffered enormous sacrifices for it, just as we did. I can even understand why they wanted to conquer the south. It's for what they did afterwards that I can't forgive them. The repression, the vindictiveness, the mindless arrogant orthodoxy – of course I blame them for what happened to Hien, but I can equally blame your country for refusing to take her, when she could have left in safety. David's death was just an accident of war. But try explaining that to a boy who lost both parents because of them. All I did was reinforce his hatred.'

She shook her head. 'We've never taken part in anti-communist activity among the refugee communities. There aren't many refugees in Britain, there's not as much scope for it there as here or in America, and in any case it's such a waste of time. There's nothing more pathetic than those emigré groups wallowing in nostalgia and plotting to get back what they couldn't hold on to in the first place.'

'We lost the war, Mr Quinn. For a number of reasons, some beyond our control, and I don't much admire the Americans for the way they let us down in the end. But we lost it. What hope is there of reconquering anything now? It can't lead to anything. Eric is too good for that, there's too much talent and promise in him to waste himself that way.'

She took a long breath, and sat back in her chair.

'To be honest, I don't know if they're thugs or militant anti-communists or just insecure kids playing at grown-ups in a world they don't understand. But now they're talking about a large demonstration, some sort of action against a visiting Vietnamese official. I'm frightened. It sounds violent. That's why I've come to you. I don't want Eric to be mixed up in that kind of world, Mr Quinn. And I don't know what to do about it.'

She stopped, and in the silence that followed a rush of memories tumbled into my mind: of David, the last time I'd seen him, his poor mangled features barely recognisable as I held a handkerchief to my nose, before they closed the lid on his coffin. The local area commander I'd questioned, down to a skinny patrol sergeant and the last outpost he'd checked at before his death. A radiator hose, they'd mentioned, confirmed by a quick inspection of the wreck, a nervous embassy driver at my side. For greater anonymity David had rented a car in Saigon, to avoid using his own – with its diplomatic plates – and he had paid the price. It was clear enough how he'd died. I was beginning to understand why.

There was Hien too, that pale dim memory, fragile as a ghost. David had failed her, by getting himself stupidly killed, and I had failed her too, through not understanding the depth of her need and her despair. No wonder she had been so desperate to leave, carrying his child, and felt so rejected. Perhaps this was a way to make amends.

Mrs Tran sat quietly watching me. She looked exhausted, almost gaunt, as if her story had taken too much out of her, yet beautiful still, even desirable in her anguish. Careful, I told myself. This was neither the time nor the place. But I couldn't help feeling a surge of excitement at the way this beautiful, tragic woman had reappeared in my life. It was a long time since I'd had anything to do with Vietnam and its diaspora of struggling, suffering exiles, but one way or another I knew I would have to help her.

She spoke up, as if reading my thoughts.

'I know this isn't your problem, Mr Quinn. You've been very patient with me. But I'll have to go back to England soon, and if I can't get Eric out of this situation I don't know what I'll do. Anything, any advice you can give me, if you can recommend anyone – I haven't got much money, but I'm quite prepared to pay for any help –'

I held up my hand.

'That won't be necessary, Mrs Tran. I was just thinking. I still have a couple of contacts in the Vietnamese community, maybe I can find out something about that group of his. But first I'd like to meet Eric. Will he be in the restaurant tomorrow?'

'Yes, he's usually there from twelve to three. It's the Dai Nam, just off John Street.'

She handed me a photo, of a youth, in jeans and a check shirt too big for him, clowning with a friend in a backyard. Two wings of thick dark hair framing a high forehead, a boyish grin, a strong jaw, the eyes staring at the camera as if issuing a challenge. A handsome face, not yet a man's, but with toughness in it. Intelligence too.

'He doesn't look very Asian,' I said. 'In fact he doesn't even look Eurasian, except for the eyes.'

'People sometimes think he's Italian. Apart from his hair he takes more after David.'

I pushed my last memory of David away.

'How did your husband die, Mrs Tran?'

'He had leukemia.'

'And your sister? I know this is painful, but I need to know that, before I see Eric.'

'I understand. I told you, we – we ran into a storm. She was swept overboard. Eric was down with me in the hold. She was seasick, she'd gone up on deck –' She looked at me, her eyes pleading. 'Please, Mr Quinn, don't mention that when you see him. He had nightmares for a long time afterwards.'

'I won't.'

We finished our tea and I stood up. I switched off the lights, locked up and walked with her to the lifts.

'Are you going back to Marrickville? I can drive you if you like.'

'Thank you, but I can take the train. I've kept you long enough from your family.'

'I live alone. It's no problem.'

Her eyes were luminous in the half-light, that scent of jasmine giving warmth to the sterile corridor. I smiled at her.

'You don't mind if I pretend that we knew each other in Saigon, when I talk to Eric?'

'Of course not.'

She looked at me.

'My sister was right, Mr Quinn. You are a kind man.'

'Your sister didn't know me very well, Mrs Tran. May I call you Hao?'

'Of course. I meant to ask –'

'And I'm Paul.'

Downstairs on the footpath I renewed my offer, but again she declined, and I didn't insist. We shook hands again. This time she didn't withdraw her hand so quickly.

'I'll call you when I've seen Eric.'

I watched as she walked off towards the station, looking lonely and beautiful, and very courageous.

Chapter Four

The Dai Nam restaurant in Cabramatta was a large barn of a place, all tiled floor and formica-topped tables, but you don't judge an Asian restaurant by its décor. It was after two, but most of the tables were still taken up with locals, which suggested the food must be good. I found a spare table near the door and looked around.

Two waiters were at work, a girl and Eric. By chance it was Eric who came to serve me. He was shorter than I expected, but well built, with broad shoulders and a slim waist, and just as handsome with that high round forehead, a slightly uptilted nose and a strong jawline. He wore his hair long, as Hao had said, tied at the back in a small ponytail, and he had a ring in his ear, but he was neatly dressed in T-shirt and jeans. He walked with a purposeful air and seemed to know what he was doing.

'What would you like?' he asked briskly, but politely. There was a dark quality to his eye, an inner wariness, like a colt, ready to bolt.

'What would you recommend?' I said. 'I only want something light.'

'You could try the *chả giò,* they're very popular, or *chạo tôm*, they're made with grilled prawn paste wrapped round sugar cane sticks, they're also very good.' He had a deep melodious voice, with a touch of Yorkshire perhaps, in which a few Australian vowels were beginning to creep.

I chose the *chả giò*, the small crisp spring rolls which you eat, hot from the deep fry, wrapped in a lettuce leaf with a sprig of Vietnamese mint and dipped in *nước mắm*, the Vietnamese fish sauce.

'Better make that a double order, with a pot of green tea.'

Eric had pronounced the Vietnamese words correctly, in the southern accent, and I took care to do the same. He shot me a quick glance and went back to the kitchen, still with his serious expression. Only when he passed the girl did he smile briefly, and I looked at her. She was Eurasian too, though in her case the Vietnamese was more marked, and pretty in a waif-like way, with large dark eyes in a pale sallow face, and she smiled back at him. In the background an older Vietnamese man came out from time to time to stand at the counter, short and stocky, with the kind of dissipated, pouchy face I'd seen in the past in Asia, on some brutal police officers.

Eric brought the tea, and soon after came back with my order. He set it out neatly on the table, the lettuce and Vietnamese mint on a separate plate, the fish sauce in a small bowl.

'You're Eric, aren't you,' I said as he was about to go. He looked at me in surprise.

'How do you know my name?'

'My name's Paul Quinn. I'm a friend of your mother.'

He stared at me briefly.

'My mother's dead.'

'I meant your adoptive mother. Your aunt. Mrs Tran.'

He stood uncertainly for a second, then pulled a cloth from his belt and began to wipe a nearby table

'I didn't know she had any friends in Australia. She's never mentioned you.'

'I knew her a long time ago in Saigon. We've only just caught up.'

He continued nervously wiping, giving me sideways glances.

'I suppose she told you that I'm up to no good.'

'Not at all. Why would she do that? She mentioned that you'd had a spot of trouble, but she said it wasn't your fault.'

'Are you a cop?'

'Certainly not. But I would like to have a word with you. Any chance of seeing you when you get off? She said you're here until three.'

He stood straight, and looked at me.

'Did she send you here?'

'No. But she told me about you, and I thought I'd come and see you. I knew your father in Saigon.'

For a moment that shook him. Conflicting emotions crossed his face, hope, wariness, a touching vulnerability. Over his shoulder I could see the older man looking in our direction. Then he collected himself.

'Alright. Meet me here at three then. I'll get your bill.'

The spring rolls were excellent. I left a generous tip, then went out to explore. Cabramatta when I'd first gone there in the early eighties had looked almost derelict, one of those down-at-heel outer suburbs you bypass on your way somewhere else. But the large numbers of Indochinese refugees who had settled there since had transformed the place. The main street, John Street, which had been in a terminal state, was now a thriving shopping strip, filled with people, lined with modern shops of every description. Most of the people were Asian, Vietnamese, Chinese, Cambodian or Laotian, like the shop signs, where English was in a clear minority. That didn't worry me, I'd always felt at home in Asian crowds. I wandered through crowded arcades, stuck my nose into grocery stores, smelling the familiar smells, listening to the jabber of voices, and tried to work out how to handle Eric. I could see it wasn't going to be easy.

Eric was cleaning up when I got back to the restaurant. He went into the back room and came out again in a denim jacket several sizes too large. He said a few words to the girl, the older man looked at me again, and then he came out on the pavement.

'Where would you like to go?' I asked. 'Anywhere we can sit and talk, where you don't have to do the waiting?'

He smiled briefly, and it was like a ray of sunlight passing over a darkened landscape. I began to understand what his aunt saw in him.

'I don't have much time,' he said. 'I have to be at a friend's place at four, and I have to go home first and pick up a few things.'

'Let me drive you. We can talk in the car.'

He gave me another wary look, but let himself be steered towards the large car park at the back of the shops, where I had with difficulty found a spot for my ageing Peugeot 405. He gave it an appraising glance.

'Nice car,' he said. 'Is that the GTi model?'

'No, the standard. But it goes fast enough.'

'How high have you had it?'

'Hundred and seventy. Kilometres of course, not miles. Only a couple of times, out in the country. The cops are pretty savage here, I wouldn't want to lose my licence.'

The car was hot from the sun and we stood outside while I switched on the engine and the air-conditioning, watching the people moving in and out of the car park, with that air of life and bustling, natural energy you find with Asians. At the back of the car park stood a large multi-level building with shops at its base and advertising banners on its walls. I pointed to it.

'That's what I like about these people. Fifteen years ago they came here destitute, and now they own half the place.' I read out one of the signs, in large white letters on a red background.

'*Công Ty Nhặp Cảng Bạch Hổ* – Bach Ho Import Export Company. Bach Ho means White Tiger, doesn't it?'

'Do you speak Vietnamese?'

'I used to.'

Eric looked at the building for a moment.

'I know that man,' he said. 'Mr Bach. The man who owns that company. Mr Ho Xuan Bach. He's the one who got me the job in the restaurant. He's a friend of the owner.'

'Is that the man I saw inside?'

'Yes.'

'What's his name?' He shot me another look.

'He's Mr Khanh. Mr Vo Khanh. Why do you want to know?'

'His face seems familiar,' I said, making it up as I went. 'Was he ever in the army, in Vietnam?'

'The Marines,' Eric answered reluctantly. 'The South Vietnamese Marines.'

'Maybe that's it. I met some of them.'

He was getting edgy, and I changed the subject. We got inside the car, and made our way in fits and starts towards the exit. I searched for ways to open him up. He was cagey as a young animal, not sure how far to trust me, more than twice his age. He began to give me directions.

'What were you doing in Saigon?' he asked suddenly.

'I worked in the embassy there for a while. Towards the end. I was there when your father died.'

'He was killed by the communists.'

'I know.'

'My mother worked in the embassy.'

'I met her a few times.'

He was silent for a moment, apart from his directions.

'She was killed by the communists too.'

'Your aunt told me she had died. I was very sorry to hear that.'

We turned into another street, lined with fibro houses in threadbare gardens, some unpainted, with rickety front fences and cracked concrete paths. This was the other face of Cabramatta, the behind-the-scenes reality, where unemployment was two or three times the national average. Eric directed me to a stop outside one of them.

'What was he like?' he asked.

I paused, thinking out my next move.

'I liked him,' I said. 'But I'll tell you about him another time. Is this where you live?'

'Yes.'

'You said you have to go somewhere by four.'

'That's right.' He stirred himself. 'I'd better go and change. Thanks for the lift.'

'I'll wait for you.'

'There's no need –'

'It's alright, Eric. I've got plenty of time. That's what I came for. To see you.'

He hesitated. 'Alright…you'd better come in then.'

He got out and led the way up the path, into a hallway and a front sitting-room. Two young Vietnamese men sat on a sofa watching a kung fu video on a large television set, the most expensive item in the room. Eric spoke to them, they said hello and nodded at me. I nodded back and sat in an armchair to one side. Eric went inside and they went on watching the video.

I discreetly examined the two men. One was short, dressed in baggy trousers and what looked like several oversized shirts, and had long hair which he kept smoothing out with both hands like a girl. The other had a crew cut and wore a tight grey sweatshirt and commando-style army pants, and flexed his biceps from time to time, showing off several tattoos. On the walls were tourist posters of the old Vietnam, scenes of the Central Highlands, and a South Vietnamese flag, the three red bars on a yellow background, carefully pinned to the wall above a small altar. Underneath were a couple of captions printed in Vietnamese: *Đả Đảo Cộng Sản, Mặt Trận Phục Hồi Việt Nam Cộng Hòa* – Overthrow the Communists, Front for the Recovery of the Republic of Vietnam.

'Nice day,' I said to the young men, and they looked at me briefly and nodded.

'Want a beer?' said the taller one.

'No thanks. I'm just waiting for Eric.'

'You friend of Eric?'

He spoke with a strong Vietnamese accent, the final consonants half-swallowed.

'Friend of his aunt.' I looked around the room. 'You guys live here too?'

'Yes. This our home. You like?'

'Not bad. Many of you live here?'

He smiled but didn't answer. I wondered if he understood much English. Like Hao I didn't see much harm in them. They looked friendly enough, but wary, and without social manners – Vietnamese or Australian. The detribalised youngsters that one heard about in the Vietnamese community, the *bụi đời* Hao had mentioned. I felt sorry for them. I couldn't see much future for them, other than as factory-fodder. A fractured grasp of the language, no sense of belonging, dreaming of a past they hardly remembered. Fertile ground there for trouble.

Eric returned, with wet hair and dressed in another assortment of T-shirt and jeans, and the denim jacket. He carried a zip-up nylon bag.

'Are you guys going to Binh's?'

'No, we go with Nam,' one of them said. 'We see you there later.'

'Alright.' Eric looked at me, uncertain how to introduce me. He decided it wasn't worth the effort. We went back to the car, where Eric began once more to give me directions.

'Weekend in the country?' I asked, pointing to the bag.

'Just going away for a few days.'

'Where to?'

'Just a – I'm not sure. A friend's got a farm.'

'Should be fun. Got good weather for it.'

I thought about my next question.

'Anything to do with that group your aunt mentioned?'

'What did she tell you?'

'Just that you're mixing with a group that's pretty anti-communist, and she's worried about it.'

'She has no cause to be.'

Eric directed me towards Fairfield, a nearby suburb, while I pondered over my approach, that was about as subtle as a bull. Was it the generation gap? I did much better when interviewing applicants.

Presently we arrived in another street, lined with apartment blocks this time. We pulled up outside one of these, with a ramshackle gate and newspapers strewn about the stairwell.

'This is where I have to meet my friend,' he said. 'Thanks for the lift.'

'Listen Eric –' I tried one last time. 'I'm sorry we haven't had much chance to talk today. I'd like to see you again. Maybe I can help, after your aunt goes back to Britain. How long are you going to be away at your friend's farm?'

'A few days. I'm not sure.'

'How about coming to my place next Sunday, with your aunt? We could have a barbecue, or go to the beach.'

'I'm not sure I'll be free.'

'Think about it. You can bring a friend if you like.' I tried my last card. 'And I can tell you more about your father.'

He turned, avoiding my eye, then suddenly blurted out:

'You're not hitting on her, are you?'

'Who, you aunt? Certainly not! What on earth gave you that idea?' I wasn't sure whether to laugh or feel indignant.

'Because I won't stand for it, you know. She's a…she's had a hard life, and I won't let anyone hurt her.'

'I'm glad to hear it! Rest assured, I don't want to hurt her either. I like her too. But if you want to help her, the best thing you can do is listen to her. You know how she cares about you.'

He nodded, half-convinced, and got out of the car.

'Don't forget next Sunday,' I called out.

He turned and gave me that quick, enchanting smile.

'If I'm back.'

———————————

I rang Hao soon after. She must have been expecting my call, as she answered almost at once.

'How did it go?' she asked. 'Have you seen Eric?'

'Yes. Everything's fine,' I said. 'I liked him.' Exaggerating a little, on both counts. But there was something there, beneath that prickly exterior, and with luck I'd be seeing him again, which was what I'd been aiming for.

'Oh good. I'm so relieved.' She gave a small laugh, and I felt a little guilty at my deception.

'He was a bit wary of me, but that's to be expected,' I went on more truthfully. 'I've invited him out for next Sunday, if you can come. I thought we could go to the beach, have a picnic maybe. It should be easier to talk then. Will you be free? I doubt he'll come just for me.'

'No – that's fine, thank you very much, Paul.'

'I have to go out of town, tonight and tomorrow. A family gathering, up in the Hunter Valley, a couple of hours away. I'll be back Monday at the latest. Let me give you the number.'

I gave her the phone number, and my home number as well. I was briefly tempted to ask her along, but pushed the thought aside. Why would she want to go away with me, overnight, a total stranger? Instead I said:

'Would you like to have dinner with me on Tuesday evening?'

'Tuesday?' She sounded hesitant.

'Somewhere in town,' I went on quickly. 'We can talk more about Eric then. I could pick you up around seven. We could make it another day if you like.'

'No…Tuesday would be fine. Thank you. You're very kind, Paul.'

Was I? I remembered Eric's warning.

Sunday afternoon saw me sitting with a cup of coffee on the veranda of my sister and brother-in-law's house, halfway between Cessnock and Kurri on the old highway, in the lower Hunter Valley. They owned a small farm there, where Geoff was growing a vineyard in his spare time. He was an accountant, Cathy a retired teacher, and they were celebrating their thirtieth wedding anniversary, surrounded by friends and children and their first grandchild. I envied them at times their solid happiness, the comfort and friendship they spread about them. That feeling of ease with themselves that happily married people have. I remembered my own marriage, and how I had chafed in its confines.

'I had a call from Rachel yesterday,' said Cathy. Rachel was my daughter. 'She wanted to come up, but she couldn't.'

'That's right. She's got exams this week.'

'She sounded well. How's Sandy?'

'Fine I expect. I haven't really spoken with her for ages, apart from quick words over the phone when I call Rachel. She's thinking of remarrying, did you know?'

'Rachel mentioned it.'

'He's a lawyer – a nice man, Rachel says. He's been married before. He should be good for her.'

Cathy, nine years older than me, had watched over me since our parents had died when I was still little, and the break-up of my marriage seven years before had saddened her. She'd liked Sandra, and she'd been concerned about the effect a divorce might have on Rachel, whom she adored. Marriage was sacred to Cathy, at least where children were concerned.

'And you, Paul? How are you getting on? You seem a bit quiet.'

'I'm fine. Just a bit of work on my mind.'

Cathy and I had always been close, but I'd never been good at explaining myself, even to her. Ironic, for a man who'd lived by prying out other people's secrets. That had been one of my problems with Sandy – we hadn't communicated enough. Cathy understood me most by signs and implications, after the event.

'Why do you work so hard? You've got enough money, you could afford to ease up, or do something else.'

'I think of it sometimes.'

'Ever think of remarrying?'

'Sometimes. But I haven't found anyone I really care enough about.'

Until now, I thought, as Hao's face suddenly swept into my mind. Stop it! I told myself sharply. You're getting carried away like a teenager. You've just met the woman, you hardly know anything about her, for all you know she has another man in her life, or else she's still grieving for her late husband. You'll help her sort out her problem, and give her adopted son a hand, and then she'll go home and that's the last you'll see of her. But I couldn't get the look of those eyes out of my mind, nor that lithe figure, and those legs. Cathy looked at me curiously, but said nothing.

In the early evening I drove back to Sydney, after the festivities and the hugs and the fresh country air had cleared the last of the champagne fumes. Through Cessnock, Kearsley, the old mining towns changeless over the decades, the pubs and the banks still the dominant buildings, a little neater nowadays and more self-conscious with the coming of the tourists to the wineries. Hobby farmers splitting up the old dairy farms. Brunkerville with its name like an American Civil War battlefield. Pretty country still, mostly unspoiled. Over the Heaton Pass and down the toboggan run to Freeman's Waterhole and the freeway junction.

Two days before I saw Hao again, a week until I had another chance to talk to Eric, if he hadn't taken fright. Time going by, before long she'd be back in Britain.

I'd better not waste any of it.

Chapter Five

Nghiem was the first person I went to. He was a gentle, frog-faced man I'd first met in Saigon in the last weeks of the *ancien régime*, and recontacted later in Sydney in the early eighties, when he'd resettled there and I was trying to set up some access to the Vietnamese target. An engineer by training, and a former Colombo Plan student in Australia, he had been one the first to be allowed in after the fall. Nghiem had looked askance at my attempts to draw him into the net – not everyone welcomes an approach from a spy – but we had remained friends, though I hadn't seen him for some years. I guessed he'd retired.

I still had his number and rang him the next morning in Lindfield, where he lived with his Australian wife Ann and the youngest of their four children. He sounded glad enough and didn't object when I invited myself round after work.

'I'm doing some consultancy work and I need your advice.'

A cover works best mixed with the truth. I thought it best not to reveal my true purpose at this stage.

'It's about the Vietnamese community,' I explained that evening in his sitting room. Ann had offered me a peck on the cheek and a cup of tea and discreetly withdrawn. I wondered how much Nghiem had told her of my past approach.

'I have a client who wants to do business in Vietnam, and needs to recruit some assistants locally. People he can trust, whose heart is in Australia even if they were born in Vietnam. But I've lost touch, and I don't know where to start. Can you give me a few clues? Who to talk to, who to avoid, that sort of thing?'

'I don't have much to do with them any more,' Nghiem said.

'Maybe some basic information, for a start. What's the community these days? A hundred thousand?'

'In Sydney? Oh less than that. Eighty at most, if you include the Chinese from Vietnam as well. Maybe he should look at those, if he's interested in business.'

'Maybe. But not counting them? Just ethnic Vietnamese?'

'I don't know. Maybe fifty thousand.'

'Where are they mainly? In Cabramatta?'

'There, and Fairfield. They're mostly southerners there, and Buddhist, and a lot of the Sino-Vietnamese have settled there too. The northerners and the Catholics congregate more around Marrickville, and you've got Bankstown as well, which is a bit of a mixture.' Nghiem paused to think. 'I'd say Cabramatta's your best bet. That's where there's the most business activity. Have you been there lately? It's amazing how the place has grown.'

'You read some alarming statistics in the press, all that unemployment.'

'I know. That's worrying.' Nghiem's kind face wrinkled in concern. 'But that's mainly the uneducated, the ones who came here without their families, the farmers and the fishermen. Some of them have a hard time assimilating, so they stick too much together.'

Nghiem came from what used to be called the mandarin class: his father had been a senior official in the north, under the French, there were lawyers and doctors in the family. People like Hao. I remembered the refugees I'd met in the camps, queuing up to be interviewed by immigration and UN officials (and by more devious types like me). Many of them had been simple folk, straight from their villages, with little education and no concept of the outside world. And the youngsters, the draft-dodgers, ducking the new war which the communist Vietnamese were now waging in Cambodia, after driving the Khmer Rouge out in 1979, or who were simply sent out by themselves, as young as twelve or thirteen sometimes, to serve as spearhead, an anchor for a family to follow. You could see there the seeds of some long-term problems. Yet many of those had done well, some becoming millionaires, and not all the former mandarins had been so successful.

'What about these gangs you read about? How serious are they, really?'

'You know what the press is like,' Nghiem said. 'A lot of it's exaggerated. There's a problem there alright, but I don't know much about them.'

Like most of his kind Nghiem had little time for the rougher elements in the Vietnamese community.

'One thing I am worried about is those extremists,' I went on. 'You know, all those ex-military types, who want to turn Ho Chi

Minh City back into Saigon. They're the last thing my client needs. Any sign of them to look out for?'

Nghiem gave me a patient look. I remembered the way he'd shrunk back when I'd asked him years ago to introduce me to other Vietnamese.

'Those you'll know soon enough. But I wouldn't worry too much about them. They're not as strong as they used to be. A lot of Vietnamese go back to Vietnam on visits nowadays and that's taken the wind out of their sails…sorry Paul, I wish I could be more helpful.'

'No, thanks Nghiem, you've been a great help.'

I took my leave of Ann, who looked secretly relieved.

'If you really want to know more about those people,' Nghiem said on the doorstep, 'why don't you ask Jack Lipton?'

He was next on my list. But Jack and I were both busy the next day, and I had to wait until Wednesday to see him. Once again I was conscious of time flying past.

Chapter Six

Hao looked even prettier on the Tuesday evening when I picked her up at the cousins' house – a mean little box with a concrete front yard where I got a hard stare from the inhabitants. She wore a dark brown knee-length dress of some soft material with a pattern of small dots and a refreshing lack of frills and flounces, and she had let her hair down at the back, held together by a ribbon. She also looked much less tense, as if our first meeting had taken a load off her mind. I felt eager as a teenager on his first date.

'Thank you again for going to see Eric,' she said as I drove towards the city. 'I'm really grateful for what you're doing.'

'It's still early days. Let's see what happens on Sunday. I was mainly trying to establish my credentials.'

I told her about our meeting, leaving out Eric's trip out of town. I needed to earn that boy's trust, and one way was to show him I could keep my mouth shut.

'I liked him, overall. He's blunt, and direct, and there's a lot of honesty in him. He warned me off in no uncertain terms if I don't behave myself with you. I had to assure him my intentions were strictly honourable.'

She gave a small incredulous laugh. 'My goodness! You did have a frank discussion.'

'When do you have to go back?' I asked.

'Soon. I've taken six weeks off, all my holidays, and I can take another two weeks if I want, but after that I'll have to go back, or risk losing my job.'

She told me she worked in a chemical plant near Leeds. She was personal assistant to the managing director.

I took her to Wolfie's, on the waterfront at Circular Quay. It's in the Rocks area, the oldest part of Sydney, and one of the best places in all Australia to take a pretty woman out to dinner. Nineteenth-century tenements, sandstone warehouses converted into loft apartments. We sat on the terrace out front, facing the Opera House, with the harbour in the background and the Bridge hanging over us on our left. Hao let me choose the menu: octopus salad and grilled barramundi, with a light Semillon.

'I think I met your father once,' I said. 'In early April, just after the fall of Hue and Da Nang. He told me the Americans were backing the wrong horse with Thieu, that Thieu should step down while it was still possible to negotiate with the communists.'

'That sounds like him.'

Nguyen van Thieu, South Vietnam's president almost to the end, had resisted any thought of compromising with the communists.

'What happened to him afterwards?'

'He was arrested, and sent to re-education. He died later that year, in Bien Hoa.'

I was appalled. Bien Hoa was a large prison on the outskirts of Saigon, which had been given a new lease of life by the communists, when they'd set up their vast programme of re-education for those who'd had the misfortune to be on the losing side.

'Why?' I cried. 'He wasn't on Thieu's side. He wanted an end to the war, he was a neutralist.'

'Not neutral enough, apparently.' She gave a dry laugh. 'Oh, I don't mean they set out to kill him. They probably just wanted to teach him a lesson. He'd been too critical of the communists too in the past. But he was old, and he had a weak heart. He died of illness, and neglect.'

'Why didn't he get out with the Americans?'

'He didn't want to leave. Vietnam was his country. Right to the end he thought he could still play a role, help salvage something from the ruins.'

She explained. Her father, although originally from the north, was a Buddhist, and had come south as a young man, in 1949. He didn't know much about communism. The people who had been most anxious to flee in 1975 had been the northern Catholics, who had come south in 1954, at the time of partition, at the end of the first war, against the French, and they'd already had a taste of communism. Her mother was from My Tho, in the south.

'Where is she now?'

'In America, with my older brother Nhan. There were three of us, Nhan, myself and Hien. Nhan also went into re-education. They gave him a hard time. He'd been an officer in the army. Originally he was a student at the Faculty of Sciences. That's how I met

44

Khiem, my husband, he was teaching there and they became friends. After Nhan graduated he was drafted and sent to the military academy, and he joined the Rangers. He wasn't like my father, he wanted to fight! He tried to escape after the fall of Saigon. His unit kept fighting for two days in the delta – but he was caught and sent north, up near the Chinese border. He was still in the camps when we got out. That's why my mother didn't come with us. She wanted to wait for him. He was lucky to survive. A lot of his friends died in the camps.'

'How did he get out?'

'He was brought back south when the Chinese attacked in the north, after the invasion of Cambodia in 79. They put him in a camp in the Central Highlands, but he escaped back to Saigon. We'd already left – a month earlier! After that Nhan went back to the highlands to join the resistance there, but he soon found that that was hopeless. So he came back to the delta and got out by boat. The Americans took him at once, with his record. Finally our mother was allowed to leave too. They live in San Diego. I went to see them once, not long before Khiem died.'

They'd had a hard time in Saigon, during those lean years: selling off their furniture, doing odd jobs, sewing, a bit of teaching, working in the fields. Her father in prison, no news of Nhan, for a long time they thought he was dead.

'I don't know how we would have managed without Khiem. Fortunately they let him keep his job, he'd never been in the army.' She shrugged. 'But we survived, and some of us got out in the end. There aren't many families in the south that haven't lost someone because of the war. Or in the north for that matter.'

I remembered the stories I'd heard in the refugee camps. The years spent in re-education, the hand to mouth existence of a society reduced to poverty, people thrown out of their jobs, their homes, their children denied university places, forced into new economic zones, persecuted and harassed. No wonder they wanted to escape. By the late 1970s the south had become a vast escape factory, there wasn't a canal or stretch of river without its clandestine boat-yard, everything that could float was being turned into a boat, despite all the authorities' attempts to stop them.

Not everyone succeeded. Some made it in one hop to Pulau Bidong off the Malaysian coast, a night and a day in a sixteen-foot tub with two inches of freeboard, twenty or thirty people crammed knee to shoulder – hundreds on the bigger boats. Others drifted for days or weeks at sea, preyed on by pirates, their engines dead, half-dead themselves of thirst and hunger before they were picked up. Even those were the lucky ones. For all those who made it to safety there were countless others who failed, never managed to get out, or simply died at sea, like Hien.

Our food came, cutting across these grim reminiscences. Hao gave me a speculative look.

'What about you, Paul? What kind of life have you had over the past twenty years?'

'Nothing as hard as yours. A couple more postings after Saigon, Colombo and Kuala Lumpur. That's when I went to Hawkins Road, in '81. I probably just missed you. I visited a few refugee camps when I was in KL. In between, long spells at home. I got married, to an Australian girl, Sandra. My daughter was born in Colombo. After KL I got tired of it and left to go into business. That was hard work. Don't ever think money's easy to make in business. My marriage broke up. But I stuck it out, ended up owning a couple of shops. About three years ago I sold out and went into my present business. I had a friend who wanted a partner. He quit soon after and since then I've been on my own, with Vivien.'

'You sound very enterprising. Why haven't you remarried?'

'Once bitten…'

She smiled. 'No girlfriends?' Vietnamese can be persistent interrogators.

'A few. None current.'

What about you, I thought, but didn't say. Hardly the question to ask, so soon after her husband's death. I poured her another glass.

'It's from the Hunter, where I was on Sunday. Near where my sister lives.'

'Tell me about her. You know so much about me now, and I hardly know you.'

So I told her more about myself. Not everything, nothing about my former occupation, but about Sandra, and Rachel, eighteen, in her final year at a private girls' school in Melbourne, coming up to see me during the school holidays.

After dinner we walked along the waterfront, around Circular Quay, all the way to the Opera House and back. It was warm, the place was animated, in other circumstances I would have been tempted to hold her hand, but this was clearly out of the question. Don't rush things, I told myself.

'How old are you?' she asked.

'Forty-five. My birthday's in February.'

She did a quick calculation on her fingers, mumbling to herself in Vietnamese.

'You're a Tiger,' she said.

'That's right.'

Tyger, Tyger, burning bright, In the forests of the night.[2] I'd always related to Blake's tiger, though not I fear in the way he intended.

'And you?'

'I'm a Horse. My birthday's in August. I was born in 1954.' Nearly 41. Older than I'd first thought.

'Is that a good or a bad thing?' I asked. 'Tigers and Horses.'

She laughed. 'It depends. If the Tiger's a woman it doesn't work very well. But when the Tiger's a man and the Horse is a woman that can be a lucky combination.'

'I'll take that as an omen,' I said, suddenly elated. 'What about your name? *Hảo*, that's rather unusual.'

'It's short for *Minh-Hảo. Hòang thị Minh-Hảo.* That was my maiden name.' She said it in the northern accent. It sounded like a cat singing.

'*Minh* I know, it means 'intelligent'. But *Hảo*?'

---

[2] Tyger, tyger burning bright
In the forests of the night
What immortal hand or eye
Could frame thy awful symmetry…

…
Did he who make the Lamb, make thee?'
William Blake, English poet and mystic, 1757-1827

'Oh. It means *good*, or *beautiful*.'

'Intelligent and beautiful. Hm.' I made a play of inspecting her. 'Your parents must have had second sight.'

'I wouldn't say that. They called my sister *Hiền*, which means gentle, and she could be fierce as a wildcat when she was angry. We had some terrible fights when we were young...'

She tailed away, as if the memories were still too painful, even after all that time. I changed the subject back to Eric.

'I've started doing some research on the Vietnamese community,' I said. I told her about my meeting with Nghiem. 'I'm seeing another friend tomorrow night. Australian this time, but he's got a Vietnamese wife, and he knows his way around the Vietnamese community. Why don't you come too?'

'Are you sure? I'd like to, but I don't want to get in the way.'

'You won't. If anything it will probably help.'

When I drove her back to Marrickville I got out of the car and walked with her to the front door. I was tempted to kiss her, but stuck my hand out instead. We shook hands formally.

'Thank you for such a pleasant evening,' she said.

'Do you really have to go back so soon?'

She gave me a look from under her eyelids, looking for a moment remarkably like Eric. Then she turned and went in.

Chapter Seven

Jack Lipton was a very different type from Nghiem. Ex-military, a former Warrant Officer with the SAS, he had served three tours of duty in Vietnam with the Australian Army Training Team, before settling down as an assistant to the Military Attaché in the embassy, where I had first met him.

There was more to Jack than bluff military virtues. A short, chunky man who looked as if he could hold his own in a brawl, he was also a first-rate linguist, having topped his Vietnamese course in Australia before first going to Vietnam, and spoke it almost like a native. And he'd picked up a wife along the way, a sweet-faced Vietnamese woman called Sen.[3] Long retired from the army, they now lived in Strathfield, where he kept his hand in interpreting part-time for the Vietnamese community, and sometimes for the police. I'd always got on well with Jack, and they received us warmly when I took Hao there the next evening, armed with flowers for Sen and a bottle of Scotch for Jack.

'Why don't we see you any more,' he cried.

Jack was much more helpful, assuming at once that I was working for my old outfit.

'I can't help you much with the gangs,' he said. We spoke in his study, beer in hand, while Sen entertained Hao in the kitchen. 'They're very secretive, and the police have a hard time cracking them. But if it's the right-wing movements you're interested in I can tell you a bit.'

'They're mostly ex-military, and by and large they're not involved in crime. Here and there they attract some youngsters, the

---

[3] There was a story to this, which few people knew. Sen was the widow of a close friend of Jack's, a Vietnamese Special Forces sergeant who'd been fatally wounded alongside Jack in a firefight with North Vietnamese infiltrators on the Ho Chi Minh Trail. Jack had reportedly fought his way out single-handed, carrying his friend's body back to base. Afterwards he'd looked after the widow and her children, and finally married her and brought them to Australia. A mutual friend had told me. Jack never talked about it.

bụi đời you mention, and that's where you might get some overlap with crime. But otherwise they're a different area. They're only interested in politics. Most of them don't amount to much, two men and a dog, and they're getting long in the tooth, but some of them are more serious and they can be a nuisance. I don't know much about that man Vo Khanh you ask about, but he sounds just the type. I hear they're planning some big demonstration against a VIP coming out from Vietnam. A guy called Loc, I think. One of the new men coming up in the party.'

That was what Hao had said too.

'Tell you what,' Jack said. 'I know someone who might be able to help you. He keeps a close eye on that kind of thing.'

'A Vietnamese?'

'Yes. I'd have to ask him first, he's a bit wary with strangers. But you can trust him, he won't talk.'

'Any chance of seeing him this week? It's rather urgent.'

'I'll give him a ring and let you know.'

He nodded towards the kitchen.

'Nice woman you've got there. Has she got anything to do with this?'

'No,' I lied. 'She's just a friend I knew long ago in Saigon.'

I thought I'd have some apologising to do to Jack, if the truth came out. But something stopped me from telling him, some hangover from the old days, when you didn't tell people more than you had to.

When I drove Hao home I walked her again to the front door. We shook hands once more, but I took a chance this time and kissed her on the cheek before she could draw away. She didn't recoil, or throw her hands up in horror, but she gave me that look again before she went in.

I was too busy at work over the next couple of days to think much about these matters, and although I was tempted to ring Hao I resisted it. Best to wait until Sunday, I told myself. And on Saturday

Jack rang me. His friend had been away. But Jack had now spoken to him, and he'd agreed to see me.

'His name's Quang,' Jack said. 'He lives in Bankstown. He's expecting your call. It might be best if you go by yourself, the first time. He's a bit leery of people he doesn't know.'

'I understand.'

Jack gave me some details. In his fifties, a northerner, had lived a long time in the south. Very bright, worked as a financial consultant in town. Not married, but had a daughter in France.

'Bit of an odd bird,' Jack said. 'He worked for the communists at one time in Saigon, after the fall, knows a lot about them. I wouldn't be surprised if he's still in touch. But he's OK. He publishes a newssheet for the community, preaching reconciliation. Hasn't made him many friends. He's even had some death threats. I think you'll like him. He's like you in some ways. A bit of a loner.'

I rang Quang that evening, and arranged to meet him on Monday.

I also rang Eric. He didn't sound very thrilled, but he said he'd be there the next day.

Chapter Eight

Sunday morning was one of those late summer days when Sydney comes into its own. It's not a very pretty town overall – lack of planning, and the greed of the developers, have seen to that. But it has the harbour, and a sub-tropical climate, and on a sunny day in March, with the boats out in force and a stiff breeze to chase away the smog, you could be forgiven for thinking it's still one of the best places on earth.

We met at eleven, at the ferry terminal at Circular Quay, not far from where I had taken Hao to dinner. I had picked her up once again at the cousins' house and Eric had come by train, bringing a friend as I had suggested. I recognised the waitress from the restaurant. She was older than I'd first thought, twenty-two or twenty-three, a little over-dressed in skin-tight jeans with high-heeled boots and a red vinyl jacket, but she looked sweet, and likeable, and seemed very attached to Eric, looking up at him as if he were the older of the two.

'This is Hong,' he said awkwardly, with his arm protectively around her. He wore his usual assortment of T-shirt and jeans and oversized jacket, and I guessed he didn't have a large wardrobe. 'My aunt you know, and this is…Mr Quinn.'

'Hi, nice to meet you Mr Queen,' Hong said, in that unbecoming mix of Vietnamese and westies accents I was getting to know.

'Call me Paul,' I said. 'You too Eric. I'm very glad you could come, both of you. You look very pretty like that, Hong.'

I gave her my best smile, and she smiled uncertainly back, while Eric looked suspicious and Hao gave me a quizzical glance. She by contrast looked almost sedate in slacks and sandals and a plain cotton shirt, with her hair in pigtails on either side like a young teenager. I was tempted to follow Eric's example and put my arm around her waist, just to see the look on his face, but didn't quite dare.

We took the ferry to Manly, across the harbour and over near North Head, one of the two giant headlands that guard the entrance. It's a half-hour cruise and the best way to see Sydney. As we pulled away from the wharf we stood outside to look at the view: the saw-toothed roofs of the Opera House on our right, the Bridge hanging massive and dark on the left, ahead of us the main harbour in all its glory, lined with luxury suburbs, alive with yachts and small boats. It was a stirring sight, but I had work to do, and when the women moved out of earshot I turned to Eric.

'How was your week away?' I asked. 'When did you get back?'

'On Thursday. We only went for a few days.'

'Where did you go?'

'Up in the hills somewhere – I'm not sure exactly.'

'Very far out?'

'About an hour and a half, I guess. I didn't check the time.'

He seemed no keener on answering my questions than at our first meeting, and only the press of people stopped him from moving away. But this time I wasn't going to let him off so easily.

'Where – up in the Blue Mountains, near Katoomba?'

'No…further north, I think. Past Windsor, up that way.'

'Beautiful country up there. But pretty rough when you get off the roads. What kind of farm has your friend got?'

'He's not really my friend. Just someone I know.'

'Is he Vietnamese too, like your other friends?'

This time he didn't answer, and I left him alone for a moment. We were ploughing through a light swell, a race was taking place nearby, all sails out like butterflies or tropical flowers. A large yacht slid close and heeled over to change course, the crew scrambling to their new positions.

'That's what I'd like,' I said.

'What's that?'

'One of those.' I pointed to the yacht. 'I keep dreaming of taking off one day and going sailing up in the Whitsundays. Up in Queensland, near the Great Barrier Reef.'

'What's stopping you?' he asked in his blunt fashion, and I laughed.

'Money, for one thing. Those boats don't come cheap. And I'm not ready yet to throw my hand in…So, what did you do on that farm of yours?'

'Nothing much – bushwalking, a bit of horse-riding, that sort of thing.'

'You must have walked through a lot of bush to get your arms in that state. What happened, did you fall off a horse?'

He had taken his jacket off in the heat, and his forearms were covered in scratches, and a couple of bruises.

'What's your birth-sign, by the way?' I asked.

'I'm a Cat. Why?' He looked surprised at my question.

'Just curious. What's this?'

I had noticed a tattoo on his upper arm, under the hem of his sleeve. I lifted the hem with a finger. He moved his arm away, but not before I had caught a glimpse, what looked like a buffalo's head, seen from the front and lowered as if charging, with sweeping horns and plumes of smoke coming out of its nostrils. It was scabbing and looked fresh.

'Some secret society badge?' I asked facetiously. He shot me a dark look and pulled his sleeve down.

'Hey, what went on up there?' I went on. 'You didn't have that last week.'

'Nothing! It's just a tattoo. Look, what's with all these questions anyway? Stop treating me like a suspect! I don't have to tell you everything I do.'

'Of course you don't. You're a legal adult, you're free to do what you want. But I'm curious about that group you're mixed up with. What's wrong with that? I'm only trying to help you.'

'I don't need your help! I only came because of my aunt anyway. Why did you tell her I'd gone out of town? It was none of your business.'

'I didn't! What makes you think I did? I thought I'd leave that to you.'

He looked disbelieving.

'She rang me on Friday. She kept asking where I'd been.'

'Believe me, I didn't tell her anything! But you should have told her. You know how she worries about you.'

'I don't want her mixed up in this.'

'Mixed up in what, for God's sake? What's so mysterious about what you're doing?'

He glared at me, still suspicious. Hao glanced in our direction, alerted by the sound of our raised voices. I shook my head slightly and she looked away. The girl hadn't noticed anything.

'Anyway, you said you were going to tell me about my father,' he said reproachfully.

'So I did. And I will. But first I want you to tell me more about that farm.'

'That's blackmail!'

'Yes it is. But it's for your own good, Eric.'

'I can't!'

'Why can't you? What's so secret about it?'

'We're not supposed to mention it.'

'Who's we? That group of yours?'

He nodded reluctantly. I felt like an interrogator beating a confession out of a suspect. But I wasn't going to stop now.

'Anyway, it's nothing much. We just get together –'

'Where, at the farm?'

'No, that was the first time. In town sometimes, of an evening.'

'Who's your leader? Vo Khanh?'

'Yes. But he wasn't at the farm, he had to stay at the restaurant.'

'Alright. What did you do up there?'

'I told you. We went for bushwalks. Had some discussions. About Vietnam, in the old days, and what the communists have done – all the people they've killed, or put in prison, like my grandfather.'

'Were many of you there?'

'Not many. About a dozen.'

'All Vietnamese?'

He nodded again, unhappily. 'Apart from me. But they seem to trust me.'

'Any firearms?'

He looked uncomfortable.

'Come on Eric. I need to know. It's just between you and me.'

'I fired a rifle a couple of times. Really, that's all there was to it! Stop questioning me like this! There's nothing wrong with what we did.'

'Maybe not. But there are laws against private armies in this country.'

I relented. I could see I was pushing him to the limit, and I didn't want to break whatever slender thread of trust remained between us.

'Alright,' I said. 'Now I'll tell you about your father. I would have told you anyway. But thanks for talking to me so frankly. I won't tell your aunt. What has she told you about him?'

'Hardly anything,' he said miserably. 'I don't even know his name. She says she can't remember. I think his first name was David, I seem to remember my mother saying it when I was little, but I'm not even sure.'

'You're right,' I said. 'His name was David. David Harper. He worked in the embassy, in Saigon. The Australian embassy. Did you know that?'

'I wondered, after you said you knew him.'

'I replaced him there when he was killed. He was a diplomat. A second secretary in the political section.'

'What's that? Some kind of spy?'

I smiled wryly. Out of the mouths of babes…

'No,' I said reassuringly, with the ease of the practised liar. 'That's just a general name, for the part of an embassy that deals with official relations between the two countries.'

'How – how was he killed?'

'He'd gone down to the countryside, to the Mekong delta, on some embassy business. He came back late along a dangerous stretch of road and his car was shot up by the Viet Cong. It was just an accident of war.'

I remembered Hao's phrase.

'I was in Saigon when it happened,' I went on. 'Doing language study. I didn't know him before I went to Vietnam, but we became good friends there.'

'What was he like?' He wasn't interested in my reminiscences.

'He was – how can I best describe him to you.'

I had thought more about David in the past few days than in the previous ten years, but I still had to force my mind to remember him.

'He was two years older than me. Fair-haired, a bit taller, very handsome. Very popular with the girls too, as I remember. I didn't know your mother so well. I know now he was planning to marry her before he left Saigon, but of course he died before that. What else. He got on well with Vietnamese, his house was always full of Vietnamese friends, and he gave some of the best parties in town. I remember that too. He was full of life, always getting into the thick of things, he hated standing still and doing nothing. He was intelligent, courageous, quick-witted –'

I was gilding the lily a little. David had been all of those things, but he'd also been superficial at times, not always concerned with the effect he had on others, and a bit slapdash in his work too, as if he was too busy keeping up with life to have much time for detail. I guessed there'd been a few broken hearts in Saigon when he'd settled on Hien. But I wasn't lying when I said I had liked him. There was something infectious about that boyish enthusiasm. And I wanted to give Eric a picture of his father he could be proud of.

Eric had put his sunglasses on and was looking straight ahead, unseeing. I put my hand on his shoulder, feeling the rock-hard bone, the strength of young muscle. He wasn't big, but he was built like a bricklayer.

'I know it must be very sad for you not to have known him,' I said, trying to find the right words. 'But he was a fine man. At least you know that now.'

'I don't know anything about him,' Eric said. 'I don't even have a photo of him. I think my mother had some, but they were lost on the boat.' He was silent for a moment, coping with his emotions.

'I don't know much about his family. I think they came from South Australia, and he was an only son. But I might be able to find out more if you want.'

'How?'

'From the Department. The Department of Foreign Affairs, that we worked for. They should still have some record of him, perhaps even a photo.'

I was thinking of course of my old employer. My friend Roger Bentinck might help. 'It would mean going to Canberra. Would you like me to do that?'

'Yes please.'

'Good. It may take some time, but I'll be happy to. In return I want you to do something for me.'

'What's that?'

'Learn to trust me. I'm not trying to harm you. Very much the opposite.'

Chapter Nine

We had arrived. The ferry rocked in the swell as we passed near the Heads, then slid into smoother waters before docking at Manly wharf. We disembarked and I took them first to the Ocean Aquarium, where we gaped at the sharks and the giant stingrays, then along the Corso, the pedestrian mall, to the ocean-side and the beach. The streets were packed, the shops were doing a roaring trade. We bought seafood and pizzas and ate lunch at a table near the seawall, facing the beach. The sun was hot, the surf looked fresh and inviting, but none of the others wanted to swim and instead we walked along the esplanade to the southern end of the beach, then followed a winding road that skirted the headland. Hong dragged Eric away to look for seashells and Hao and I went on ahead.

'What were you two talking about on the boat?' Hao asked. 'He looks so subdued.'

'I was telling him about his father. It made him feel sad. But I think it did him good.'

'I thought you were quarrelling. Did you know he's been away most of the week? Up on a farm, he says.'

'Yes, he mentioned it.'

'Do you think it's alright? Is it something to do with that group?'

'I'm still trying to find out. But I wouldn't worry too much. He's a sensible lad, he knows what he's doing.'

I hated lying to her, and wished I didn't have to. But I still felt I had to earn that boy's trust, and I didn't want to alarm her unduly. There was too much I didn't know yet. Let me find out what I could first, from that friend of Jack's.

Eric and Hong caught up with us and walked ahead, hand in hand. This time I didn't hesitate, and took Hao's hand too. I felt her stiffen a little, and thought she'd withdraw it, but she relaxed and left it there, soft and trusting like a child's.

'How do you find Hong?' I asked. 'She seems a bit old for Eric.'

'Only by a couple of years. I like her. She's an orphan too, she told me. Or at least her mother's dead. Father unknown. Probably some American soldier, unless it was one of your embassy colleagues. She's some kind of relation to the man who owns the restaurant.'

'Who? Vo Khanh?'

'I think that's his name. She calls him uncle. He brought her out when she was very young, and she's been working for him since. It's a pity I have to go back. Otherwise I might be able to help her. She speaks Vietnamese of course.'

'What about Eric? Does he still speak it?'

'Not so much any more. He still understands quite a lot. English took over once he started going to school. He tells me he's relearning it.'

'Didn't you speak Vietnamese at home? You and your husband?'

'We did, some of the time. But you know what children are like, in a foreign country, they often feel embarrassed about their mother tongue, especially if they feel insecure. Besides, Khiem spoke such good English, and we wanted to make sure that Eric learnt it properly.'

'How did they get on?' I asked. I wanted to know more about her husband, but didn't want to ask directly. 'Eric's rather cut up about David, but in a sense Khiem was his real father, having brought him up.'

'They were very close. Eric loved Khiem. They spent a lot of time together, before Khiem fell sick.'

'I suppose, not having any children of your own –'

'I suppose so. But Khiem would have loved him in any case. He was a kind man.'

Kinder than I'd been, I thought, remembering my own marriage, and the harsh words I'd exchanged with Sandra before we broke up.

'Was Khiem sick for long before he died?' I went on.

'Not very long. He had AML. Acute myeloid leukemia. It's usually very fast. He was in treatment for a few months, chemotherapy, and that seemed to work, but then he had a relapse, and after that it was very quick.'

'It's a cruel way to go.'

'He was very brave about it. Even at the end, when he knew he was going to die. He never complained.'

'Hard on you too. You must miss him still.'

She was silent for a moment.

'He deserved better than to die like that.'

I sensed I'd gone as far as I could. We stopped, and leaned against the parapet that separated the road from the rocks and the surging surf below, looking back over the long sweep of beach that curves north to the headland at Queenscliff, all overgrown with ugly forties-era apartment blocks like an outcrop of toadstools. Beyond that more headlands, dwindling away into the distance, each one marking off another golden beach. It was a beautiful view, and the ugly buildings were too far off to spoil it. I thought about her husband, and how hard it is to compete with the dead.

As if to prove it she took back her hand.

'What about you Paul? Do you miss your wife? You must have loved her once, even if you did end up in divorce.'

'I thought I did. But we started to grow apart fairly quickly. I don't think we were really suited to each other. She didn't like my job much, for one thing. Oh, she liked the glamour of it at first, the embassy life, but you soon get tired of that, and she didn't like all the sacrifices that went with it. She used to complain that I worked too hard.'

That was one thing I couldn't explain. The demands of embassy life were hard enough on spouses, but those of intelligence work were in another dimension. How could you expect your wife to share the thrills of a clandestine car pick-up with a secret source you met once a month at night, while she stayed home by herself until three in the morning, worried sick that you'd been picked up by local security and were being worked over with rubber hoses – or worse, having it off with one of the embassy girls? It was a wonder more marriages didn't end in divorce.

'Were you ever unfaithful to her?'

I looked at her, startled by the question, not sure at first if she was teasing. But then I saw she was serious. She shook her head with a rueful smile.

'I'm sorry. I shouldn't have asked. Besides, it's different for men, isn't it?'

'Is it?' I laughed awkwardly. 'I'm not so sure. No, I don't mind telling you. As a matter of fact I wasn't. But that didn't make it a happier marriage. Maybe I would have if I'd met the right person.'

She considered that.

'Or the wrong one,' she said.

Afterwards we caught a ferry back to Circular Quay, the jet-cat this time, taking half the time. I retrieved my car and drove them up to my flat in Mosman, an old three-bedroom apartment with a view over Balmoral beach. We pottered about for the rest of the afternoon, drinking soft drinks and eating the cake I'd baked that morning. Hao wandered around, examining the various mementos I'd brought back from abroad.

'You'll recognise these,' I said, leading her to four wooden panels hanging on a wall, inlaid with mother-of-pearl in classical Chinese designs, birds and flowers, and polished rather than lacquered in the modern manner.

'The Four Seasons,' she said, running her fingers along the wood. 'They're beautiful.'

'Almost the only thing I brought back from Saigon. I bought them soon after I arrived. I was so worked up when we left I could hardly be bothered packing. But these I wasn't going to leave behind.'

'You're lucky. My parents had a beautiful collection of old furniture. But we sold most of it afterwards, to buy food and medicine for my father, and when we left we changed the rest for gold or dollars. That was more practical. But even that we lost on the way.'

We stood out on the balcony, leaning against the railing, while Eric and Hong lay on the floor inside listening to Beatles records. His manner wasn't unfriendly, but he kept avoiding me, as if afraid I might harass him with more questions.

'Have you decided yet when you're going back?' I asked.

'Not yet. I keep putting it off. But I'll have to do something soon. I can't stay with the cousins forever. And I have to get back to work.'

'You could stay here.'

As soon as I spoke I knew I'd said the wrong thing. She didn't say anything, looked down at her hands, then across to where Eric and Hong were sprawled on the carpet. It looked as if they'd been kissing.

'I mean it,' I persisted. 'You've seen the flat. There's more than enough room, you'd have your own room, your own bathroom, I wouldn't get in the way. I could even get you a car if you wanted.'

She shook her head.

'I can't, Paul.'

'Why? Are you afraid I'll make a pass at you? I'm very attracted to you, Hao, that must be pretty obvious by now, but I'll keep my distance, I promise. No strings attached.' Even as I spoke I knew I'd find that promise hard to keep. 'And if you're worried about what the cousins will think, to hell with them! You're old enough to lead your own life, you don't owe anyone anything, except maybe Eric, and he'll understand. Look, think about it. Just so you can stay a while longer, and we can see this thing through with Eric. Please?'

She looked at me then, as if thinking it over. She shook her head again.

'It wouldn't work.'

I wanted to argue further, but I could see it was no use, and I let it drop. After a moment she stood up and went inside.

A few minutes later I drove them back, Eric and Hong first, to Central Station, then back to Marrickville to take Hao home. The strain between us was almost palpable. Bloody hell! I kept telling myself. Why hadn't I kept quiet, and let nature take its course? But sometimes you have to push nature along, if you want to get anywhere. When we got there she walked ahead of me to the gate. Her thanks were as formal as her handshake.

'I'm sorry. I didn't mean to hurt your feelings. But can't you just think about it?'

She shook her head again and went inside before I could make an even bigger fool of myself.

Chapter Ten

I took to Quang at once when I went to see him on the Monday evening. He was a typical Vietnamese political intellectual: a tall, thin man in glasses with an intelligent face and a gentle manner, very sharp, very knowledgeable. How practical was another matter. He received me courteously in the sitting room of his flat, on the third floor of a neat apartment block in Bankstown. The room was littered with books and papers, on the chairs, the floor, on every available surface, and the desktop computer on a corner of his dining table looked like it received heavy use.

'Jack tells me you were in your embassy in Saigon,' he began. He spoke good English, in the staccato, sing-song rhythms of a northerner, with a noticeable French accent.

I gave him a sanitised résumé of my career.

'But you're interested in the Vietnamese community, he says. Doing research for a client.'

'That's right.' I had tried to work up a better cover story to explain the detailed probing that I would have to do from now on, but I couldn't think of anything that sounded convincing. It was probably time to come out with the truth. But first I had some questions of my own.

'I understand that you worked for the new government in Saigon, after 1975,' I asked.

His eyes glinted with amusement behind the glasses.

'And you want to know if I'm still working for them? Rest assured, Mr Quinn, I'm not. I've never been a communist. I worked for them because they asked me to, and I thought I could do something for Vietnam. I quit when I saw the way they were ruining the country.'

'What were you doing for them? Please call me Paul.'

'I worked for the Ho Chi Minh City People's Committee, as they've renamed Saigon. As an economics planner. Have you heard of a man called Dang van Loc?

'Is he the one who's coming soon to Australia?' That was the name Jack had mentioned.

'That's him. He's now a Deputy Premier in Hanoi. Then he was vice-chairman of the HCMC Committee – a kind of deputy mayor.

I worked for him for about a year and a half after 1975. Before that I was with the Bank of Vietnam. He's a good man. We could have done some good things together. But he didn't call the shots, and he was overruled when the doctrinaires from the north took over. He's a southerner himself, from Ben Tre. Have you ever been there, Mr Paul?'

'No. It's near the mouth of the Mekong, isn't it?'

'Yes. Under communist control for most of the war, even under the French. He's a real revolutionary, from the earliest days. And yet he helped me escape.'

'From Vietnam?'

He nodded.

'Surprising, isn't it! But there are many surprises in Vietnam, even under the communists. Loc's an intelligent man. He could see it wasn't working. So he sent me abroad, on an official mission. To France, and then here. I came here to ask for aid, Mr Paul. I asked for asylum instead. Your government was kind enough to grant it.'

He smiled with gentle irony, clearly enjoying himself.

'I still keep in touch with him from time to time. Indirectly, through friends. He's a moderate, in communist terms. If Vietnam is to get out of the mess it's in it can only be done with people like him. Not by trying to overthrow them, as those hotheads in the Vietnamese community here keep saying.'

'Jack mentioned you'd received some death threats.'

He gave a derisive laugh.

'They seem to think anyone who doesn't hate the communists is a traitor. But they're dinosaurs, Mr Paul. They live in the past.'

He seemed to like calling me that. Maybe it was his sense of humour.

'All they can think of is restoring the old order. As if they had any hope! No, the only way forward is through compromise, and evolution. We need to install a multi-party system in Vietnam, a genuinely democratic society, but we can only do it with the help of the communists themselves. So we have to come to terms with them. Otherwise we'll just keep going in the same cycle of hate and conflict, and nothing will ever change...'

There was a messianic light in his eye, and I headed him off before he launched into a lecture. I'd met people like him before, in

Saigon and later among the refugees, idealists who thought they could hold back the tide, somehow appeal to people's better nature, or who wanted to play the part of conciliator, and ended up getting caught in the middle, and crushed, like Hao's father. I wished him better luck.

But that wasn't why I was there, and I decided to trust him. After all he had taken me on trust himself, on Jack's recommendation.

'I'm interested in one particular group in the Vietnamese community,' I said. 'But I know very little about it.'

'May I ask the nature of your interest?'

'Yes. But if you don't mind I'd like to keep it between us. I didn't tell Jack the full story.'

He gave me a searching look, then nodded his agreement. 'Rest assured, anything you tell me will be in strict confidence. I expect the same in return.'

'Of course.'

I gave him a brief version of the truth, keeping Hao and Eric's names out of it. I spoke of a friend, who had a young relative who was involved in that group, and who was concerned about it. He asked if my friend was Vietnamese. I said yes, but assured him it was someone I trusted fully, and I hadn't told my friend about our meeting. He accepted this.

'Do you know a man called Vo Khanh?' I asked. 'He runs the Dai Nam restaurant in Cabramatta, and he's a former officer in the South Vietnamese Marines.'

Quang's eyes twinkled again.

'Of course. He's well known in the community. He's one of those people I was telling you about, who want to overthrow the government in Hanoi and restore the old order. I sometimes see him at meetings. He has a reputation for violence. Lately I've heard that he's trying to organise some demonstrations against Loc's visit.'

I pulled out a sketch I had made of the tattoo on Eric's arm. Afterwards I had remembered seeing it before, on one of the young men I had met at the house in Cabramatta. Quang smiled when I told him where I'd seen it.

'That's a mad buffalo,' he said.

'That's what I thought. What does it mean?'

'You haven't heard of the Mad Buffaloes? That's what they used to call one of the Marine battalions in Vietnam. *Tiểu Đoàn Trâu Điên*. The Mad Buffaloes Battalion. Because of their fighting spirit. When they attacked, they kept charging like mad buffaloes until they reached their objective. That was their sign.'

'Is that the name of this group then?'

'Possibly. I hadn't heard the name being used here. But it makes sense, if Vo Khanh is at the head of it. What else do you know about them?'

'Not much. It seems they hold meetings, from time to time. And they may have a training camp out in the country, somewhere in the hills north-west of Sydney.'

I told him what I'd learnt from Eric, conscious that I was breaking my promise to him. I didn't have much choice, if I was going to get anywhere. He took it all in, but couldn't add any more.

'Do you know a man called Ho Xuan Bach?' I asked. 'Also known as Bach Ho. He's a prominent businessman in Cabramatta.'

'I don't know him personally. You're right, he is a wealthy businessman. Is he involved in this?'

'I don't know. But he knows Vo Khanh.'

'That probably doesn't mean anything. But I can check it out.'

He smiled at my look of alarm.

'Don't worry, Mr Paul. I'll be discreet. I have my own friends too in the community. If what you say is true, your young friend would be well advised to stay out of that group.'

'That's very kind of you, Quang. And please call me Paul.'

'In return I'd be grateful for anything else you can find out. I am worried about what they may do during Loc's visit.'

Quid pro quo. I'd never met a source who didn't want something in return, if not cash then at least a favour.

'I should have something in a couple of days.'

I made sure I took one of his newsletters when I left.

Chapter Eleven

At this point I started to make some mistakes.

The first was not to tell Hao at once everything that I'd learnt, even if it meant breaking my promise to Quang, and to Eric. I was thinking of doing just that, when she herself rang, and her news pushed mine aside. She'd been on the phone to her office in Leeds, they had a crisis on, they'd asked her to go back urgently. She was booked to fly home that week-end.

'So soon?' I cried.

'I'm sorry.' Her voice softened. 'I did think about your offer, Paul. But it wouldn't have worked. You don't know me, you know nothing about me...'

'I know enough.'

'Really. It's better this way.'

I wanted to argue, but there was no point.

'What's going to happen with Eric?' I asked.

'I've just spoken with him. He's assured me everything's going to be alright. He's promised to stay out of trouble.'

'I hope so. You don't mind if I keep an eye on him after you've gone?'

'Of course not. But I've already put you to so much trouble – you've been so kind –'

Not kind enough, apparently. I asked about her flight, and she told me she was leaving on Saturday, but when I asked if I could see her before she became evasive. I didn't insist. It was clear she didn't want to see me. Feeling rather bitter, I decided I'd handle Eric alone.

That was my next mistake.

It was too late to do anything that night, and the next day I was busy at work, but the following evening I drove once again to Cabramatta. The restaurant was much quieter this time, Eric was serving alone, without Hong, but Vo Khanh was at his post beside the counter and he gave me a dirty look as I walked in. Feeling somewhat defiant I took a table and waited. After a while Eric came up to me, looking unhappy.

'What are you doing here?' he asked. 'Haven't you found out all you want?'

'It's alright, Eric,' I said. 'I just want to have a talk.'

'Well I don't want to talk to you. Sunday was enough, thank you.'

Hardly an auspicious beginning. But I pushed on.

'You know your aunt's going back to Britain this weekend?'

'She told me. Why, what's it to you?'

'What it is to me is that she was very worried about you just a week ago. She asked me to help you. And now she says everything's going to be fine. What have you been telling her, Eric?'

'Nothing! All I said is that I can look after myself. Why should you care anyway? Why do you keep barging into other people's affairs?'

He was getting agitated, his voice rising in irritation.

'Because I'm worried about you too. And because I don't think you're being honest with her. Did you tell her what you were doing at that farm?'

'That's none of your business.'

'Maybe not, but it's an important question, Eric. Did you? Or are you still hiding the truth from her?'

He said nothing, and I tried a softer approach.

'Look, I didn't come here to argue with you. But this is serious. What if something happens to you when she's gone? I'll do everything I can to help you, I promise, but it may not be enough. And this time she may not be able to come back. Then she'll be really worried.'

He stayed silent, his expression wooden. I had no way of telling if I was getting through.

All might have been well if Vo Khanh hadn't chosen that moment to butt in. But suddenly he appeared at Eric's side.

'You OK, Eric?' he asked. He had a rough, gravelly voice which went well with his looks. I stood up and held my hand out to him.

'Mr. Vo Khanh? I'm Paul Quinn. I'm a friend of Eric's aunt.'

He ignored my hand and I let it drop.

'We closing now,' he said.

'I know. I'm going. But first I think you should know that she is very worried about him.'

'I do not want to discuss. We closing now,' he repeated.

Close up he looked even more unpleasant. His eyes were bloodshot, whether from drink or tiredness I couldn't guess, and he had a sullen expression which boded no good. But it was too late to back out now.

'She's worried because of some of the people he's mixed up with. People I think you know. I'm trying to make sure he doesn't get into trouble because of them.'

'I do not know what you are talking about.'

'People who wear this!' I seized Eric's arm and pulled up his shirt sleeve. I was getting annoyed myself and heard my voice getting too loud. 'People who go to secret training camps in the hills and play with guns. People who talk big about fighting the communists but are better at organising violent demonstrations in Australia.'

His face became ugly.

'I not speak with you, Mr Quinn! Go away! We are closing now.'

'I'll go in a minute. But first hear me out.'

'Mr Quinn, this not your business! Eric is big boy now. He decide who his friends are. He don't need you to tell him. Go away!'

'Mr Khanh, I'm not interested in your Vietnamese affairs. If you want to fight the communists and reconquer Vietnam go ahead! If you can! But don't try to use Eric to do it. If you don't leave him alone I will tell the police.'

'Police have nothing to say! I not break the law. Eric a free man. This not Vietnam, and you are not big white man telling us what to do! Go away!'

He glared at me, his colour darkening with anger. He was almost a head shorter than me and running to fat, but stocky and still muscular, and he gave an impression of barely contained violence. He moved closer to me, rolling on his feet like a street-fighter, and I stepped back. I had no wish to tangle with a mad buffalo on his own premises.

'I'm leaving now, Mr Khanh, but I'll be back. If you don't leave Eric out of your activities I promise you I won't give you a moment's peace.' I turned to Eric.

'Eric, I'm sorry it's come to this. I think you're headed for big trouble if you continue to associate with people like him. And I'm not going to stop until I've made sure you're safe. I promised your aunt, and I'll keep that promise. I'll see you again soon.'

Chapter Twelve

Hardly a step in the right direction, I told myself angrily on the way home. All I'd achieved with that stupid confrontation had been to antagonise Eric further and make an enemy out of Vo Khanh.

But I had not a clue what to do next. The last thing I wanted was to go to the police. That would only mean dragging Eric into trouble, and that was precisely what I wanted to avoid.

I decided to go and see Mr Bach. That was my next mistake.

In fairness it didn't seem like a bad move at the time. It was on the Wednesday morning, three days before Hao was due to leave, and I hadn't yet heard from Quang. I didn't want to leave any stone unturned in my attempt to rescue Eric before she left. What I'd overlooked was that some stones are better not turned.

I rang him first thing the next morning. The White Tiger company was listed in the phone book. He wasn't keen to see me at first, but I pushed, saying that if he didn't I'd have no alternative but to go to the police. Whether that did the trick, he agreed to see me that morning. I went there at once, taking time off from work.

Mr Bach received me politely. His office was on the third floor of the building at the back of the carpark. It was little more than a cubicle, at the end of a long room which seemed to serve as a kind of clearing office, but Asian businessmen don't always flaunt their wealth. Three young people were working there, all Vietnamese, two girls and a hard-looking man with a pock-marked face, answering the phones which kept ringing.

The young man led me to Bach. He was an elderly, dignified gentleman, short and a little stout, with steel-grey hair carefully brushed back and knobby cheekbones like little apples. He looked like a well-dressed garden gnome. He offered me a seat and a cup of green tea and asked me what the problem was. He had a dry, nasal voice and spoke good English, with an accent.

'It's about Eric Tran,' I started. 'A young man you helped get a job in Mr Vo Khanh's restaurant.' I gave him the story of Eric's life, up to the time of his arrival in Australia. Mr Bach listened calmly, nodding from time to time.

'As a result of these personal tragedies Eric has become a little unsettled. He's come to Australia in search of his father's memory, and he blames the communists for the death of both his parents. He is a highly personable and intelligent young man, but I think he is also impressionable and emotionally vulnerable.'

'What has now happened is that Eric has fallen in with a group of young Vietnamese who are strongly anti-communist.'

I told him what I knew of the Mad Buffaloes, and Vo Khanh's involvement. I tried to do it in such a way as to minimise what Eric had told me.

'My concern is that Eric is coming increasingly under their influence. I'm afraid that if he stays with them he may be drawn into activities which are against the law in this country.'

'My reason for coming to see you is simply this: you know Eric personally, and you recommended him to Mr Vo Khanh. From this I assume you are well acquainted with Mr Khanh and that he regards you with respect. I have come to ask you to use what influence you have over Mr Khanh, and over Eric, to ensure that Eric is not drawn into those activities and severs his relations with that group.'

I felt like a lawyer trying to defend his client in a hostile court. There was something of the judge about Mr Bach, an icy detachment. His eyes were upon me, unblinking, and although he didn't comment while I spoke I was sure he'd absorbed every word.

'What you have told me is very interesting, Mr Quinn,' he said at last. 'I did not know all these details about the young man. All I knew was that he had a Vietnamese mother, and seemed very interested in Vietnam. May I ask what your interest is in all this, Mr Quinn? Are you a friend of Eric's?'

I explained my involvement, and gave him something of my own background.

'It's not his fight, Mr Bach. Whatever Mr Khanh and his group have against the present government in Vietnam, Eric should not be drawn into it. That's why I'm here. I like him, I think there is a lot of potential in him, I'm very happy to see that he's interested in both Vietnam and Australia, but I do not believe that his present associates are doing him any good. That is why I have come to you. His aunt is about to go back to Britain, and both she and I would like to see this question settled before then.'

Once again he paused before answering, as if judiciously weighing up the options.

'Unfortunately the problem isn't so simple, Mr Quinn,' he said. 'Eric Tran is a free person, he is I believe over nineteen, which makes him a legal adult. And so of course is Mr Vo Khanh. Personally I am not involved in Mr Khanh's activities, but I understand his feelings, and those of his friends. They suffered enormously from the communists, Mr Quinn, and while I do not approve of violence, I cannot blame them for wanting to express their feelings against the present government there. I regret that I do not think I can help you. I will speak to Mr Khanh of course, and tell him of our discussion. I will also try to speak to Eric. But I've talked with Mr Khanh, and from what he tells me you yourself have no influence over Eric. If anything your own behaviour last night has destroyed any standing you might have with him. I will speak with them both, but I cannot guarantee the outcome. And my advice to you, Mr Quinn, is to stay out of Vietnamese affairs. Vietnam has already suffered far too much from foreign intervention in the past, starting with the French, and Vietnamese should be left to sort out their problems among themselves. It is very arrogant of others to want to do it for them.'

There was no doubt that much of what he said was correct, but the icy tone in which he said it, and the note of contempt for anyone who wasn't Vietnamese, including myself, made me angry. If he was so concerned with being Vietnamese, what was he doing here in Australia?

'Eric is only half Vietnamese,' I pointed out. 'He is also half Australian. And he belongs to a new generation. He shouldn't be drawn into the conflicts of the past.'

'That is for him to decide, ultimately. We are all children of our past, Mr Quinn, whether we like it or not. As I said, I will speak with him. But I cannot go beyond that, Mr Quinn. And I suggest that you yourself should refrain from trying to make him do something he clearly does not want.'

That made me even angrier. Who the hell was he to take the high moral tone? He still looked outwardly the dignified elderly gentleman, the Asian wise man, but there was something a little devious about him which I didn't like. I doubted that he would do anything very effective, and knew that my mission had failed.

Chapter Thirteen

It was after one when I got back to the office. Work had piled up in my absence, and Vivien was beginning to fret at my lack of attention. But I kept going over that meeting in my mind. It was clear that I would have to see Eric again, no matter what Bach had said, to make at least one more attempt at convincing him. First I needed to hear from Quang. I knew I should ring Hao, but I thought I'd better wait until I knew a bit more. She'd only think I was using it as an excuse to keep on seeing her.

At five Quang rang me. He said he had something, 'on that matter we discussed', and asked if I could come round that evening.

'Quang,' I said, 'can I bring someone with me this time? It's the mother of the young man I mentioned. I'd like you to talk to her directly.'

He sounded hesitant, and I went on.

'She's totally reliable. She's the one who first approached me. I'm sure you'll enjoy meeting her. Jack and Sen got on well with her.'

'Alright. But please don't tell her anything about me until I've had a chance to see her.'

We made a date for seven.

Unfortunately Hao proved much harder to convince. She was home when I rang, and she listened to me, but she clearly didn't want to change her mind.

'I can't come, Paul. And besides, Eric has told me about last night. You shouldn't have done that! It's not helping him at all.'

'But Hao, you don't know what's involved –'

'Please, Paul! I know you're trying to help, but it's not necessary. I trust Eric.'

'Alright! But this man's going out of his way to find out about Eric's friends, and I think you should know about it. Whatever Eric says. Can I see you tomorrow, or Friday?'

'Paul – please – I told you – it won't change anything –'

'At least tell me when your flight is. So I can come to see you off.'

'There's no need –'

'I'll find out from the airport anyway. There can't be that many flights to London. Please, Hao. I need to see you again, at least one last time before you fly out of this place.'

'Alright –' She gave me the details. Did I imagine it? There seemed to be the ghost of a smile in her voice. 'I'll see if I'm free–'

I felt crestfallen as I made my lame excuses to Quang.

'Did you give her my name?' he asked again anxiously.

'No, Quang, don't worry. All she knows is you're a friend of Jack's.'

Reassured, he told me what he'd learnt: there was indeed a group, calling itself the Mad Buffaloes, and Khanh seemed to be their leader, with a younger man called Binh. It was small, probably no more than a dozen, secretive, and fiercely anti-communist. Quang's informant hadn't been able to find out a great deal, but they held regular meetings, in Cabramatta and Fairfield, where they discussed politics – a kind of indoctrination session.

'I'm told my name is occasionally mentioned,' he added wryly.

He also confirmed that they had a kind of training camp on a farm north-west of Sydney, where they did military-style training, with firearms. He didn't know who owned it. Binh seemed to be in charge, though Vo Khanh sometimes attended.

'It does sound as if my young man is getting involved in some pretty strong stuff,' I said.

'You should get him away from them as soon as possible.'

Quang sucked his teeth a bit when I told him what I'd done. He was too polite to tell me to my face, but I could see he thought I'd made a mistake by going to see Bach. I had to assure him I hadn't mentioned his name, or revealed that I knew much about the group.

'There's something I don't entirely trust about Mr Bach. Have you been able to find out much about him, Quang?'

'Not a lot yet,' he said, but what he'd learnt was interesting. Bach was certainly a successful businessman, with a hand in several businesses besides his Bach Ho Import-Export Company, and he also owned some real estate – including the building where the Dai

Nam restaurant was located. He'd also been back to Vietnam on business, though as Quang remarked that wasn't unusual these days. Nghiem had told me the same thing.

According to Quang's source, Bach had helped Vo Khanh finance his business. It could be that Vo Khanh in fact was just a front man.

'That wasn't the impression he tried to give me today,' I said.

'No. But here's something else.'

According to his source, Vo Khanh wasn't the only person involved in the Mad Buffaloes. It seemed there was someone else, someone senior to him. Someone they called *Bác*, `uncle', like *Bác* Ho, the way they used to call Ho Chi Minh.

'Whether it's Bach or not I don't know, but it would make sense, don't you think? Vo Khanh's very brave no doubt, but I don't think he's got the brains or the patience to organise something like the Mad Buffaloes by himself. So there could well be someone else behind him. And running an organisation like that takes money. That farm, weapons…It would be amusing, wouldn't it, Mr Paul? From *Bác* Ho to Bach Ho.'

He chuckled at his own pun, all excited at the idea of uncovering a plot. Vietnamese are born conspiracy theorists.

'Why would he want to be involved with the Mad Buffaloes, if he's trading with Vietnam?' I asked.

'Who knows? He may have strong convictions of his own, that he doesn't want to show in public. That could explain why he keeps his distance. He wouldn't want to hurt his image with the communists, if he's doing business with them. I'll try and find out more about him. What he did in Vietnam before coming out.'

He reflected for a moment in silence.

'Meanwhile what worries me is what they may do during Loc's visit. You remember the man I mentioned to you?'

'Yes, the one you worked for in Saigon. But that's to be expected, isn't it?'

'Certainly. Whenever there's an official visit from Hanoi you get a demonstration. But this one looks like it could be rather big, and it could turn violent. Can you get some details from that young friend of yours, Paul? I really think I ought to warn Loc.'

'Can't his embassy do that?

'Yes, but he's more likely to listen to me, if I can get a message to him.'

'Well, I'll try,' I said, not very hopefully. 'When's Loc due out?'

'I'm not sure. It looks like early May.'

He smiled. 'My source also told me the Mad Buffaloes recently recruited a young Eurasian who works in Vo Khanh's restaurant. That wouldn't be your young man, would it?'

'You're too sharp, Quang.' It was time to come clean. 'You're right. But if I tell you about him, it has to be in the strictest confidence. I don't want him hurt in any way.'

He nodded, and listened in grave silence as I gave him Eric's background.

'Unfortunately,' I went on, 'he won't listen to me. I can't get it into his head that I want to help him, and that he's heading for trouble. And his aunt goes back to Britain this week-end, and after that I may lose all contact with him. But I'll try and see him again tomorrow. I'll let you know how I get on.'

Chapter Fourteen

This time I was really worried. If Quang's source was correct, then not only was Eric keeping bad company, but I very much doubted that Bach would do anything to save him. It was time to bring Hao into the picture. But when I rang the next day all I got was one of the cousins telling me in a rusty voice: 'She not home'. Time was running out. I couldn't wait any longer, and decided to go and see Eric again, even if she took me to task for it afterwards. It was getting too late for niceties.

That was my final mistake.

Once again that evening I went back to the restaurant in Cabramatta. They had more customers this time, Eric was there, with Hong, and so was Vo Khanh, standing at his usual place near the counter. Hong gave me a smile and Eric another nervous look, but Vo Khanh quickly barred my way.

'Go away!' he said angrily. 'Why you come back? We not want you here!'

'I've come to see Eric, not you!' I said rudely. I was tired of his overbearing ways.

'Why you bother him like this? He not want you! Leave us alone!'

'You leave Eric alone, and I'll leave you alone! I told your friend Mr Bach yesterday, and I'm telling you again. Your Vietnamese politics have nothing to do with Eric.'

People's heads were turning towards us, but I didn't care. I knew there was no risk of Vo Khanh calling the police.

'Why you go and see Mr Bach? Is none of your business!'

'I'm making it my business! Who are you trying to fool with your little games? *Tiểu Đoàn Trâu Điên*. Mad Buffaloes indeed! More like stupid buffaloes! *Tiểu Đoàn Trâu Ngu*!' My Vietnamese was coming back fast. 'You lost the war twenty years ago, Mr Khanh, do you think you can win it back now? So stop dragging him into your problems, and I'll leave you alone. But not until then!'

He was quivering with fury, but I was past caring myself.

'I'll see you outside, Eric, when you've finished. I'll wait in my car.'

I waited an hour for Eric to come out. I had parked up the street this time, close to the restaurant. I was afraid he might duck out the back way, but in due course he emerged. He walked along through the pedestrian mall but I drove round and caught up with him on the other side. I slowed down beside him.

'Go away!' he cried, and I heard the anguish in his voice. 'You heard him. Why are you harassing me?'

'We need to talk, Eric,' I said. 'Come on. I'll drive you home. Then I'll leave you alone.'

I leaned over and pushed the door open and he grudgingly got in.

'Why do you keep pestering me like this?' he said as I drove off.

'Because you don't know what you're getting into, Eric.' I tried a more reasonable tone. 'That man's a thug, and you're letting yourself get dragged into something which has nothing to do with you. Let him fight his little wars if he wants, but why should you waste your time on him and his group?'

'They're my friends! They've looked after me.'

'So what? You're working for him, aren't you? You're earning your pay? You don't owe him anything else! All that talk of fighting the communists is outdated, Eric. It's prehistoric!'

'You have no right to tell me how to live my life!'

'Somebody has to, when you make that kind of mistake. Your father's dead, and so's your uncle and at least one of your grandfathers. Whether you like it or not I'm probably the nearest thing to a male relative you have in this country.'

'You're only doing it to get close to my aunt! Why did you ask her to come and live with you? That really upset her!'

As I'd guessed. Why did she have to tell him? I really must have got under her skin.

'Look, I only suggested it so she'd be able to stay longer. She couldn't stay with the cousins forever!' I took a breath. 'And besides, what's wrong if I am attracted to her? She's a very attractive woman! Don't tell me you object to that!'

He said nothing. For the first time it struck me that he might be a little jealous.

'In the meantime I think you're heading straight into trouble with that gang of yours.'

'You don't know about the communists! They killed my father. They killed my grandfather! My mother died because of them! Don't preach to me about forgiveness!'

We'd reached his house. I pulled up outside, and tried one more time.

'Look, Eric,' I said more gently. 'I understand. But not this way! They're not all like that. And you can't solve the past with more violence. You'll only end up destroying yourself.'

'They're not thugs! They're my friends, and they've done more for me than you'll ever do! Stop pestering me like this! And stop pestering my aunt too. I know what you want! You just want to fuck her! Well go fuck yourself! She doesn't want you, and I don't want you! So piss off!'

He got out of the car, slamming the door behind him. The front door to the house opened and one of the young men looked out, attracted by the noise. With a sinking heart I watched Eric storm inside.

For an ex-spy who was supposed to be good at handling people I'd made a right mess of things: Eric, Vo Khanh, Mr Bach, even Hao on the personal front. Only Quang stood by me, and only his innate courtesy and the Vietnamese reluctance to make you lose face had stopped him from telling me straight out what a fool I'd been to go and see Bach.

I knew why I had, of course. I was getting my wires crossed, like David. I had no doubt now why he'd been in such a hurry to get back to Saigon. Hien had rung him that fateful morning, virtually asking him to come back that night. Hao had told me that on the way back from Jack Lipton's. Hien had been beside herself with guilt and anguish over it. It had taken all of Hao's tenderness and skill to make her see it wasn't her fault.

But that was what had led David to his death. He'd got his wires crossed, letting his heart rule his head.

And now here I was doing practically the same thing: in my anxiety to sort the problem out before Hao left – and in the process maybe win her back – I had let my heart take over my judgement, rush me into situations I should have avoided – and all I'd succeeded in doing was to drive her away.

I soon got my come-uppance. And in the process, an unexpected reprieve.

Chapter Fifteen

On Friday evening I stayed back at work. I still hadn't been able to reach Hao, and I was getting desperate. I knew I'd see her the next day at the airport, but I could hardly tell her what I'd learnt in a few words as she boarded the plane! Vivien had taken the afternoon off. After a week of functioning at half speed there was plenty for me to do. A couple of clients rang with last minute requests for the following week, and that kept me busy for an hour or so, ringing round our stable of part-timers, then I started on paperwork. There was nothing to tempt me to go home to my empty flat.

By nine o'clock I was ready to leave. The cleaners had gone, the building was quiet. I heard the whine of the lift, but took no notice. People often came back after hours. When it stopped at my floor I wondered who it could be. I wasn't expecting any visitors.

Then the outer door creaked open and I went out to investigate.

The first blow came at me from nowhere. I put my hands up, but a punch in the face sent me reeling, a kick in the guts doubled me over. Before I could react two pairs of hands had pinioned my arms while a third began to work me over.

The next few minutes passed in a savage blur of beating. I struggled as best I could, and tried to call for help, but they held me too tight, and there was no one to hear. I wriggled and twisted to dodge the worst of the blows – the one who was doing the punching slammed his fist on my skull and cried out in pain, but then he changed places and another took over. I lashed out with my feet but he moved in closer and began to beat a tattoo on my ribs, occasionally varying it with a punch to the head. Before long I was too groggy to know what I was doing. My lips were split open and my eyes began to close.

Tyger Tyger burning bright. What does a clever Tyger do when cornered? I'd been told that if you got caught in a fight and there was no way out, the best thing to do was pretend to pass out. This I did, and it worked, to the extent that they got tired of holding me up. Instead they let me fall to the floor and started to kick me. There was a swishing sound, a sudden lash of pain on my back. I curled up into a ball, tried to protect my head. The kicks kept coming, the chain lashing at my back. I heard myself scream. Something hurt in my side and my back was on fire. I tasted blood in my mouth.

The blows stopped. Vaguely I heard rummaging, the crash and thump of furniture thrown about, papers flying. A chair fell on me.

'Stay away from us! Bastard! Fuck! Next time we kill you!'

A few more kicks, a sharp stab of pain in the ribs. I cried out again. Then silence.

Clever little Tyger, curled up on the floor, feeling sorry for himself.

When I came to I couldn't move at first. I lay panting on the carpet, feeling its rough texture under my hands. One of them felt as if it might be broken. My mouth had stopped bleeding but I ached everywhere and my back felt on fire. I rolled over, and the chair which had been lying on me fell off with a clatter. Painfully I sat up. My eyes had puffed up, all I could see were two slits of light, and there was a thumping in my head.

Later I pulled myself up, bending over to ease the pain in my side. I was cold and my legs were starting to seize up. I fumbled my way to the wall and switched on the light. The room was a shambles, and my office next door wasn't much better. Everything that could be moved had been upended, the filing cabinet lay on its side, the records I'd spent the afternoon sorting out lay strewn about on the floor. Even the screen of Viv's PC had been smashed in. Only the pot plant on the window-sill had been spared, but the jug had been thrown at the wall and water had soaked into the carpet.

I tried to go to the washroom outside but had to sit down again. There was no way I could make it home on my own. I thought of who I could ring: Vivien, Quang, or Hao? There was only one person I wanted to see.

Dimly I groped for the phone with my good hand. The plug had been ripped from its socket and it took another bout of groping to put it back in. By some miracle it still worked. I rang her number. After ringing it all day it was burnt into my brain. After a long while one of the cousins answered. He sounded displeased.

'Who that? What you want?'

'Hao,' I managed to say, between a gargle and a croak. My mouth was swollen, I had difficulty moving my lips. 'Please. I must speak with Hao. Mrs Tran. Urgent. It's Paul Quinn. Very urgent.'

'She in bed. Already late. She leave tomorrow.' He sounded angry. I had no idea of the time.

'Please. I must speak with her. Emergency.'

Oh God, I thought. Let her answer, let her come to the phone, let her not be too angry with me for waking her up on her last night here. I need you, Hao.

'Wait!'

I waited, for what seemed an age. Finally she came to the phone.

'Paul? Is that you?' Her voice was cold and distant. 'Do you know what time it is?'

'Sorry. Can't tell,' I mumbled. My watch was broken, the hands stuck on nine.

'It's after ten! What do you want? You really shouldn't have gone to see Eric last night! I've spent all day calming him down.'

'Explain later. I need help.'

I felt myself slipping.

'Are you drunk?' I heard the disbelief in her voice.

'No! Not drunk! Hurt. I need your help, Hao! Please! No choice. I can't move.'

Something in my voice must have got through. She was silent for a second or two, then when she spoke again it was in a different tone.

'Where are you?'

'My office. Can you come? Please? Just you. No one else. Take a taxi. I'll pay.'

She was a practical woman. When she realised I couldn't talk much she asked no more questions, simply said she'd come at once. I had to stop her before she set off, to give her the code to the street door downstairs, so she could get into the building.

While waiting I tried to clean up the mess. I managed to close the venetian blinds – I didn't want curious looks from across the street the next morning – but moving about was too painful, and after righting a couple of chairs I turned the lights out and sat down again on the floor. I wanted to sleep. But I forced myself to think.

There had been three of them. Three dark shapes, their faces covered in scarves or handkerchiefs, dimly glimpsed in Vivien's darkened office before they pounced on me. I wouldn't be able to identify them, but I knew by their shape and their way of walking that they were Vietnamese, and the accent in those words had left no doubt. Perhaps one of the young men at Eric's house had been among them. They must have come in earlier, before the front door was locked, and waited on one of the floors, or in the toilet.

I also knew that none of them had been Eric, and was grateful for that small mercy. I was getting tired of him and his problems, but that would have been too much to take.

I dozed off a little, thinking of Rachel, and when she was next due up on her holidays. That helped take my mind off the pain. The lift brought me back to the present. A moment later Hao stepped into the room. She fumbled round until she found the switch. Then she caught her breath and stood still.

'My God! Paul! What on earth –'

'Sorry for the mess,' I said, and managed a lopsided smile. I had to tilt my head back to see her. She had dressed hurriedly, in dark slacks and sweater and plain shoes, her hair pulled back in a pony-tail. She wore no make-up and her face was pale and strained. She looked like a million dollars.

She knelt on the floor and took my hand in hers. I flinched and she saw the state it was in.

'Who did this to you? Was it Eric?'

'No. Not Eric. Tell you later. Can you help me get home?'

'You need a doctor! You need to go to a hospital. Let me call an ambulance.'

'No. No doctor. No ambulance. Just take me home. I'll be alright.'

'But you can't –' It took a while to dissuade her. 'Please. For Eric. No hospital. No police. Can you drive?'

'Yes. I have a car in Leeds.'

'Ring Quang. The man I told you about. Number in my coat pocket. He'll know what to do.'

She looked round at the mess, dismay and incredulity on her face.

'Paul, I'm so sorry about this.'

'Dear sweet Hao. I don't think I could have made it to the airport tomorrow.'

I felt absurdly happy.

Chapter Sixteen

The rest of the night went by like a bad dream. I was too stiff to move and Hao had to help me down to the basement car park, and at the other end practically carry me up the stairs to the flat. She led me straight to bed and made me lie down on my side. She put a blanket tenderly over me and went out to ring Quang.

'He's coming,' she said. 'He's bringing someone.'

In an awful parody of some secret dream she helped me undress. She hissed quietly when she saw the state of my back, but she set about cleaning it and applying antiseptic with calm efficiency. People who had survived refugee boats had seen worse. She gave me painkillers from the bathroom cabinet and I dozed off.

Later there was Quang, looking down at me with concern in his eyes.

'I told you these people were rough,' he said with a wan smile.

'I didn't expect them to be quite so rough,' I mumbled. My face was too stiff to smile back. He too wanted me to go to hospital, but understood when I refused.

'Because of that young man?'

'It wasn't him who did this. But I don't want him involved. If the police come in he'll only get into trouble.'

Quang's friend was an elderly Vietnamese with a shock of white hair on a large round head, who smiled at me and looked me over. He took my pulse, shone a light into my eyes, gave me a couple of injections. He carefully explored my hand, my back and my rib-cage. He had gentle hands, and I went to sleep before he'd finished.

When I woke up again it was broad daylight and Hao was dozing in an armchair near the bed. My chest was strapped up and my right hand in a splint, and my head felt full of cotton wool. I made a sound and she looked at me in alarm.

'You'll miss your plane,' I said. I had no idea of the time.

'I've already missed it.'

'Oh God! I'm sorry. I didn't mean to be such a nuisance.'

'It was my fault. I should have listened to you.'

'What are you going to do? What about your job?'

'I rang them. I used your phone, I hope you don't mind. They said they'll keep it open. But I don't really care. I can find another.'

She wore the same clothes as the night before. Even in my doped up state I could see she was exhausted.

'Can I take up your offer?'

'My offer?'

'Stay here for a few days, until you get better?'

As if I'd say no.

She fed me more tablets and I drifted back to sleep, to be woken again when Quang returned with his friend. Quang also looked as if he hadn't slept much, but his friend smiled when he saw I was awake. I took a closer look at him. He was a short, sturdy man in his early sixties, with the lined face of someone who had seen a lot of hardship, but a patient, understanding look in his eyes. His English was barely comprehensible and Quang had to interpret.

'He doesn't think your hand is broken – just badly bruised. And your ribs should be alright if you lie still for a few days. It's probably just a bruise, or at worst a cracked rib. But if it doesn't improve you should go to a hospital.'

'Then I'll just have to get better, won't I,' I said, more bravely than I felt.

The friend shone his torch again into my eyes, took my pulse, made me count his fingers.

'How's your head?'

'Sore. And I get headaches.'

'You'll have to stay in bed for a few days anyway. In case you have concussion.'

'What about my office? I need to ring my assistant –'

'I'll do that,' Hao said. 'You just rest. *Anh* Quang, we shouldn't tire him too much.'

'Don't worry, *Em*, I won't let him get tired.'

Anh Quang, she had called him, Big Brother Quang, and *Em*, he had replied, Little Sister. Quang gave me a roguish smile.

'You didn't tell me she was your friend.'

'Do you know her?'

'I knew her family in Saigon. I met her father a few times. A good man, if a little impractical. I was sorry when he died.'

'And her husband? Did you know him?'

He gave me a bland look. 'Yes. I knew him too. You're in good hands with her, Mr Paul. I can see now why you're so concerned about her nephew.'

It seemed I was in good hands with his friend too. According to Quang he'd been one of the best army surgeons in Vietnam in his day. And he knew the communists too – six years in the camps, before they let him out. He wasn't allowed to practise in Australia. His English was too poor, and he couldn't be bothered requalifying. 'So please don't tell anyone. He only came because I insisted.'

Quang sat down. 'I can't stay long. But this is serious, Paul. It's the first time they've attacked a non-Vietnamese. Are you sure you don't want to go to the police?'

'Absolutely. But now I really want to find out more about them. When's that friend of yours coming out? The politician from Vietnam?'

'Loc? Soon. I haven't tried to contact him yet. I want to find out more about what they're planning. There's something I don't like about all this, Paul. Vo Khanh, and Ho Xuan Bach. Something doesn't feel right.'

'Be careful. You've seen what they did to me.'

I was exhausted when he left. Hao stuck her head in briefly, asked if she could borrow the car.

'Of course. But I need to see Eric.'

'I've rung him. He'll be here later. You need more rest first.'

Eric came late that afternoon. I heard Hao's voice sharp in the sitting room, and then she came in, looking angry.

'Eric's here,' she said. 'Are you fit enough to see him?'

'Yes. But Hao – it might be best if I talk to him alone.'

She looked about to argue, then nodded and walked out. Eric came in, looking chastened and uncomfortable. I guessed she'd given him a good talking to.

'It was your friends who did this, wasn't it?' He nodded glumly. 'I thought I recognised one of them. The young man at your place, who had a tattoo on his arm.'

'I didn't mean this to happen. I'm sorry.'

'Are you?'

'Yes. I never thought they'd go so far. I told them you were bothering me, asking questions about the Mad Buffaloes, going round to the restaurant, and they said they'd fix it, they'd scare you off – but they didn't tell me they were going to beat you up like this.'

'Well, now you know what kind of people they are.'

'My aunt said you don't want to go to the police.'

'That's right.'

'Why not?'

'Because I don't want to get you into trouble. You've already been questioned once, if the police bring you in again on something like this they may well try to cancel your visa and have you sent back to Britain, and I don't want that to happen. But they have to be stopped.'

He stared down at me. I couldn't tell what he was thinking, except that he didn't seem to be enjoying it.

'For that I need your help.'

'How?'

'By telling me everything you know about them.'

He didn't say anything, looking down at me with his dark serious eyes. I let him stew in his silence for a while.

'Come on,' I said. 'Sit down, and let's talk about this.'

He pulled up a chair and sat next to the bed, still looking glum.

'You're asking me to rat on my friends,' he said. 'I know what they did was wrong, but you're asking me to betray my friends.'

'It's not your friends I'm worried about. It's the people behind them. People like Vo Khanh, and Mr Bach. Think about it, Eric. I'm not trying to get your friends into trouble. But if this is what they do to someone who simply asks questions, what will they do to their real enemies? Next time someone could get killed. And it could be someone like your aunt. So I want you to tell me all about them. Who they are, and what they're up to. And I don't want you to tell them. Do you think you can do that?'

Still he didn't answer, and I used my trump card.

'It's not an easy thing to do, Eric. It takes courage, and a sense of what's right and wrong. Your father had courage, and so did your mother, and I know they'd be saying the same thing to you. So go away and think about it. And come back when you're ready. And Eric?'

'Yes?'

'Let's keep your aunt out of it. This is just between us.'

He nodded, and left soon after, still looking sombre. Hao came back.

'What have you said to him?' she asked. 'I've never seen him so grim.'

'We've just had a good talk. Can you pass me the phone? I need to ring Viv. Otherwise she won't know what's hit her when she walks in on Monday.'

'I've already rung her. We've been round and cleaned up the mess.'

'You went to the office?'

'I didn't think it was fair to leave it to her. She wanted to come and see you but I told her you were still under sedation. She's coming by this evening.'

'You're a bit of a wonder,' I said. 'I can see why they want you back in Leeds.'

Chapter Seventeen

By Tuesday I was starting to get about. I wanted to be back on my feet before then but Hao and my personal physician both insisted I needed more rest, and practically forced me to stay in bed – and later sit fretfully in an armchair – while Hao cosseted me and people dropped in with expressions of concern: Vivien of course, several times, to report on progress at work, Cathy down from the Hunter Valley as soon as Vivien had rung her, Jack Lipton and Sen, alerted by Hao, the people next door. Vivien had also phoned Rachel, who rang back at once. She had tests on that week, but she said she'd be up on the Friday.

'Dad, who was that who answered the phone?'

'That? Oh. Just a friend, who's helping to look after me. Maybe she'll still be here when you come.'

'She sounded foreign.'

I'd have some explaining to do.

To each of them I gave the same story: a random attack in the street, by some yobs who had objected when I'd tried to stop them breaking into my car. Only Vivien knew the real story, and not much of that either: that it was the work of some Vietnamese thugs, angry that I'd been sticking my nose into their private affairs. She had agreed to keep quiet, for fear of getting Hao's nephew into trouble – I assured her he wasn't involved – but she was shocked and outraged by what she saw as an affront to civilisation. Not everyone would have been so understanding.

Even with Hao I was economical with the truth. She knew of course that it was members of Eric's group who had attacked me, and she was very angry with him – he had the sense to lie low most of that week – but she accepted my explanation that it wasn't his fault; and while she knew by now that Quang was conducting his own investigation into their activities, and I'd told her about the farm, I'd made no mention of Loc, nor of firearms, nor of my request to Eric. There'd be time for that when I knew more myself. I saw no point in alarming her unduly.

Our relationship was slowly changing. From patient to nurse, to something more like friendship, and perhaps deeper still. We didn't talk about it, but I sensed she was aware of it too. When she looked at me sometimes I thought I detected a softness in her eyes. At other times she seemed to be quietly assessing me, as if she had yet to reach a decision. I kept my distance. It was a long time since I'd shared my living quarters with a woman, other than Rachel when she came to visit, and as I started to mend I felt once again that familiar stirring in the blood. But this time I wasn't going to rush things. I'd already spooked her once, I didn't want to lose her a second time, however tenuous the link still between us.

Meanwhile at the office things were happening. On Sunday Hao had gone back with Viv – they had become allies - and together they had repaired as much of the damage as they could. Apart from tossing everything upside down my assailants had done little lasting damage. By Monday things were almost back to normal. Vivien rang to reassure me and told me what they'd done. She regarded Hao with something like awe.

'She's coming back later today. Would you mind if she helped with the interviewing? We're having a lot of responses to Saturday's ads.'

'Has she done this sort of thing before?'

'No, but she's very good, Paul. She's much more than a secretary. She runs the whole office for them, back in Leeds. I'm sure she'll be alright.'

'Oh alright,' I grumbled. I was in no shape to argue.

Later Viv reported. 'She did those interviews marvellously,' she enthused. 'Much better than I could. She's a real treasure, Paul, I'll be sorry when she's gone.'

So will I, I thought, not wanting to think that far ahead.

On Wednesday Quang came back, without his friend the unlicensed doctor. Loc was due in the first week in May, and large-scale demonstrations were being organised in both Sydney and Canberra.

'By the Mad Buffaloes?'

'Not just them, the whole community. But they're involved alright, they're right in the thick of it. They really are barking up the wrong tree, you know. They should be supporting him, not attacking him. If anybody's got a chance of changing things in Vietnam it's him, and people like him. But they're blinded by their hatred and their resentment.'

'You like him, don't you,' I said.

'Well, he's such an unusual man, for a communist. Did I tell you that he lost most of his family in the war? He was badly wounded himself once, in a B-52 raid. But he bears no bitterness, he doesn't hate the Americans. He saw it as an inevitable part of the struggle. I remember him telling me, it's all history now, we won, that's what matters, now and the future. It's up to us to make it work. If he'd had his way there would have been far less of all this re-education.'

He was getting carried away again.

About the Mad Buffaloes there wasn't much to add. Vo Khanh was just what he appeared to be, an unreconstructed hot-head.

'It's Ho Xuan Bach I'm worried about,' he said. 'I'm pretty certain now that he's behind them. He's attended a couple of meetings, and one of his assistants is also involved, that man Binh I told you about. Have you heard anything from your young man?'

'Not yet. I had a good talk with him, and he seemed to take it seriously, but he hasn't come back to me.'

'Let me know when he does. I'd like to ask him some questions. Did you know that back in Vietnam Bach was doing good business with the communists, before he escaped? He got out in 1981, organised a large boat with all his family and friends, made it out to Pulau Bidong off the Malaysian coast, over two hundred and thirty in all. But before that he'd managed to stay in business, working with the army, it seems he even helped them prepare for the invasion of Cambodia in '79, he had a factory that made military equipment, tents and things like that. That's how business goes, deep down, they always follow the money. He must have managed to get a lot of money out, because as soon as he came to Australia he started up again in business, buying up real estate. He's very clever. But it's his role in the Mad Buffaloes I want to know more about. Let me know when you hear from the young man.'

That afternoon Eric rang me. Hao was out, we spoke freely.

'I can't do it,' he said. 'I know what they did was wrong, but I just can't.'

'Have you said anything to them?'

'Only that I'd come to see you. I said my aunt made me. I didn't tell them what we talked about, I just said they shouldn't have done it, they'd gone too far. They said they only wanted to frighten you, but you fought back and – things got out of hand. They said they didn't mean to hurt you like that.'

That wasn't the way it had felt.

'They said they won't bother you again. But I can't betray them, Mr Quinn – Paul. I hope you understand.'

There was an unusual note of apology in his voice, as if he really felt sorry for what had happened.

'Well, I hope you can still come round, at least while your aunt's here. My daughter's coming up, I'd like you to meet her.'

'I'd like that.'

Soon after there was another phone call. This one was for Hao, from her office in Leeds. She was still out and I offered to take a message.

'It's probably easier if I call again later.' A man's voice, English, managerial, a little bossy but otherwise pleasant, with that flat smooth tone which gives nothing away. 'Are you the friend she's been looking after? I understand you've had an accident.'

'That's right,' I said cautiously.

'How are you now? Getting better?'

'Improving slowly. Who shall I say called?'

A slight hesitation.

'Tell her it's George. She'll understand.'

'Will do. I'm Paul.'

'Thank you Paul. I hope you get well soon.'

I passed Hao the message as soon as she returned. She didn't say anything, and when George rang again that evening, at my suggestion she took the call in the study. It lasted a good half hour, When she came out she looked troubled and a little angry.

'Everything alright?' I asked.

'Yes,' she said shortly. 'It was just my office, They wanted to know when I'm getting back. I told them I didn't know yet.'

Going by her expression, I thought there must be more to it.

By chance Eric was there on the Friday when Rachel arrived, having caught an afternoon flight and a taxi from the airport. She gasped at the sight of my face, gave me a hug a little too tight for comfort, and looked enquiringly at Hao and Eric. I introduced them.

'Hao's been kind enough to look after me since my incident. You don't mind using the study? I've given her the second bedroom. Eric's just visiting.'

They smiled politely at each other and made the right noises, and then Hao withdrew, taking Eric with her. And the questions began.

'Who is she, Dad, and what's the connection? You've never mentioned her before.'

'She's just a friend, to coin a phrase. Someone I met a long time ago in Vietnam. No, don't go fantasizing, she was never my girl-friend, and Eric isn't my natural son. Things are exactly what they seem.' Liar, liar! 'She's visiting from Britain.'

She stared, clearly not believing me.

'Are you sleeping with her?' she asked with all the tact of a sixteen year old.

'In my condition? I have enough trouble sleeping on my own, thank you very much!'

'Well...you know Mum's remarrying.'

'You told me. Bernard, isn't it? What's he like?'

She told me. Balding, bear-like, and kind. Should make a good stepfather.

'What about you, Dad? Thinking of remarrying?'

'You're the second person who's asked me that in a fortnight. What's wrong with you women, can't you bear the sight of a man on his own?'

She saw through my bluff with the sharpness of a professional poker player.

'She'd be good for you.'

'Really? Maybe she has other ideas. And how would you cope with a Vietnamese step-mother?'

'In this day and age? Come on, Dad. Just because you sent me to an expensive girls' school. We're not all racists in the stockbroker belt.'

That evening we had a companionable meal together, cooked by Hao, with several Vietnamese dishes which Rachel certainly enjoyed, and their wariness slowly dissipated as they talked while doing the dishes. I expected more caution with Eric, and they took their time sniffing each other out: the rough-looking lad with the suspicious eyes, the cool-eyed red-head with the imperious tilt to her chin. I foresaw clashes and was pleased when they sat and talked on the balcony.

'Bit of alright, your daughter,' he muttered to me before she walked him to the bus stop.

'He's yummy,' she confided when she came back. 'Are you sure he's not my half-brother?'

'You'd like that, wouldn't you!'

Before the week-end was out she and Hao were talking like old friends, and when it came for her to leave she spontaneously gave Hao a hug. 'Thank you for looking after my Dad,' she said. 'He does some silly things at times, but he's the only one I have and I wouldn't want to lose him.'

Chapter Eighteen

On Sunday the weather turned nasty, cold squalls from the south whipping up the harbour and rattling the windows. Eric came round again but we stayed indoors, until late afternoon when I drove Rachel to the airport. I wasn't sure why he had come, to see his aunt or Rachel, and there was a worried look about him. When I asked what was the matter he shook his head. He spent much time talking with Rachel.

'He's nice,' she said again as she kissed me goodbye in the car. I was still too ugly to show my face in public. 'They're both nice. I hope she stays.' So did I, but I didn't hold much hope.

When I got back Eric was still there, and Hao made a strange request.

'Would you mind if I did a *cúng*?' she asked. 'For Hien. It's her birthday today, and I always do one for her.'

She explained. Pronounced 'coom', with a short 'oo', the way they say 'come' in Yorkshire (*coom 'ere loov*), a *cúng* is a votive feast for the dead, carried out at birthdays and anniversaries or other special occasions. I watched as she set the dining table up as a small altar. She had made odd purchases over the past two days, for which she wouldn't accept any money, and now their purpose became clear. On a table-cloth she set out a number of dishes and plates, all in threes: three plates of fruit, lychees, mangoes, and small sugar bananas, three dishes of food – caramel pork, a lacquered duck, and three salted duck's eggs, plus a dish of the sweet tapioca dessert called *chè*. 'That was her favourite dessert,' she said. In front of them she put three bowls of uncooked rice with three sets of chopsticks, and three small cups of green tea, with an empty glass in front of them.

She went into her bedroom, and reappeared in Vietnamese dress, the first time I'd seen her in it. It was a dark blue *áo dài*, the long, close-fitting tunic with long sleeves and a tight bodice which is worn, slit from the waist down, over long silken trousers – black in this instance, and black high-heeled sandals. The *áo dài* was embroidered with a design of twigs and blossoms. She looked exotic and delicate and very elegant, but she wasn't concerned with effect. Behind the display on the table she placed a small framed photo of a Vietnamese girl. The photo was cracked and not very clear but there was no doubt who it was.

'It's my only photo of her,' she said. 'I got it from my mother. We lost all we had on the boat. You don't mind, Paul? You're being very understanding.'

'It's the least I can do.'

'You can join in if you like.'

She had also bought a packet of joss-sticks, the long incense sticks which Vietnamese use at these ceremonies. She lit several, gave me three to hold, and three to Eric, and we stood side by side in front of this improvised altar, Eric in the middle, holding the incense sticks between our palms in the traditional attitude of prayer. We bowed three times, then put the incense sticks upright in the glass, where they continued to smoulder, shedding ash on the table-cloth. Eric and I stood back but Hao went down on her knees and did the three *lạy*, the three deep bows of prayer and humility, her hands on the carpet before her and touching the floor with her forehead. When she stood up her face was streaming with tears.

I put my arm around her shoulders. 'I'm sorry,' she said. 'I don't normally get so emotional. But there's something about this year – I don't know – something special, as if she's trying to tell me something...'

She dried her tears, Eric looking on awkwardly. He too seemed moved by it all, though no doubt felt it unmanly to show it. She went into her bedroom to change.

'Do you remember much of your mother?' I asked him.

'A little. It's all very vague. I'm not sure how much I remember and how much I make up.' He seemed lost in thought. 'Can I give you a ring during the week? I want to ask you something.'

'Why not now?'

'I...I need to think about it.'

Hao came back, in a loose jumper over a skirt. We helped her clear the table. She packed some of the food for Eric.

'Take that back with you,' she said.

Vietnamese are very practical with votive offerings to the dead: they don't throw them away, but after a decent interval to allow the dead to partake of them in spirit, they eat them. As they always choose the best quality for their *cúng*, this is a treat for the living as well.

After Eric left she sat next to me on the sofa. She looked very beautiful, even with no make-up, her hair held back with a ribbon and her face still pale and puffy. I touched her forehead. Her skin was warm, and she looked tired and sad. I thought guiltily that I'd imposed a great strain on her. She had not spared herself, working in the office and looking after me, and the weeks spent with the cousins couldn't have been easy either. I felt a surge of warmth. She sat with her legs tucked up beneath her, showing a bit of thigh, her knees like pale ivory.

I kissed her. Her lips were cool and unresponsive at first, then softened as she leaned into me. I caressed her face, her neck, let my hand wander to her knee. For a moment I thought she was going to respond – she moved her leg, as if to make it easier – then suddenly she pushed my hand away and went out of the room.

'I can't – I'm sorry –'

I looked after her with a sinking feeling. Not again, I thought dismally. Why did I always have to rush my fences? This time I wasn't going to let it end like that. I waited a moment, then got up and went after her. Her bedroom door was ajar. I knocked softly and looked in. She sat on the bed with her back to the wall, her knees drawn up to her chin and her head in her arms.

'Can I come in?' I asked gently. 'I won't do anything. I just want to talk.'

She nodded. I sat on the edge of the bed, careful not to touch her.

'I'm sorry,' I said. 'I didn't mean to frighten you, or upset you like that.'

She shook her head.

'It's alright. It's not your fault.'

'You probably think I'm a bit of a beast,' I went on awkwardly. 'Some kind of sex maniac who can't keep his hands to himself. Please don't think that. Of course I want to make love to you. You're one of the most attractive women I've ever known. But it's not just that, you know. There are so many other things I like about you. Your honesty, your kindness, your strength, your smile – I love you, Hao. The last thing I want to do is to make you unhappy.'

She shook her head, still not looking at me. 'You're one of the nicest persons I know.'

I sat in silence, not daring to believe what I'd heard.

'I mean it. You've been so good to me, and I've been unfair – I like being here with you –' She moved forward and rested her forehead on my shoulder.

'If I tell you something, will you promise not to tell anyone? Ever? Not Eric, or anyone else?' she said.

'Of course.'

'And will you promise not to hate me, or think badly of me?'

'How could I ever do that? What is it, Hao? Is it something to do with Hien? Something that happened on that boat?'

An idea had come into my head, an idea that sent a chill through me. She nodded and spoke, so low that I had to strain to hear her.

'Yes. I told you that she died at sea, in a storm. But she didn't die. Not then. There was no storm. She was kidnapped.'

'By pirates? Is that what happened? Your boat was attacked?'

'Yes.'

'Oh God! I am sorry!'

Haltingly, she told me the story. It was a story I'd heard so many times before, in the camps in Malaysia and Thailand, that nothing in it surprised me. Thai fishermen, turning their hand to piracy when easy prey came their way, or more vicious organised gangs ranging up and down the Gulf of Thailand, searching for refugee boats in distress, connected to each other by radio. RPM, we called it in our reports, compiling the routine statistics. Rape, Pillage and Murder. How many women raped, girls abducted, had anyone been killed...

This one was as bad as they came.

'It was our second day at sea. We'd had engine trouble, we'd drifted north, too far off course, up into the Gulf of Thailand. There were three boats. Thai. They came in the afternoon. First one, and then two others. They were well organised, they had radios, and loud hailers, and they had guns. We knew what they were, we all knew about pirates, but there was nothing we could do. One of the men on our boat had a gun, and wanted to shoot at them, to scare them off, but the others stopped him, they were afraid that the pirates would shoot us all – they came aboard. The men had made us hide, down in the hold, we wore old clothes, and we put grease

and dirt on our faces to make ourselves look ugly and old – but they
– they dragged us out, and – and –'

'You don't have to tell me.'

'I want to say it. I've never told anyone – only Khiem knew, and
the doctors – I want you to know. So that you can understand why
I'm – like this.'

I held her hand. There was nothing I could say.

'They took us on one of the boats – about eight of us. All the
young women. And they kept us there. All that night. There were
many – I don't know how many – men from the other boats as well
– they took turns at us –'

She stopped, and I waited, silently. She started again, more
calmly.

'I don't know how many times I was raped. Ten, fifteen times
maybe. I could hear Hien scream, and fighting back – and the others
– I was pregnant, and I started to bleed. I think that's why – why
they sent me back, the next morning, with one or two others, but
they kept Hien – and the others – and then they left – I could hear
Hien scream…'

'Some of the men tried to stop them. But they beat them up, very
badly. One man was killed. And then that afternoon, the afternoon
of the third day, we were rescued, and taken to Singapore. I was still
bleeding.'

'Did you ever find out what happened to her?'

'No. When we were rescued we tried to tell them, on the ship,
and in Singapore, we made reports, and talked to the UN, Khiem
went to the American embassy, the French, the British, the Thais.
And later, through the UNHCR[4], they tried with the Thai
authorities, but nobody ever found out what happened. We couldn't
even give them the boat numbers, they'd all been blacked over.'

I remembered a girl I'd interviewed once, in Songkhla in
southern Thailand, where I'd gone to visit a refugee camp. A
Vietnamese girl, eighteen or nineteen, who'd been abducted with
her two sisters off a boat. A very similar story. Thai fishermen, or
pirates. They'd kept her three days on board, alternately raping her
and her sisters and throwing them scraps of food, and then, when

---

[4] United Nations High Commission for Refugees

she started to weaken and looked as if she might die, had thrown her overboard. She'd survived by taking off her long trousers and using them to make a rough kind of float, tying the ends and filling them with air, and staying afloat. Later another Thai boat had picked her up and brought her to shore. Sometimes in all that savagery you got a small, inexplicable act of mercy. Perhaps, being Buddhist, they thought they could achieve some redemption that way.

What I remembered most about her – this was three weeks later, when I interviewed her in the presence of an older woman – was how angry she looked. She had survived physically the worst of her ordeal, apart from a bad case of sunburn, which gave her a comically angry look – and I thought, thank God she's tough. She'll survive. She's one of those who'll make it. One of the lucky ones. Like Hao, of her sisters she had no news, and wondered if they were still alive. What I remembered most about myself, on that occasion, was how ashamed I felt, simply at being a man.

Yet only now did I begin to understand something of what they'd gone through. Sometimes suffering is almost harder to look on than to endure. Once it's over, the victims – those who aren't dead – somehow learn to cope, better perhaps than some others, relatives or onlookers. But now I could see the ravage that that experience could inflict. Deep inside, where it didn't show, and you didn't talk about it. Except one day, much later, when some clumsy stranger made you relive it all.

'I think she's dead. I've been praying that she's dead. But I don't know.'

'I expect she is. If it's any consolation. So long after, if she were still alive you'd have known by now.'

'The UN tried, we even tried to go to Thailand ourselves, but the Thais wouldn't give us visas.'

'You'd know, she would have got a message out, one way or another, if she were still alive. I'm sure she's dead too.'

The alternative was almost too horrible to contemplate.

'That's why I can't have any children, Paul. I was four months pregnant. I had a miscarriage, and almost died. I was bleeding. There was no doctor on the ship but we had one with us, and he operated on me, in the sick bay. The ship took us straight to Singapore, but I had an infection, I had to go to hospital. They did a hysterectomy, they took my insides out. Khiem – Khiem was so upset, I thought he would go mad, but there was nothing he could do. They even killed a man, when he tried to save his daughter. They had the guns.'

'What happened to Eric? Did he see all this too?'

'No. They kept the children in the hold, while they – while they did those things. And some other people on the boat looked after him. On the boat and later in the camp, until I got better. We said his mother had fallen into the water, and drowned. Please put your arms around me, Paul, and hold me.'

I held her for a long time, as she wept softly. Tears had come to my eyes too, I wanted to howl, with rage and grief. After a while she lay down exhausted and went to sleep. I put a blanket over her, made sure she was comfortable, and went to my room.

During the night the storm intensified, became a gale, tearing at the windows and the balcony. I lay awake, thinking over what Hao had told me, unable to put those images out of my mind, occasionally getting up to check the windows. I put my ear to Hao's door, but couldn't hear anything.

I must have slept. A sound woke me, I looked towards the door and saw Hao there, a darker silhouette just visible in the darkness. I sat up, felt more than saw her come round to my bedside.

'I can't sleep. Paul, can I come in with you?'

I pushed the covers back and made room for her beside me. She wore a long T shirt and not much else. She was shivering.

'Just let me lie with you. Please. Don't do anything. I don't want to be alone.'

'You're not alone, Hao. Not with me here.'

We shifted awkwardly until we found the best position, on our right sides, her back towards me. I put my arm around her, felt the shivering gradually stop. I stroked her head. I wore my usual sleeping gear of old T shirt and gym shorts, and occasionally felt her legs brush against me. I pulled mine back as far as I could, not trusting my reactions. She stirred a little, gradually her breathing became more regular, she went to sleep. I stayed awake a long time. Towards dawn I fell asleep.

The phone ringing in the sitting room woke me. Hao had turned and lay heavy on my arm, her breath soft against my cheek. I freed myself cautiously and she stirred but didn't wake up. I felt an immense tenderness for her. I kissed her gently on the temple and hurried out to see who needed me at that hour of the morning.

It was Jack Lipton, and his voice was rough with anguish.

'Paul? Something dreadful's happened. It's Quang. He's been murdered.'

PART II

Need to know

Chapter Nineteen

The drive to Canberra didn't take very long any more. Once upon a time it was a real expedition, crawling along on the old single-lane highway at the speed of the slowest vehicle as it meandered through the hills and every little country town, you felt at times that a horse would get you there faster. But the road had been much improved in recent years, the curves straightened and the roadway widened and bypasses built around the towns, you could do it now in just on three hours if you were quick getting out of Sydney: two hours down the Hume freeway to Goulburn, two hundred kilometres to the southwest, then a swing to the left on the Federal Highway for the last stretch, past the small village of Collector and around the north-western corner of Lake George before snaking off into the hills that lead to the Australian Capital Territory. A fairly boring trip overall, Lake George itself the only interesting feature, a wide shallow depression between two ranges of low hills which some years looked like an inland sea, at others dried up completely to become a flat expanse of pasture.

There was water in it that year and somewhere along its western shore I stopped to rest and collect my thoughts. The weather was fine, there was little traffic, I had made good time on the highway, taking liberties with the speed limit until I got close to Goulburn: it was the site of the Police College and the cops were pretty vigilant there. Nearby a kestrel hovered in search of its prey, further back a flock of white sulphur-crested cockatoos and pink-and-grey galahs had risen and wheeled against the sun, the first time I'd seen those two birds fly together.

Any other time I would have enjoyed it greatly. I've always loved the dry inland country. But this time there was too much on my mind. It was twenty-four hours since Jack's phone call, and nothing since had brought any joy.

Our quarrel had started almost from the moment I hung up.

Jack's call had come as a terrible shock, though not a total surprise. Ever since my beating I'd known it couldn't end there. But I had never expected anything so brutal. Even Jack, tough old soldier that he was, had taken it hard. The police had called him in to interpret and go through Quang's papers and he'd formally identified the body.

'It must have happened in the early evening.' His voice quivered as he gave me what details he could. 'A neighbour found him last night. His door had been forced, and he'd been stabbed. It looks as if he put up a fight – there was blood everywhere, everything was upside down –'

'Do they have any idea who did this?' I asked.

'Not yet. But they'll be talking to anybody who knew him.' He paused, as if to weigh his words. 'Listen,' he said heavily. 'I shouldn't be telling you this. They found your name and address among his papers. They'll probably want to talk to you too. I didn't tell them I'd introduced you.'

'Thanks. I'll tell them what I can, of course, but I doubt that'll help very much. I hardly knew him.'

'Tell me this has nothing to do with what we talked about.'

'I don't see how it could,' I said, telling the first of several lies that day. 'I only asked him some questions. Don't worry about the connection. He knew Hao's family in Saigon, I can say that's how we met.'

Hao had come in on the tail end of our conversation, straight from bed, and she rushed into my arms when I told her the news. 'Oh no!' she cried. 'He was such a good man! Who could have done such a thing?'

'I don't know.' I'd known Quang for less than two weeks but I'd grown to like him a lot in that short time and I felt a great sense of loss. 'Listen. I need to speak to Eric.'

She looked at me in alarm.

'What? You don't think –'

'Of course not! But he may have heard something, through that group of his. And there are things I want to ask him.' Despite the shock my brain had started to function. 'Can you ring him, please? I don't want to call him myself, in case someone else answers the phone.'

'Paul, what is it? Is there something you haven't told me?'

'I'll explain. But first we need to get hold of him. There may not be much time. And for God's sake go and put some clothes on. What would Eric say if he saw us like this.'

I meant it half in jest, but my tone must have stung her. Her face coloured, a hurt look came into her eyes, before I could say anything she went into her room. When she reappeared she had changed into jeans and a dark sweater, with her hair pulled back from her face and a severe expression. By then I'd also thrown on a few clothes.

'Hao, I'm sorry –' I began, but she cut me off.

'You're hiding something, aren't you, Paul. About Eric and his group.'

I sighed and nodded.

'Yes. It's more serious than I said. But I promised Eric I wouldn't say anything without his permission, and I don't want to break that promise now. Wait until he gets here. Then you can ask him.'

'Why did you promise him? You knew I was worried about him!'

'Because that was the only way, Hao! Otherwise he wouldn't have told me a thing! In the meantime we need to get our story straight about Quang.' I told her what Jack had said, and explained what I wanted her to tell the police when they came. She listened, her face set and angry.

'And don't tell them about the break-in in my office either. I don't want Quang or Eric linked to this.'

'Why all these complications? Isn't that the police's job, to know about all this?'

'I think there's more to this than a simple murder. But we'll talk about that later. Will you please ring him? And don't mention my name on the phone.'

We were about to argue again when Eric himself rang. He was calling from a phone box – sensible lad. He had just heard the news, and wanted to be sure he'd got it right. He fell silent when I confirmed who it was.

'I want to come and see you,' he said. 'You know, the things you asked me.'

'You'd better come straightaway. But don't tell your friends you're coming to see me. Do you want to talk to your aunt?'

'No. I'll wait until I get there,' he said gloomily.

I passed this on to Hao.

'Don't be too hard on him,' I said. 'The only reason he didn't tell you was because he knew you'd only worry more.'

'And that's why you both kept that from me? Aren't you forgetting he's also my nephew?'

'I'm not forgetting anything, Hao! For God's sake, the whole thing's happened because I've been trying to help him! As you asked, remember? Please have some trust in me!'

'And what about Quang? Did you promise him too?'

'Yes! He found out some things which were disturbing but he was very secretive about them and he made me promise not to tell anyone. He didn't even tell *me* everything! Look, you had your chance, Hao, I asked you to come, remember? And you didn't want to because you were angry with me! So don't blame me for all this secretiveness!'

We were still arguing when Eric arrived. He seemed genuinely shaken by Quang's death. They'd only met briefly in the flat but he'd been impressed by Quang and now he was disturbed by some of the things he'd heard. But before he could say anything Hao took him away into her room, where I soon heard her giving him the rough edge of her tongue. When they re-emerged Eric gave me an accusing glare.

'Why did you have to say anything? You promised –'

'I know. I'm sorry. But a man's been killed, a very decent man who should still be alive. So it's time to stop playing games. Eric, I want you to tell us everything you know, everything that's happened. Will you do that?'

He nodded, and we sat in the lounge, with me facing them like a headmaster confronting a couple of wayward students.

'We're going off on another camp,' he said. 'That's what I wanted to tell you yesterday. Only – I wasn't quite ready yet.'

'It's OK. I understand.' It had taken Quang's murder to bring him to that point. 'Tell us about this camp. Where is it? Up at the farm again?'

'Yes. We're going up on Wednesday, coming back Friday I think.'

'Do you know what it's about?'

He nodded again, uncomfortably.

'Come on Eric! This is serious. We're not going to tell the police, this is just between us. But we need to know what's going on.' Hao started to say something but I waved her quiet. 'So don't hold out on us, please.'

'OK. We – there's only a few of us going. We're not supposed to tell the others. Binh said we'd been specially selected.'

'Who's Binh?'

'He works in Mr Bach's office. He's the one who told me you'd been there.'

I remembered the hard-looking young man who'd escorted me to Bach's office. Quang had mentioned him too.

'There was a meeting on Saturday. They talked about someone coming from Vietnam. One of the leaders, someone called Loc. The group's organising some big demonstrations against him, here and in Canberra. Mr Khanh was there too. Afterwards Binh kept a few of us there. That's when he told us about the camp. He said it was for special training, not to tell the others because they'd get jealous, we'd been picked because we're the best. That's what he said.'

'OK. Thanks, Eric.'

Hao made to speak again but I held up my hand. She stayed quiet, her lips pressed together.

'First things first. Did you hear anyone mention Quang? Before or after the murder?'

'Not before, no. Someone said all traitors should be eliminated, on Saturday, but that was just talk, you know, the kind of thing they say at these meetings. Only this morning – when we were watching the news, one of them said good riddance. He said that's one communist gone, at least. He wasn't a communist, was he Paul?'

'No, he wasn't. But he knew them, he understood them, which is more than that group will ever do. Was that when you first heard about the murder?'

'Yes. We were watching some programme on TV, and someone said to turn on the news, and there they were talking about it. At first I didn't know who it was, but then they showed his picture and I recognised him –'

'Who said good riddance? Was it Binh?'

'No. He was there too but he didn't say anything. I think it was Lam. You don't know him. He was one of those who beat you up.'

I sat back. 'Thanks,' I said again, and stopped to reflect about all this. Hao spoke up.

'Now we must go to the police,' she said firmly.

Eric looked up anxiously and I held my hand up again.

'No, wait. I've got a better idea, if Eric feels up to it.'

'What's that?'

'I'd like him to go back first, attend that camp up at the farm, and find out what's going on. Then come back and tell us about it. After that we can decide whether to go to the police.'

'But why wait?' she argued. 'What do you think you'll learn that way?'

'I'm not sure. But maybe more about what they plan to do to Loc.'

'Why should you care so much about this man? Who is he anyway?'

'He's a deputy premier in the Vietnamese government, and a friend of Quang's. His full name's Dang van Loc.' I told them something of what Quang had told me. 'It's alright, Eric. There are good and bad communists, just like everything else, and he's one of the good ones. If your friends really want to do something for Vietnam they're picking on the wrong man.'

'But what you're asking Eric to do is dangerous, Paul! You're asking him to take risks for someone he knows nothing about –'

'There are no risks. All Eric has to do is act naturally. As he's been doing. Just don't tell them about this discussion. If they ask why you came here today tell them you rang your aunt and she asked you to come because she was upset about the murder. You can even say you met Quang here once, and he questioned you about what you were doing and you didn't like it and didn't tell him anything. All you have to do is go off to your camp, do what they ask you to do, don't ask too many questions but keep your eyes and ears open, and above all sound enthusiastic about what they're doing. Keep on hating the communists for what they did to your father and mother. And when you get back, tell us what happened.'

'You want me to spy for you.'

'Not just for me, Eric. There's someone in Canberra I want to talk to about this. Someone I trust. He'll know what to do.' I looked at Hao. 'He's the man you spoke to when you rang Canberra, remember? Believe me, he's good.' And to Eric: 'Actually he knew your father too. He'll be even more interested when I tell him about you.'

'It's not fair, Paul!' Hao burst out. 'You're playing on Eric's feelings! You have no right to ask him to take risks like that for someone he's never heard of! Eric's just a child –'

'Eric's nearly twenty, Hao! He's not a child any more. Young men like him have been going to war at eighteen!'

'Yes, and getting killed for it! I won't have it, Paul! You have no right to tell him what to do!'

I held up my hands in surrender.

'You're right. I have no right to tell him or you what to do. But let him decide for himself, Hao. He's old enough to do that. It's up to you, Eric. I'm not forcing you. But if you want to help find out who killed Quang, and maybe prevent something worse, this is the way to do it. Talk it over with your aunt. Call me when you've decided.'

I went into my bedroom and stood staring out the window, wondering if I knew what I was doing, whether I wasn't leading Eric into real danger, as Hao feared. For a moment I was on the point of going back to tell them I'd changed my mind, I agreed with Hao. But then Eric knocked and called me and I went back to the lounge. Hao sat very still with her lips firmly pressed together, and Eric had a worried frown, but when he spoke there was a new firmness to his voice.

'I'll do it, Paul.'

I looked at Hao.

'Hao? Is that OK with you?'

'Don't ask me, Paul! As you say, Eric's a grown man!'

'Alright. Thanks, Eric. I know you can do it. But just to be safe, you'd better not come back here. If anyone asks, just say we had an argument and you don't want to see me any more. Instead, when you have something to tell me, ring your aunt, say you want to see her but you don't want to come to the flat. She can meet you somewhere and you can tell her and she can pass it on to me. Hao? Would you mind doing that?'

'Whatever you say, Paul!' she said. 'You're the mastermind!'

'Look, it's not for very long – a couple of times maybe, when you get back from your camp. Meanwhile I'll talk to this man in Canberra and after that we'll have a clearer idea what to do. Then maybe we can go to the police.'

I took Eric through it again, to make sure we both agreed, while his aunt looked on, unhappy but resigned. I left them together then came back as Eric was getting up to leave. I walked with him to the door.

'Are you OK with all this, Eric?'

'Yes,' he said. 'Don't worry. I can do it, Paul.'

'That's the spirit. Just don't do anything foolish, alright? Act natural. You'll be fine.'

What I used to tell my sources, when they had doubts. I'd never lost one as a result. But there was always a first time.

By comparison the police visit was almost a relief. It came in the late afternoon, in the shape of Detective-Sergeant Emerson, from Bankstown police station. He was a polite, careful man in his late thirties in a neat brown suit, who didn't miss very much. By then I'd had a chance to catch up on the news, and rung Vivien in the office to tell her we wouldn't be coming in. Hao had retreated into her bedroom after Eric left but she came out to meet him and he questioned us in the sitting room, the two of us facing him, an arm's length apart on the settee.

'What happened to your face, Mr Quinn?' he asked curiously. 'You look as if you've been in a fight.'

I gave him a sheepish smile. 'Just a scrap. I tried to stop a couple of idiots from breaking into my car and they turned on me.'

'Did you report it to the police?'

'No. I managed to fight them off and they didn't take anything. It hardly seemed worth the trouble. All I got was a few bruises.'

'You should have, you know,' he said sternly. 'Incidents like that should always be reported! You look as if you got a good working over.'

'Well, I landed a few punches myself.'

He eyed me suspiciously, then turned to Hao.

'You're staying here, are you Mrs Tran?'

'She's a houseguest,' I said quickly. She nodded and blushed faintly. 'She's visiting from Britain. Mrs Tran and I are old friends, we knew each other in Saigon, a long time ago.'

'Oh, you were in the army then.'

'No, I worked in the embassy, just before the end of the war. In 1975. That's when we met.'

He explained that he was making inquiries into the murder of Le Minh Quang, and asked if we knew him. It was the first time I'd heard Quang's full name. When I asked how he knew that, he said that my name had been among Quang's papers. I nodded wisely, as if that explained everything. He seemed satisfied with our explanation of how we came to know Quang, but then asked if we knew who his other friends were, or if we knew anyone who might have wanted to harm him. I said no, and then he looked at Hao.

'Mrs Tran?'

She seemed to hesitate briefly before shaking her head, and he gave her a more probing look.

'Are you sure? Mr Quinn?' He turned to me again.

'No. I liked him, but I hardly knew him, I don't know who his friends were.'

'Mrs Tran? You're sure there's nothing you can think of?'

This time she was more positive. 'No, nothing, Sergeant. I've only been here a few weeks, I don't know the Vietnamese community in Sydney very well, apart from my late husband's relatives, and they had no connection with him.'

'Thank you. And just for the record, can you tell me where you were yesterday afternoon and evening?'

'Certainly. We were here. My daughter was up for the week-end visiting from Melbourne. I drove her back to the airport about five and then came straight back.'

'Anyone else here with you?'

'Only my son – my adopted son,' Hao cut in firmly before I could speak. 'He lives in Cabramatta and had come out to see us.'

'What time did he leave?'

'I don't know exactly. Paul? It would have been about eight, I think. He stayed for dinner.'

'Can you give me his details?'

'Of course.' She gave him Eric's name and address. 'I doubt if he can help you much, Sergeant. I think he met Mr Quang here once, but otherwise they didn't know each other.' She spoke with a steady clear voice, and he seemed quietly impressed by her manner and ease in English. I guessed the Vietnamese he met in his job weren't usually so articulate.

'Thank you. You've been very helpful. Please let me know if you think of anything else that might help us. This is a shocking murder and we want to do everything we can to catch those responsible. And Mr Quinn, next time you get into a scrap like that, please report it at once to the police. We may not be able to catch the culprits straightaway, but at least it helps us with our statistics.'

'You're right. I'm sorry. If it ever happens again you may be sure I will,' I said. He looked slightly mollified.

It was nearly six when he left. The end of a long and dispiriting day. I went into the kitchen to look into the fridge, though I didn't feel much like eating. Hao was there, standing at the kitchen counter, and I spoke to her back.

'Thanks for backing me up, with that policeman,' I said. 'I'm sorry if I was pushing you earlier, when Eric was here. But I really think that's the best way to do it. It's alright, Hao. It'll work out, you'll see.'

'You like pushing people around, don't you,' she said. 'You like to have things your own way.'

'Only when I know I'm right. Sometimes it's the only way to get things done.' She turned, and looked at me steadily. I should have seen the signs. The deep shadows under her eyes, the air of strain –

selfishly I'd been more concerned about myself and my little plots
than her welfare, but she looked on the edge of exhaustion.

'Let's not fight, Hao,' I said pleadingly. 'It's been a bad day, we
should be helping each other, not quarrelling.' I made to put my arm
around her waist but she pulled away.

'Don't!' she snapped.

'I'm sorry!'

'You think that – that because I crawled into your bed last night
you can treat me like some – some kind of bar-girl –'

'Hao, of course not!'

'What happened last night –'

'Nothing happened last night! Don't you remember? You were
lonely and miserable and you came to me for comfort! What do you
think, that I was going to take advantage of that? What kind of a
monster do you think I am? I love you, Hao!'

'Don't say that!'

'But it's true! Why, don't you believe me?'

'You don't know me – you know nothing about me –'

'So you keep saying. But what you told me last night, didn't that
tell me anything?'

'There are other things – things I haven't told you –'

'Well tell me now then!'

'I can't –'

'Why not? Oh, let me guess. You don't like men, is that it? Well,
that's hardly surprising, after what happened to you.'

She shook her head.

'So what is it? Have you got someone else, is that it? Is there a
man, a lover, waiting for you in Leeds?'

She looked down.

'There – there is someone –'

'Oh Christ! Now you tell me!' I sat down, suddenly deflated. To
think that I'd been so naïve, so self-absorbed as to imagine I was
the only one who mattered to her. 'Who is it? Is it that man, who
rang the other day? George?'

'I don't want to talk about it.'

'No. Of course not! Why should you! It's not as if we had
something going between us, is it!' I suddenly felt very bitter.

'So what are you going to do?' I asked. 'Go back to him?'

'I don't know!' she cried. 'Stop asking me all those questions! I have to go back anyway! My visa's going to run out soon.'

'You could get an extension.'

'No I couldn't. They told me in London when they gave it to me that I wouldn't be able to extend once I came here. If I want to stay longer I'd have to go back to England and reapply from there.' She looked despairing. 'Anyway, what does it matter. Another month or two, I'll still have to go back in the end.'

It matters to me! I wanted to cry out. Instead I burst out angrily.

'Well, don't let me stop you! I've told you how I feel, but if you want to go back to your friend go ahead. I'm not holding you prisoner here. You came to my help, you've been very good to me, but I'm better now, thanks, I can look after myself from now on.'

I stood up. She looked almost unbearably beautiful, her face pale and drawn, her eyes lustrous with intensity. I thought if I didn't get a grip on myself I'd break down in front of her.

'Now if you don't mind, Hao, I have a phone call to make. Don't worry. I'll look after Eric, I'll make sure nothing happens to him.'

She looked as if she was about to say something else, then changed her mind and went out.

It was now nearly seven. I waited until I'd got myself under control, then rang Roger Bentinck, my former colleague in Canberra. I caught him at home in Red Hill, one of Canberra's premier suburbs. He had just come in from work and sounded glad to hear my voice.

'I was about to give you a call,' he said.

'Roger, I need to see you urgently.' I started to tell him what had happened, but he cut me off when I mentioned Loc's visit.

'I know about that,' he said quickly. 'I can come up tomorrow afternoon –'

'It's better if I come down. I can be there early.' I needed to get away from that flat.

We made arrangements for ten, and I hung up. I thought of eating, but I'd lost all appetite. I went and stood for a moment outside Hao's door. I could hear her moving, and what might have been her blowing her nose. I thought bitterly of how much things had changed over the past twenty-four hours. I went to my room and tried in vain to sleep.

When I left early the next morning her door was still shut. I wanted to go in and say goodbye, but thought better of it. Instead I left a short note on the kitchen counter to say I'd be out for most of the day. I walked out on tip-toe.

Chapter Twenty

The Australian Secret Intelligence Agency – ASIA – had its headquarters in one of the wings of the Edmund Barton Building on King's Avenue, half-way between Lake Burley Griffin and the new Parliament House on Capital Hill, on Canberra's south side. The EBB as it was called was built in the shape of a hollow square, the office wings suspended above ground and held aloft by a series of round towers which also served as lift wells. I entered one of these and took the lift to the first floor, the only one marked with a button. There I emerged into a small lobby painted in muted pastel shades, where an elderly guard in a blue uniform studied me from behind bullet-proof glass. Apart from the guard nothing much seemed to have changed over the years. I filled in a form, received in exchange a Visitor's badge which I clipped to my lapel, the guard picked up his phone. A moment later a side door opened and Roger Bentinck came out, smiling in welcome. He gave my face a critical look.

'Christ!' he said. 'You look as if you've run into a wall!'

'You should see the other fellow,' I quipped back, not very originally.

'Good to see you anyway. Come on in.'

We shook hands and I followed him inside. He hadn't changed much either since we'd last met, a neat fair-haired man about my own age, with watchful eyes in a youthful boyish face. He led me along carpeted corridors lined with closed office doors. Here and there red lights winked, to warn of my presence. When I was still working there the doors would have been open and no lights would have winked. But it was an iron rule in the Agency: once you left you lost all access, no matter how trusted you'd once been or how polite they were about it.

'I've arranged a meeting in our small conference room,' he said as we turned another corner. 'A couple of people want to see you.'

We went up a flight of stairs to a large waiting area, with more shuttered doors. Here the carpet was thicker, the silence even more secretive. This was the senior directorate, where the top brass sat. Bentinck had been a desk officer when I'd left the Agency but he'd climbed fast and was now Deputy Director-General in charge of operations, second only to the D-G.

Roger opened one of the doors and ushered me into a narrow windowless room with wood panelling and sliding maps along one wall, and a conference table with chairs along both sides. At the far end of the table stood a tray with cups and milk and sugar and a small percolator. 'Help yourself to coffee. I'll get the others.'

He closed the door behind him, returning a moment later to let in three others.

'You remember Bill Forsythe,' he said, introducing the oldest of them, a tall fleshy man in his early fifties with hooded eyes and the beginning of a stoop. 'The Director-General.' Forsythe smiled and held out his hand.

'Of course we were all much younger then,' he said in a rich actor's voice. 'How long's it been? Ten, twelve years? You haven't changed a bit.'

'Neither have you, Bill,' I lied, remembering the lean hawk-faced man of my youth. But I also remembered those eyes, which gave him a faintly menacing air, and that politician's ready smile. Forsythe had always been a smooth operator.

'Congratulations,' I said. 'I saw your appointment in the papers.'

'The price of fame,' he said. 'You can't stay hidden in this job.'

Forsythe introduced the others: Keith, a tall man in his mid-thirties with a sombre face, and Samantha, a leggy and very pretty brunette with intelligent eyes and a slightly wicked smile. No surnames. Another routine precaution.

'Keith is head of our South East Asia Branch and Sam runs the Indochina desk. We've had a few changes since you left, and one of them is a number of women coming up through the ranks. They make damn good case officers.'

'Paul's one of the old guard,' Bentinck cut in jovially. 'He'd probably be in my job if he'd stayed.'

'Don't believe him,' I said. 'He always was a flatterer.'

The others made appreciative noises and helped themselves to coffee, then Forsythe took a chair near the end of the table and the rest of us grouped ourselves around him. Samantha produced a note pad. Forsythe asked how I was doing in Sydney, then got down to the business in hand.

'So, Paul, tell us what's been happening lately,' he said, with another smile. 'And how you came to get in that state. Roger's briefed us but there's a lot we don't know and we'd like to hear how it looks from your end.'

'Of course. That's why I'm here,' I said, returning his smile. I had come there at my own request, not to ask for help but to offer it, and I didn't want anyone to pretend otherwise. These people were arch-manipulators, skilled at exploiting a situation. I took a sip of coffee and looked at them all.

'It's probably best if I start at the beginning,' I said. 'It's not a long story but there are several angles to it. Do you remember David Harper?'

'Harper? Of course,' said Forsythe. 'He was that young officer who was killed in Vietnam. The only man we ever lost in the field.'

'Right. And I took his place in the embassy.' I turned towards the two youngsters, who would have been at school at the time. 'Saigon, 1975.' I looked again at Forsythe and Bentinck. 'I've spent the past fortnight getting to know his son.'

Forsythe's eyebrows rose, but he didn't say anything, and I told them the story, much as Hao had told it to me at our first meeting – of Hien, and Eric, and how Eric had grown up in Britain with his adoptive parents, and how he had come to end up in Cabramatta with a group of Vietnamese anti-communist fanatics. Everything leading up to Quang's death, bar a few details about Hao and Hien's kidnapping, which was none of their business. They listened quietly, like the trained listeners they were, while Samantha took notes. When I finished there was a moment of silence. The youngsters looked at Bentinck and Forsythe, and these two looked at me. Finally Forsythe spoke.

'Thank you, Paul,' he said. 'It's a very moving story. You're certain that Eric is David's son?'

'Absolutely,' I said. 'I don't remember David very well, but you only need one look at Eric to know it. And she wouldn't have made up a story like that.'

'She? Mrs Tran?' asked Roger.

'Yes. His aunt. She's totally reliable, believe me.'

'Where is he now? At that house in Cabramatta?'

'Yes.'

'And Mrs Tran? Is she staying there too?'

'No. She's staying with me.'

Roger gave me a quick look but neither he nor Forsythe said anything, and I let it hang there. The other two kept quiet. Standard group behaviour: when the top brass was around you kept your mouth shut unless you had something worth saying. Except that I hadn't always had the sense to shut up.

'Presumably she knows you've come here?'

'Yes. I told her I wanted to speak to someone in Canberra. I didn't go into details.'

'But she'll have put two and two together.'

I shrugged. 'I couldn't very well avoid it. I had to give her some reason why I didn't want to go to the police straightaway, as she wanted me to.'

Forsythe nodded. From his point of view, the less people knew the better.

'So, tell us why you've come to us then, Paul,' he said. 'What you'd like us to do.'

See what I mean? When I'd spoken to Bentinck the night before he'd been very keen for us to meet, and so it seemed had Forsythe and the others. But now they were trying to make it look as if I was the one who'd come for help. It was time to set the record straight.

'What you do's up to you, Bill,' I said gently. 'I've only come to you for one thing, and that's to tell you what I know.'

They looked at me in silence and I went on.

'Until Quang's death I wasn't sure what to do. My main concern was getting Eric away from that bunch of crazies, the Mad Buffaloes. But Quang was starting to get suspicious, that there was something else behind it all, something more sinister perhaps, and when he died it struck me that he might well be right. If so, I don't think it's something the police can handle. All they'll want to do is find his killer, but if there is something else behind it I doubt they have either the resources or the skills to find out. That requires intelligence work, of a fairly specialised kind. That's why I asked Eric to go and attend that training camp in the hills, and report to me afterwards. You're the only guys I know who can handle that sort of knowledge.'

'It's really ASIO's job,' cut in Keith. 'Anything to do with security –'

'I know. But I've never had much dealing with ASIO. Whereas I know you guys. This is right up your alley. You've got the knowledge, of Vietnam, who's who there, of the whole situation, or if you haven't you should. I don't know much about this man Loc, but from what Quang told me he's one of the good ones, and if something nasty happens to him it could affect the whole future of the country. Now you can tell me that's no longer my business, and you'd be right. My aim is still to get Eric out from under. But it is your business, or should be. That's why I've come to you.'

ASIO, the Australian Security Intelligence Organization, whose offices were across the lake, had prime responsibility for anything to do with security in Australia, and ASIA in theory had to hand anything in that line over to them. But there had always been some leeway, and ASIA was allowed to run its own sources inside Australia, provided they didn't cut across ASIO's tracks. This case, if it became one, probably belonged best to whichever service first owned it.

But there was another reason why I didn't want to deal direct with ASIO. At a pinch Eric wouldn't mind working for his father's old firm, in fact he'd probably get a kick out of it. But he would balk at anything to do with ASIO, and Hao even more. Where they came from, security services only spelt trouble, repression or worse, the secret police of authoritarian states. ASIO wasn't like that, but they would never accept it.

'I could have gone to the police,' I went on. 'That's what his aunt wanted. But they'd trample all over it, and no one would ever know what that bunch is really up to. Especially that man Ho Xuan Bach. And they probably wouldn't catch who did it anyway. Whereas this way, there's a good chance of finding out, and maybe catching Quang's killer as well. In fact I can probably guess who it is, but it wouldn't do any good without proof, and there's no way the police will get it, not the way the Vietnamese work. They won't say a thing to the cops.'

I must have spoken with some heat, because they all stared at me for a moment, while I simmered down.

'If you're not interested of course I will have to go to the police,' I went on more calmly. 'They won't thank me for holding out, but I can probably talk my way out, in terms of protecting Eric. So it's up to you to decide. I've only come to give you first option. If you don't want it I'll just go to the cops as soon as I get back. Ring Detective Sergeant Emerson, and take it from there. Your decision.'

Forsythe had heard me out, pursing his lips slightly. He and I both knew, and so did Roger, that I'd had my brushes with senior management in my day, when I had insisted on speaking my mind. That had been another reason for leaving.

'You say the aunt's reliable, but what about the boy?' Bentinck said. 'How steady will he be if the going gets rough?'

'He'll be OK. Of course you never know until you try it. But he's got a lot of strength in him. And he's totally sincere, just like his aunt. He hates injustice. He was really upset by Quang's death. He'll be alright. In any case there shouldn't be any need for him to play that role much longer. As soon as he comes back and tells me what he knows, then he can pull out.'

'That might be a little premature.' Bentinck again.

'Meaning?' I knew what he meant. This was Bentinck the operator speaking.

'Assuming there's something sinister going on, and he finds out during this training session, it's unlikely to stop there. There's still two weeks before Loc's visit, if they're thinking of organising something nasty – we're not talking just demos here – it's unlikely he'll find out everything in a couple of days. Or who's behind it. That man Bach for instance. Is he going to be at the camp?'

'I don't know. Maybe. What are you getting at?'

He looked at Forsythe for a moment, as if seeking approval. Forsythe gave a nod and Bentinck turned back to me.

'This is just between us, right?'

'Of course.'

'The aunt, you say she knows you've come here today?'

'Yes. And so does Eric. But all I told them was that I knew someone in Canberra who would be interested in all this, and I wanted to get his advice before going to the police. That's all. Come on guys. I had to tell them something! They're not going to talk. Besides, she already knew your name, Roger, you're the one who spoke to her that day, when she rang the Department to get hold of me.'

'I remember. She sounded nice.'

I nodded and smiled slightly, but went on. 'I also told Eric that you knew his father. I did that deliberately. He's never known his father, he's desperately searching for something of him, that's really what's driving him, and that's what I've been working on. Hell, you can't ask a young man like that to betray people he thinks are his friends, without giving him some pretty strong reasons!'

Bentinck held up his hand.

'It's OK. I understand. But let's keep it at that, alright? What I'm about to tell you, that's strictly between us. Understood?'

I nodded. 'Of course.'

'As it happens, most of what you've told us we already knew. Sorry to disappoint you, but there you are. We've had our own source in the Vietnamese community – until two days ago, when he got himself killed. Don't be so surprised, Paul. What did you expect, that he wouldn't appreciate an audience?'

'I'm not surprised. Not really. Congratulations. He must have been a good source.'

'He was. But now we've lost him, thanks to you.'

'I didn't ask him to get killed!'

'No. But he did get killed chasing information you put him on to. Oh yes, we're as sure as you are that that's why he was killed. Because he was getting too close to something. To your friend Mr Bach, possibly. So now we no longer have a source. And this is where you come in.'

'I know what you're going to ask,' I said.

'Then I don't need to spell it out. We want you to go back and run Eric for us. Now you've got him. We don't want you to pull him out. Not until we can find out more about this whole business.'

'You realise what you're asking. You're asking me to put him at risk –'

'You already have.'

'Yes but only for a couple of days –'

'This may not be much longer.'

'He's only nineteen, for Christ's sake! What if something happens to him? His aunt would never forgive me!'

'Don't tell her!'

I looked at him for a moment, then at Forsythe, and the others. Keith What's-his-name and Samantha-with-the-wicked-smile were both very still, watching me, as if trying to guess which way I'd jump. But I knew, and Roger and Bill Forsythe knew, that I had no option. That I'd had no option from the moment I'd decided to ring Bentinck. What could I expect, coming to them with that sort of information? That they'd say thank you and just sit on it, without trying to get more? Especially now that they'd lost their best source. I must have got very rusty, not to have guessed that Quang would be working for someone like them.

Nevertheless the little devil at the back of my mind made me want to argue the point a little. Just so they didn't think they had all the cards.

'Just for argument's sake, what if I say no? What if I think it's too risky?'

'In that case you'll leave us no option. We'll have to go to the cops ourselves, in Sydney and Canberra, and also ASIO, and tell them everything we know. That will certainly put the spotlight on Eric.'

I smiled. That was pretty well what I'd imagined. The gentle art of friendly persuasion.

'OK. You've got a deal. But I need something in exchange.'

'Such as?' Forsythe asked a shade frostily.

'Protection, for a start.'

'Protection against what? The Mad Buffaloes?'

'No. The police. I don't want either Eric or his aunt to be harassed by the cops on the grounds that they've withheld information. If they withheld it, it was because I asked them to, and that was because I wanted to hand it to you. So I want a guarantee that they won't be prosecuted or pursued by the police.'

Forsythe nodded. 'We can give you that.'

'Could I have that in writing please.'

He jerked his head up a little, as if I'd questioned his word, and Roger looked at me with a glitter in his eyes.

'And how exactly do you propose we do that?' More frost.

'That's up to you too,' I said breezily. 'A letter, perhaps? From you, Bill, as D-G ASIS, to the Commissioner of Police in Sydney? My Dear Commissioner. This is to certify that Mrs Hao Tran and her nephew Eric Tran have been acting in all good faith as informants of my service, in an operation of the greatest delicacy concerning elements of the Vietnamese expatriate community in Sydney. On learning of Mr Le Minh Quang's murder I arranged for them to be debriefed at once by one of my officers to ascertain whether they had any information which might be of use to your police force in its investigation. It quickly became clear that they did not know anything that could assist you directly. I have however instructed them to make themselves available to you or your officers at any time that you may require for the purposes of this investigation, provided their role is kept strictly confidential. Yours etc. Something along those lines? Rather long-winded, but I'm sure you can work something up.'

'You really are asking a lot, Paul. You know we don't work like that.'

'Come on Bill, you work any way you want to, provided it delivers the goods. Look, I'm not trying to be difficult. But unless you give me an iron-clad guarantee that they'll come to no harm I will have to ask them to come with me to the police when I get back. I can't run the risk of getting either of them into trouble.'

Blackmail can work both ways, I thought. Forsythe looked at me steadily for a moment, his eyes becoming more hooded.

'We'll look at it,' he said finally.

'Thank you. Visas.'

'What?'

'Mrs Tran's visa. It's about to run out. Can you arrange to have it renewed, or extended? It wouldn't be good if she were forced to go back to Britain, just when Eric goes underground. If anything happens, she'll need to be here.'

'Wouldn't it be safer for her if she went back to UK?' asked Roger. 'You could be putting her in danger if she stays.'

'I don't think she's in any danger here. Not as Eric's aunt. Why would they pick on her? She's no threat to them. No, she has to stay here for this scheme to work. I need her as a cut-out to Eric.'

Fat chance of that, I thought, after last night. I was clutching at straws. But they didn't know that. Forsythe nodded again. 'Alright. We can work on that.'

'I've got her details with me.'

'Give them to Roger. Anything else? I have another meeting to go to, can we wrap this up? Roger, can we have a quick word? Nice to see you Paul, thanks for coming down, good to see you haven't lost your form.' Forsythe gave me another smile as he stood up, with rather less warmth than before. Keith and Samantha stayed with me as he and Roger left the room. I got up to pour myself more coffee, offered them some, which they declined. I needed all the caffeine I could get.

'Tell us more about this man Bach,' Keith said. 'We hardly know anything about him.'

'There's not much I can add. I've only met him once. My gut feeling is that he is part of it, maybe the brains behind it, but I can't base that on anything solid. All I can say is that he struck me as a sharp customer, and not very nice. Quang knew more about him, he must have told you.'

He shook his head. 'We hadn't heard from him for over a week. His case officer was supposed to meet him yesterday.' He brooded on this. 'You don't suppose he kept any records?'

'No idea. If he did, they'd be in the hands of the police by now.' I thought. 'Actually there is someone who might have access to them.' I told them about Jack Lipton. 'I could ask him. But I'd have a lot of explaining to do, and I doubt that he'd pass them over without getting clearance from the cops.'

Keith nodded.

'I'll ask Roger. But you see now why it's vital we keep that young man in there. He's the only lead we have into that group.'

'Sure. But he won't get you much closer to Bach. The most he can learn is what they're up to, if he's lucky. If you want more on Bach you'll have to find other sources.'

He nodded again.

'Why don't you try Immigration?' I went on. 'They should have some record, from the time he came into the country. That might tell you something.'

Keith was about to say something when Roger came back into the room.

'Right. We've had a quick chat with our legal adviser, he's drafting up a form of words now, I can show it to you before you go, Paul. But it'll have to stay here. We can't let you take it with you.'

'Okay. Thanks.' I nodded. This was the best I could hope for. 'As long as you guarantee you'll step in if needed.'

'Sure. We won't leave you in the lurch.'

'One last request, if I'm not imposing too much,' I said. He shot me a weary look.

'Photos. Or a photo. Of David. I promised Eric I'd try and get one through the Department, but of course you're the ones who have them. There must be a couple on his personnel file, some old passport photo –'

'Doesn't he have any?'

'No. They were all lost when they came out in the boat. He doesn't even know what his father looked like. I think it would do a great deal for his morale if you could get me one. And some details of his family, if at all possible.'

'About the family I'm not sure. Maybe later. But I'll see what we can do about a photo. Keith? Could you chase that up? I'll have to get back to you on that Paul, we won't be able to get one today.'

'No. I understand.'

'Right. Anything else?' He looked at the others. Keith spoke up again.

'Paul's come up with a suggestion,' he said, and told him what we'd just discussed. Roger thought about it.

'It's a thought. But we could only get at those records through ASIO, the police'd never pass anything directly to us. Let me discuss it with Bill. In any case we'll have to bring ASIO in from now on. Bill's just decided. It's too risky to leave them out.'

'Sure. As long as I deal with you.'

'They'll want to talk to you too, you know. This is right in their patch.'

I nodded dubiously. That too I'd more or less expected.

I got stuck in traffic on the way home, and didn't get back to the flat until late. I called out to Hao, but there was no answer. When I looked in her room I saw her luggage was gone. Then I found the note she had left on the kitchen counter.

Paul. I've gone back to Marrickville. Please don't try to ring me. I need to think. I'll let you know if Eric has anything for you. H.

Chapter Twenty-One

The next day I went back to work. I had no choice, if I wanted to stay in business, and it was better than staying home feeling sorry for myself. Vivien was glad to see me back, but when she asked if Hao was coming in I snapped at her: 'I haven't a clue.' She gave me an odd look and I apologised, but she had the sense not to ask any further questions.

For two days I stuck at it, doggedly forcing myself back into harness. My bruises were fading, I could write without too much discomfort. But no amount of work could wipe Hao from my mind. I knew I'd lost her, but I kept hoping against hope for some small miracle, that somehow I'd get another reprieve. As far as Eric was concerned there was nothing I could do until he came back from the hills, and then only if he took the initiative. Anything else would be too risky for him.

Bentinck rang, and I had to tell him there was nothing new. But I had another idea. When did Bach come to Australia? 1980 or 81? Through Pulau Bidong off the Malaysian coast or via some other third country, Singapore or Thailand or Indonesia? From what Quang had said he'd come out on a large boat, a sea-going cargo of some sort, and that should have attracted attention.

I tried explaining this to Bentinck, without using names over the phone.

'Maybe it was before my time,' I said. 'If you can find out the dates from Immigration, and where he was processed – why don't you ask Svensson?' Svensson had been my predecessor in that job, a pallid Swede who burnt to a painful red in the sun. 'He might remember, if he's still around.'

'He's retired. But it's a thought.'

'Or the Yanks. Have you tried tracing him with them?'

Bentinck was uneasy at discussing these things on an open line, but I persisted. 'There should be something in archives. If you can trace others from that boat, maybe you can find someone who knew him in Vietnam.'

'Leave it with me. By the way, the reason I rang. Your lady friend's visa: done. All she has to do is present her passport to Immigration in Sydney, and quote this reference –' he gave me a number. 'They'll extend the visa on the spot. Another three months.'

'Thanks. I really appreciate that.' Knowing it was probably too late. I couldn't even ring Hao to tell her.

––––––––––––––

Then, on the Friday morning, things began to happen.

The first was a phone call from Eric, in mid-morning, as I sat in my office worrying about him. He'd returned the night before, and was ringing from a phone booth near Cabramatta station. He sounded aggrieved.

'What happened with my aunt?' he cried. 'Why has she gone back to Marrickville?'

'It's a long story.' I didn't feel like telling it. 'I think she needed a break.'

'She doesn't sound very happy. I just talked to her on the phone. I wanted to come and see you but now it's too late, I have to work in the restaurant over lunch.'

'It's probably safer this way. Tell me about the farm.'

Only three of them had gone up, he said: Lam and himself and another one called Nghia. Plus Vo Khanh and Binh from Mr Bach's office. The others had pulled out.

'Paul, they're planning to kill Loc.'

'What? How?'

'They didn't say. But we did a lot of training yesterday, with guns. Pistols and things.'

He gave me some details. They'd gone up on the Wednesday afternoon, as planned, and spent that evening in discussion, and the next day they had trained for several hours on a small firing range at the back of the farm, under Vo Khanh's supervision, with a variety of weapons: pistols and revolvers and sporting rifles, including an old army .303 Lee-Enfield, cut down and remodelled as a hunting rifle. A bolt action mechanism, I remembered from my own small arms training with the Agency, with a five-round magazine – slower than an automatic weapon but much more accurate, an ideal sniper's weapon in the right hands. That sounded more serious than anything else. They even had a scope to go with it.

'I got top score on that,' he said with a youngster's pride.

'Did they say who's going to do it?'

'No, but they asked for volunteers.'

'And?'

'I offered to do it. So did Lam. Nghia piked out.'

It took a second for that to sink in.

'What do you mean, you offered to do it!' I cried. 'Do you realise what you're saying?'

'Of course I do! I had to, Paul! That's what we were there for! Besides, that's what you wanted, isn't it? You wanted me to find out what they're up to and I did! I don't want to kill the guy. But if I hadn't offered they'd pick someone else and we'd never find out. This way we can try and stop them.'

'But this is highly dangerous! Have you any idea what that involves? I think your aunt was right. It's time we went to the police.'

'No, not yet! Let me find out some more first. Come on, Paul, you asked for my help, remember? This is our chance. You said you knew some people.'

'Have you told your aunt any of this?'

'Are you daft? She'd rip my head off! No, I just said we'd done more training, preparation for the demos against Loc's visit. She didn't ask any more.'

That wouldn't stop her thinking. I did some quick thinking myself.

'We need to talk about this. Can you take time off this weekend? Without alerting your friends?'

'I can take Sunday off. I have to work tomorrow. I'll tell them my aunt's going back to Britain and she wants me to spend the day with her.'

'Has she decided to go back?' The thought hit me like a cold shower.

'She was talking about it. She said she has to go into town on Monday to make her booking. What happened, Paul? I thought you two were getting on together.'

So did I, I thought. But I'd obviously got it wrong.

'Listen. I need to make a phone call. Can you ring me back in half an hour? And find out what time the trains run on Sunday. See if there's one that can get you to Marrickville by seven thirty. Even earlier if possible.'

'Why so early?'

'We may have to go out of town.'

I hung up, and rang Roger's office in Canberra. He was at a meeting, but I said it was urgent and a moment later he came on the line. I gave him the gist of what Eric had told me.

'Right. I can come up –'

'No. I've got a better idea. I'm bringing him down on Sunday. I want you to meet him, and I want him to meet you. It wouldn't hurt to have the others there as well, Keith and Sam. This boy's about to lay his life on the line, and he needs to know who he's doing it for.'

'You can't do this!'

'It's the only way, Roger! This isn't some juvenile delinquent looking for kicks! This is David's son, he's clever and tough and very committed, and he's taken on a pretty tricky job. If you can't do that for him we might as well go to the police and let them handle it. They might just have enough to make charges stick.'

He thought about it for a moment.

'I'll have to discuss it with Bill.'

'Of course. But it's non-negotiable, Roger.'

He sighed. I knew how much they hated to lose the initiative.

'Alright! Come down early. I'll arrange something and ring you back. But for Christ's sake don't say anything to him until I've met him!'

I rang off before he could make any other objections.

Twenty minutes later Eric rang back. There was a train, he said, which got to Marrickville just before seven thirty.

'Where are we going?'

'To Canberra. To meet the people I was telling you about.'

'Really? That's cool!'

'But first we need to take some precautions. Here's what I want you to do.' I gave him instructions, made sure he understood them. 'And you'd better ring your aunt too while you're at it.'

'But this is just between us, Paul, the way you said!'

'Yes, but she'll have to know where you'll be on Sunday. Otherwise she might try to ring you in Cabramatta, when you're supposed to be with her.'

'Can't you ring her? If I talk to her she'll only ask more questions. She'll listen to you.'

He had a point.

'Alright,' I said. 'I'll call her. But if anything happens and you can't make it you'll have to call her yourself. And you'd better dress up a little too. It wouldn't hurt if you could look neat for a change.'

'I know how to dress! You're beginning to sound like my aunt!'

'I could do worse. See you Sunday, bright and early.'

I didn't ring Hao straightaway. I was too upset by what Eric had told me. The plot to kill Loc was alarming enough, but the news that she had finally decided to go back to Britain had thrown me into a deep depression. What particularly hurt was that she hadn't rung to tell me herself. Did I matter so little to her?

But Eric was right, I had to call her, even if he'd only said that to get us talking again. I waited until mid-afternoon, then swallowed my pride and rang the cousins' house. She wasn't there and I left a message. When she hadn't rung back by six I phoned again and asked if she could call me at home before seven. When she finally called, at seven thirty, I was about to go out and I had given up hope of hearing from her that day.

'Paul? I've just got your message, I've been in the shop all afternoon. Are you alright?'

'Yes,' I said, and tried to sound as if I was. 'And thanks for ringing back. I'm sorry to bother you like this. But something's come up.'

I told her briefly about Eric's call, and our planned trip to Canberra, leaving out the more sensational aspects.

'Would you mind pretending that he's spending the day with you, if anybody asks? We don't want his friends to find out where he'll be, obviously.'

'Of course. Is he alright? He sounded very mysterious on the phone this morning.'

'Yes, he's fine too. Don't worry. He's doing a great job. It's just that the people I saw in Canberra on Tuesday said they'd like to meet him, and I thought it would do him good to take him down there for the day.'

'I'm sure he'll enjoy it. I meant to take him there sometime, but we never got round to it.'

There was a pause. In the background I could hear voices, the sound of cooking, kitchen utensils. I guessed she was calling from the kitchen, with the family around.

'How are you?' I asked at last.

'Alright I suppose. Pretty depressed, to be honest. But I'm glad you rang. Did Eric tell you? I'm going back to Leeds.'

'He mentioned it.'

'I was going to ring you.'

'Can I ask a question? I know it's none of my business, but is it because of that man, that you wouldn't tell me about?'

'No! I told you! I have to go back! I haven't got any choice!'

'Well, you do now. In case it makes any difference.'

'What do you mean?'

'I got you an extension. You can stay longer if you want.'

'How did you do that?'

'When I went to Canberra. I asked my friend there if he could fix it and he did. It's all arranged. All you have to do is go to Immigration and they'll give you one on the spot. You'll need a reference number but I've got that too if you want it.'

'Why didn't you tell me?'

'I couldn't, remember? You didn't want me to ring you! Besides, what difference does it make, if you've decided to go?'

'But I don't want to go back, Paul! I want to stay!'

'You do?' I couldn't believe my ears. 'But what about that man? Don't you want to go back to him?'

'No! He – oh Paul, we need to talk!'

'We certainly do!'

The background noise had risen, sounded more like an altercation. A woman's voice made some sharp remark, there was silence, as if we'd been cut off, and then Hao came back on the line. She sounded flustered.

'I can't talk now, but can I come to see you? Are you free this evening?'

'No, I'm sorry, I have to go to a dinner. But I'm free all day tomorrow if you like.'

'Tomorrow's no good, I promised I'd work in the shop, they're short-handed.'

'Tomorrow night? Or would you rather wait until Sunday, when we get back from Canberra?'

She hesitated.

'Maybe we'd better wait until then. Can I call you tomorrow evening? Will you be home?'

'Yes. I won't be going anywhere.'

Another comment. I couldn't make out the words, but they didn't sound very pleasant.

'I'm sorry. I have to go – I'll call you tomorrow.'

She hung up before I could speak. I felt frustrated as I put the phone down. As conversations went this one raised more questions than it answered. But at least we were talking again. After the misery of the past four days it was a blessed relief.

By an ironic coincidence the dinner I went to that evening was at the house of a former girl-friend, a gentle and perceptive academic and fellow divorcee with whom I'd had a brief but passionate fling two years previously. She had remarried since, without as far as I knew telling her husband about our past liaison, but we had remained friends. Much as I liked her I could have done without it. All I could think about was that unfinished conversation. I did my best to be sociable, and my fading bruises attracted some interest, but my heart wasn't in it and Liz – that was my friend – couldn't help noticing. 'What's the matter, my love,' she asked quietly, when no one was listening. 'I've never seen you so worried. *Chagrin d'amour*?' I shook my head. 'Don't ask,' I said darkly. 'I'm just hoping I haven't fucked up my life.' 'You Paul? Surely not you!'

It didn't sound much like a compliment. But she looked concerned, and she didn't ask any more questions, and I was grateful to her for that.

Saturday was largely a waste of time. With nothing else to do I spent it mostly thinking, and waiting. But that evening Hao rang again as promised. This time she called from a phone booth, kitchen noises replaced by the sound of traffic.

'I'm sorry about last night,' she said. 'I wanted to talk longer but I couldn't.'

'I guessed you were having some problem. Is everything alright with the cousins?'

'Not really. I don't think they like me very much. Paul, you're quite sure about what you said last night? That I can stay longer?'

'Absolutely! My friend rang me specially to tell me. Why, is that what you've decided?'

'That's what I need to talk to you about. Could I come back, and stay with you again? Please? I'm sorry to be such a nuisance –'

'Don't be silly. Of course you can! Do you want to come now? I can come and get you.'

'No, I'd better wait until tomorrow. I have to pack, and I'm very tired. I've been in the shop all day. You're sure you don't mind? It's not just the cousins, you know. I really want to see you.'

'Of course I don't mind! Do you think I'd turn you away? Listen. I want to apologise for last Monday.'

'You don't have to.'

'Yes I do. I did and said some stupid things and I'm sorry if I hurt your feelings. If it's any consolation I've been kicking myself ever since.' I took a deep breath. 'But I meant what I said, Hao. I love you. It may not be what you want to hear right now, but it's the truth. So when we talk, tomorrow night or whenever, can you tell me the truth too? Tell me what you feel? I know we haven't known each other very long, but there have been times when I felt we were getting very close. At other times I wasn't so sure. Now I'm confused. There's too much that hasn't been said between us. So will you do that please? Tell me honestly what you feel? And after that I promise I won't bother you again if that's what you want. But I need to know.'

I stopped, aware I was talking too much. There was silence, while I listened to my breathing. Then she spoke.

'Yes. I will. You're right. There are things that – that need to be said. I can't talk about them now, but I will tell you. I promise.'

'Thank you. That's all I ask.'

When we hung up a few minutes later for the first time I felt hope.

Chapter Twenty-Two

On Sunday morning I was up bright and early myself. I'd told Eric I wanted to make sure he wasn't followed, and for that I had a simple plan. By seven thirty I was parked up the road from Marrickville station, watching as he walked towards me.

He followed my instructions exactly. Half way up he crossed over, without looking at me, and turned left at the next corner. I stayed where I was, watching the road. No one crossed after him, or seemed to be following him. I drove off, took up a similar position two streets away, where we repeated the process, with the same result. It was at best a basic precaution, which wouldn't have fooled experienced surveillants, but if he was being followed, which I doubted, I didn't think it would be very professional. The Mad Buffaloes didn't have that kind of resources. For good measure we went through it all again a third time nearer the cousins' house. Then, when I was satisfied that he had come alone, I drove off again, circled round and picked him up as he entered their street.

'Real spy stuff,' he said, grinning happily. He looked alert and excited, as if it was all a game. He had taken my words to heart: he wore near-new jeans that had been recently washed, a polo shirt with a collar and a canvas jacket that for once fitted him. He'd even taken his ear-ring off, though he still had his hair long. He looked like a kid dressed up to visit the relatives.

'Everything go OK this morning?' I asked. 'You had no problem getting away?'

'No. Everyone was still in bed. I told them last night I'd be spending the day with my aunt, but no one was interested. In any case we don't always tell each other where we're going. Did you talk to her?'

'Yes. Everything's fine. In fact she's coming back to stay with me for a few days. We'll be seeing her tonight, if you have time.'

'Sure. I don't have to be back early.'

He didn't say anything else, but I could see he was even happier.

I drove quickly out of Marrickville, and soon we were on the M5, heading for Goulburn and Canberra. This time I didn't try to break the sound barrier. Instead I used the time to catch up on some details.

'Tell me what they said about Loc,' I said. I was more interested in that than in their weapons training, significant though that was. What I wanted to know was what they'd revealed of their plans.

It had been skilfully done.

The discussion on the Wednesday evening had stuck to generalities, along the lines of their regular meetings in town, with the usual anti-communist themes. Binh had repeated that they'd been selected because they were the best in the group. Then he had announced that the leadership was planning a 'special operation', as he called it, against Loc. All he would say about it was that it was very secret, but he asked if they were prepared to take part in it. They all said yes, though Nghia had seemed nervous.

The next morning early Vo Khanh had taken them on their weapons training. He took this role seriously, as befitted a former Marines officer, whereas the more intellectual aspects of the job seemed to fall to Binh. This reinforced my feeling that somehow Bach Ho was involved.

Afterwards Binh had taken them for a second talk. This time he'd been more specific, though still short on detail. He'd described Loc as a top Viet Cong leader, one of the architects of the war and the repression which followed, and said his removal would strike a great blow for the resistance. Now he said they were trained guerrilla fighters, and like guerrillas they must strike at the enemy whenever an opportunity arose. Loc's visit was giving them that opportunity. He asked again if they were willing to play their part.

Again they all said yes, though Nghia's reluctance was more evident, and later he asked to withdraw. He returned to Sydney separately with Vo Khanh, after being sworn to secrecy.

Finally before leaving the farm Binh had taken Lam and Eric aside for one last talk, one at a time. Eric didn't know what he'd said to Lam, but to Eric he'd been pretty clear: was Eric prepared to avenge his parents' death and strike a decisive blow for the liberation of Vietnam? The word *assassination* wasn't mentioned, but there was no doubt what was meant. Eric had asked if it would be dangerous. Binh had assured him they were working on a plan that was virtually foolproof, and he would be protected and supported throughout. Eric had then confirmed he'd do it.

Binh had congratulated Eric, said he'd give him more details later. In the meantime he wasn't to discuss it with anyone other than himself or Vo Khanh.

'What about Quang?' I asked. 'Did anyone mention him?'

'No. And I didn't want to ask directly. But when we were talking at the end, I asked Binh if he'd ever killed anyone. He gave me a look, and said that's not a question you should ask. But then he said he'd never ask anyone to do something he couldn't do himself. That's when I said I could do it.'

I was impressed. Eric had conducted himself with great coolness throughout. I wanted to ask how he felt about deceiving his friends in that way, but thought I'd better not rub his face in it.

Instead I decided to come clean.

'Thanks, Eric. I think you've done a great job. Now it's my turn to tell you a secret. But this time it's really secret. You must promise not to tell anyone. Not even your aunt at this stage. Promise?'

'Yes.'

'It's about the people we're going to see. It's also about your father, and me too in a way.'

He listened in grave silence as I told him about the Agency, and what David and I had done for a living.

'So you were a spy after all,' he said with a touch of awe in his voice.

'Don't let it go to your head. And don't tell the people we're meeting either. They'll want to tell you themselves. And they'll probably get you to sign your life away first.'

———————

Roger had given me an address, a safe-house in Downer, one of Canberra's northern suburbs. They were already there when we arrived, Samantha looking sharp and sexy in a sweat shirt and stretch jeans. Coffee and juice were laid on and Roger democratically poured while I did the introductions. I felt like a horse-owner parading a new colt in the ring, but they must have been satisfied because Roger soon moved on to the next step.

As I expected the first thing he did was get Eric to sign some papers.

'I'm going to tell you something very sensitive, Eric. It concerns our national security, and we only tell people when we have to. It's called need-to-know. Do you understand that?'

'Yes.'

'Good. So before anything else I want you to read this form and sign it. Ask me any questions you want. But we don't go any further until you've done that. Is that OK with you?'

'Of course. Thank you.'

Eric started to sign but Roger stopped him.

'Read it first. Make sure you understand it.'

'Yes. Sorry.' Eric nodded, a little chastened, read the form more carefully, then signed it. Roger witnessed it and put it away in his briefcase.

'Now for the exciting part,' he said. 'I don't know what Paul has told you, but we are the agency that looks after foreign intelligence for Australia. We're spies, in other words.'

He proceeded to give Eric the beginner's guide to the Agency: what they were, what they did, who they worked for. This was less than I'd already told him, but Eric sat through it with rapt attention, giving no sign that he'd heard any of it before.

'We all belong to it here – Sam and Keith and I – and so did your father, and Paul here until ten years ago. In fact I knew your father, we did our training together. I was very sorry when he died. He was a good officer. He'd probably be in my shoes if he were still alive.'

As Roger had said the same thing about me at our last meeting I took that with a grain of salt. But Eric was impressed. There was none of his provocative flippancy about him, he looked grave and sober and totally reliable.

'Now we've got a lot to cover today, so I won't waste too much time talking. But first I want to say a few things, to make sure we're all on the same page.'

'The reason we're having this meeting is because you got yourself involved with a group of people in Sydney who look as if they might be up to no good. The Mad Buffaloes, as they call themselves...'

Roger had prepared well for his talk with Eric. Whatever annoyance he felt at the way I'd cornered him into it he kept well hidden. Starting with what had attracted Eric to the Mad Buffaloes in the first instance, he took him gradually through the process which had brought him to the meeting. He was careful to show sympathy and understanding for Eric's motives, and he watched Eric as he spoke, gauging the effect of his words.

'Take this man Dang van Loc,' Roger said. 'This Vietnamese leader who's coming out here. I don't know how much they've told you about him – probably that he's evil, he's a communist and therefore must be destroyed. But let me tell you something about him. So you know the kind of man they're planning to kill.'

I listened as he ran through Loc's life. Much of it I'd already heard from Quang, but there were details I didn't know. Loc was a southerner, as I knew, and he'd been a communist all his life. In 1954 at the age of seventeen he had gone to the north, with his mother and his younger brother. He'd already lost his father, who had been a leading Vietminh in the Mekong delta, and had been shot by the French. His elder brother had also been arrested by the French and had died in a French gaol.

In 1960 Loc had come south again. He was married by then, with one child, but his wife and child stayed in the north. He'd fought in the south until 1966, when he had been badly wounded in a B-52 strike. He had been evacuated secretly out through Cambodia and back to the north, where he recovered.

There was a gap of a few years, but it seemed he'd returned south in 1972, and stayed there until the end of the war. By then he was a senior cadre with the Viet Cong. He'd had another child by then, a boy. But during the American bombings of the north his wife and both his children had been killed. He also had a younger sister, who'd stayed south after 1954 and joined the Viet Cong. She'd been captured by the South Vietnamese, under the Phoenix programme, which tried to turn captured Viet Cong and run them back against their own people. She'd refused to cooperate and they'd tortured her to death.

After the communist victory in 1975, Loc, who was then very senior in the party, had become deputy chairman of the Ho Chi Minh City People's Committee – a kind of deputy mayor, as Quang had said. That was when Quang had first met him. Roger talked a bit about Quang, without revealing that he knew Quang personally. He stressed that Quang was not a communist, never had been, didn't like them very much, but had deliberately stayed behind rather than flee abroad, to help his country through a difficult transition. He had been a high official under the previous government, and because of that had had to go into re-education. Loc himself didn't approve of re-education, he thought it was unnecessarily harsh and wasteful. He'd heard about Quang and arranged to have him released and attached to his staff. They had become friends, and Quang had helped him a lot in running Ho Chi Minh City. Later, Loc had seen that things weren't working out well for Quang, and had helped Quang leave Vietnam. He himself had stayed. He was a communist, Vietnam was his country, he wasn't going to leave it just because things weren't working out quite as he had hoped. He had fallen from grace for a time, lost his job as deputy mayor, but later had come back into favour when the conservatives became less powerful in the party, and he had gradually moved up until he was now Deputy Premier for the whole country.

'Here is a man who lost his father to the French, and his brother, whose family was killed by American bombs, who lost his sister in a very nasty way to the old South Vietnamese government – and yet he has no feelings of revenge. He's never wanted revenge. He wants Vietnam and the US to be friends.'

'That's the man they're planning to kill. The top liberal among the communists in Vietnam. One of the few people there who understands the west, and wants to open up his country and maybe liberalise it a little.'

'So you'd have to ask yourself. Is that the right way to get revenge on Vietnam, and punish the communists for what they did in the past?'

Roger paused. Eric had sat riveted throughout, even the rest of us, who knew more about the subject, were impressed.

'You see what I'm getting at, don't you Eric. And why I think you've done the right thing in coming here to talk to us. We need your help, Eric. You're probably the only person who can stop this mad scheme, to kill the one man who's in a position to do something good for Vietnam.'

'Now it's your turn, Eric. Paul has told us a lot of good things about you. So we've decided to trust you. But now we need you to trust us. So I'd like you to tell us what you know about this group. How you came to join them, and what you've been doing up to now. Tell us what you've told Paul.'

This was the tricky part. But by then Eric was completely in their thrall, and he told them everything he had told me over the past two weeks, willingly or otherwise. By the time he'd finished they knew as much about the Mad Buffaloes and their leaders as Eric was ever going to be able to tell them, and more than I'd found out.

'Tell us about that last session up in the hills.'

Again more detail. Besides the .303 rifle they'd fired an M16, the standard American infantry rifle in Vietnam, and also a couple of pistols: a North Vietnamese Tukarov and a .38 Smith and Wesson revolver, which they'd learnt to strip and reassemble. But most interesting was another weapon, which only Eric had been allowed to fire: a .22 pistol, a Walther PPK apparently, with a silencer. That was a professional assassin's weapon, and Eric had become proficient with it.

'OK.' Roger called a halt. It was now twelve thirty. 'There are still a few things to discuss, but let's break off for lunch. Are you still with us, Eric?'

'Yes, most definitely.'

'Good. I need to take Paul away for a bit, but we've arranged for Sam to take you to lunch and show you something of Canberra. You haven't been here before, have you?'

'No sir.'

'You can call me Roger. We all use first names in the Agency. We'll all meet back here after lunch. Keith has something else on but he'll be back then too. Does that suit you?'

'Yes. Thank you very much.'

I bet it does, I thought as he cast a quick glance at Samantha, who gave him her slightly wicked smile.

———————

'He's really very good,' Roger said in the car. 'I hope we're not asking too much of him.'

'I hope so too! You were going at it a bit strong there for a while.'

'I wanted to make sure we had him on side. We can't afford any backsliding.'

'I'm sure there won't be any.'

Roger wanted to go to Parliament House. I took Northbourne Avenue and began the long drive south towards the lake.

'Get any more details about the visit?' I asked.

'We've got some dates now. He's arriving on the second.' The second of May. Just over two weeks away. 'That's a Tuesday. Coming first to Canberra, just transiting Sydney on the way in. One night here, back to Sydney the next day, one night there and then out again. Here he'll be having meetings with the Deputy Prime Minister and the Foreign Minister, a courtesy call on the PM, and addressing a lunch at the National Press Club.'

'Bringing many people with him?'

'Only a couple of aides. He's travelling light. Someone from their Ministry of Foreign Trade. I think he mainly wants to talk aid. And a security guy, some senior minder from their Ministry of Public Security.'

I drove through Civic, the old Canberra city centre, then followed Commonwealth Avenue over the lake and up the long slope to the new Parliament House. I parked in the underground car park and we took the lift to the top of the building and the grassy slope which overlooks the main entrance, stopping on the way for sandwiches and drinks at the cafeteria. We stood for a while looking at the view. We were facing north, back over the lake, towards the War Memorial away on the other side, with the wooded hump of Mount Ainslie at its back. Down the slope in front of us the old Parliament House stood like an old-fashioned wedding cake. Beyond, more official buildings, open spaces, further away residential suburbs, and on the far right faded khaki hills on the horizon, beyond Canberra airport. It looked very peaceful, an unlikely setting for murder.

'He'll be staying at the Hotel Canberra, just down the road.' Roger pointed the way we had come. 'We're picking up the tab.

From there he'll be coming straight here for his official calls. Driving up the road here, dismounting in front of the main entrance. Dinner that night in one of the smaller dining rooms. Only a small gathering, hosted by the Deputy PM, with a few MPs interested in trade with Vietnam. Their ambassador of course. No wives. Driven back to his hotel. Next day, lunch at the National Press Club. Then straight to the airport. He'll no doubt be spending the morning with their embassy, but we'll be providing escorts to and fro.'

'What about demonstrators? Aren't they coming in buses from Sydney?'

'They'll be kept well away.' He pointed to a roadway that cut across our front, some distance down from the main entrance. 'There'll be barriers along that road, and they'll remain on the other side. There'll be lots of police about, both here and at the hotel. I don't see anyone taking a pot-shot at him here, do you?'

I looked down at the scene.

'You think they're more likely to try it in Sydney?'

'That's my guess. The trouble is we don't have all his programme there yet. He'll be meeting the Premier and some business leaders, trying to get them interested in investing in Vietnam, and there's another meeting organised with some local Vietnamese businessmen. All closely monitored, only people with a clean slate. Interestingly, your Mr Bach is among them. He really seems to be playing both sides of the street! And New South Wales police will provide protection of course. But that's all we have, no timings or anything else yet. We don't even know where he's staying.'

'Does he know about all this? Are you going to try and warn him?'

'We'll probably do it through the Foreign Minister. They're having a separate session, behind closed doors, we're hoping to get Bill in there for a private chat.'

'Why don't you do it through his embassy?'

He hesitated. 'We think it's better if we tell him direct. Otherwise they might use it for propaganda, against the Vietnamese community here. I'm told he speaks passable English, but we'll have our own interpreter there too.'

'You'll have a job getting him away from his minders.' There was something funny about that arrangement, but I didn't seize upon it there and then.

'What about Bach?' I asked. 'Found out anything about him yet?'

'We're starting to get a few details. We found out how he got here. From Immigration, as you suggested.'

'And?' I prompted. He seemed reluctant to give out trade secrets, even to an old hand like me.

'He came out through Pulau Bidong, in Malaysia, that's where he was processed.'

'Did you manage to get hold of Svensson?'

'We did. But he doesn't know anything. He remembers the boat, more or less, but for some reason he wasn't involved in those interviews.'

'Who did him then? The Americans?'

Again that hesitation.

'Come on! I did that job too, remember? I know the drill.'

'We're still waiting for traces from them.' And then he closed up. Once again I had that uneasy feeling.

'What are you planning for this afternoon?' I asked. 'More of the same?'

He grinned.

'No. We've covered all that. Now it's just a question of detail. Meeting arrangements and so on. It shouldn't take long. You don't have to be there, if you want to take time off.'

'No, I want to be there. You're going to be discussing contact arrangements, that involves me too.'

'Not any more. We want to set up our own direct arrangements with him.'

'How are you going to do that? Through his aunt? She may not want to talk to you. I had enough trouble persuading her that it's OK so far.'

'We don't want to involve her either. We've worked something out, you'll see. It's much safer that way.'

'I don't want him put in any danger, Roger!' I said sharply.

'Rest assured, neither do we.'

'How long do you plan to use him?'

'Just a few days. All we want is information. That's all. It's all well and good knowing they're planning to kill Loc, but until we know how the information's not much use.'

'And when you've found that out? What happens then?'

Again he hesitated.

'It depends on what he tells us. Look, stop worrying! We're being very careful here, Paul. He's in more danger associating with you than anything else right now. We're moving up to Sydney tomorrow. Setting up an operational base there, with Samantha on standby, ready to meet him whenever he calls a meeting. And we've started talking to ASIO. In fact we need to set up a meeting with you there. They want to talk to you. And we're also talking to the police. Don't worry, we're making sure he's protected, we're not going to let him get hurt.'

'I hope not!'

'Now if you have no further questions we'd better get back.'

He turned away but I stopped him.

'Wait. There's one more thing. The price has gone up.'

'What do you mean?'

'Passports.'

'Passports?'

'Yes. I want two Australian passports. One for Eric, and one for his aunt if she wants one. Not straightaway, but when this is over.'

'Paul! Have you gone crazy? That wasn't part of the deal.'

'It is now. Look! I brought him to you, in good faith, so you could make use of the information he's got, and judge for yourselves how much trust you can put in him. And yes, so you could use him a little longer if need be. But this is getting a bit more ambitious, Roger, and I'm starting to have doubts about it. So this is the deal! Either you arrange for him to get a passport when this is all over, or I pull out. And I pull him out with me. And don't forget his aunt!'

What she'd say to that I could only guess. But I'd face that later.

'Come on Paul,' Roger pleaded. 'You know we can't do that! The Minister will have a fit if we ask him! Christ, it's hard enough to get a passport under alias, we can't give these things out to just anyone –'

'Not just anyone, Roger!' I said hotly. 'This is a kid whose father was Australian, who got himself killed in the line of duty, a kid who himself would have been born Australian if our government in 1975 hadn't been so shitty over Vietnam! His mother died trying to bring him out here! Do you want me to tell him how Canberra refused to accept her? That'll put a dent in his motivation! So either you go to your minister and get approval, or we both pull out and you can kiss your operation goodbye. We'll go to the cops in Sydney and they can take it from there.'

Roger listened in silence, his face set.

'OK. I'll see what I can do,' he said after a while. 'But I can't promise anything. Not about her. Why don't you just marry her for God's sake!'

'Leave my private life out of this!' I snapped. He stared at me.

'Christ, she really has got under your skin! OK. I'll see what I can do.'

'I want your word!'

'Yes! I promise! Satisfied? Bill will simply go berserk.'

Bill can go fuck himself, I thought. But at least I'd won that point. What good it would do was for me to work on.

The afternoon session went much faster. Roger left as soon as we got back to the house, to confer with Bill Forsythe no doubt, while Keith and Samantha went over the details of contact arrangements in Sydney with Eric. They were simple, and just shady enough to pass as genuine. Samantha was to be Eric's girl-friend – but I already have a girl-friend, he said. All the better. That way you've got more reason to keep Samantha secret. She'll use her real name, but she's from Sydney, here's her phone number, you met at Bondi and you've both got the hots for each other. So when you feel the need you just give her a ring, and come out to meet her. You can meet in town over coffee, or go for a walk somewhere quiet. Be prepared, she'll change her appearance a little. And you just tell her what you know. She'll give you instructions. OK with that? Don't worry, you won't be called on for any scenes of passion. Just hold hands as you huddle over a drink or walk along the beach.'

He smiled at the thought, and there was amusement in her eyes too as she contemplated having assignations with this tough looking lad with the smouldering eyes. She had taken him up to Black Mountain tower for lunch and they seemed to have become very chummy all of a sudden.

Roger came back as they were finishing up. He had a quick word with me first, his manner terse and not very friendly.

'I talked to Bill. He's not happy, but I put your arguments to him and he agreed to do what he could. We'll put it to the Minister. But not until this is over. Then we'll have a good case, and he'll probably wear it. Sorry, that's the best we can do.'

'I understand. Thanks. But I'll hold you to it.'

'I'm sure you will.'

Then he went back to Eric, all avuncular once more.

'Got everything worked out? Are you happy with it, Eric?'

Eric was happy. His eyes were dancing with excitement.

'Good. It's not too late to back out you know. What you're doing takes courage. I can see you've got that, you're a lot like your father, and from what I've been told your mother was very courageous too. So you're doing them proud. But it's not too late to pull out. No one here will blame you if you do.'

'No. I want to get on with this.'

'We're going to back you all the way. We'll have people on the ground to make sure nothing goes wrong. And we'll sort everything out with the police in Sydney. So you don't have to worry about that. But you'll be on your own for much of that time. Think you can handle that?'

'Yes.'

'I think so too. But remember. We don't want you to take any risks. Once you've found out what they're planning, get in touch with Sam. Don't lose her number. OK? You can still keep in touch with your aunt, of course you can, but you mustn't go anywhere near Paul. Not until this is over. It's too risky for you. Paul understands that too. He'll drive you back to Sydney but after that you don't have any further contact until I tell you. All agreed?'

'Yes. Perfectly.'

'Just one more thing.'

Like a magician Roger produced a large manila envelope from his briefcase, from which he pulled out his rabbit of the day.

'Paul told us you didn't have any photos of your father. These are for you.'

They'd done a good job, and the two large glossies would have done a portrait photographer proud: two full-face shots of David, taken at different times – one on his first entry into the firm, the second some time later, probably when he set out for Vietnam – making him look young and fresh and eager, like a student on graduation day. And a third smaller print, even more telling, taken at the training establishment, David doing unarmed combat, with the instructor's face carefully blacked out. Eric studied them in silence then looked up, almost too moved to say thanks.

'I can't let you keep them, not until this is over. It wouldn't be safe. But later on you can have them. Permanently.'

'Perhaps I can keep them for him,' I suggested.

Roger gave me a sharp glance, as if suspecting me of wanting to see Eric behind his back, but Eric looked at me with such a hopeful expression that he didn't have the heart to refuse.

'Alright,' he said. 'As long as they stay with Paul. It's for your own safety, Eric. You must understand that.'

He nodded, his head bent over the prints, moved almost to tears.

I let him drive on the way back. He had a licence, and I was glad to sit back and relax for a change, while I thought about what lay ahead. As far as Hao was concerned I told myself not to get my hopes up, but I was deeply excited that shortly I'd be seeing her again, and bringing her back to the flat. What happened after that I could only dream of.

Now it was Eric I was worried about. The day had gone well, better even than I'd expected. Roger and his team had handled it expertly, like the professionals they were. I thought they'd genuinely liked him as well, and I had no doubt they'd do their best to protect him. But their objective first and last was to exploit his access to get as much information as possible before Loc arrived, and perhaps go beyond that and ask him to play a more active role. I knew they wouldn't sacrifice him wantonly. But when it came to the crunch I wasn't so sure they'd put his safety first.

That was where we parted company. I was prepared to help all I could, and had brought Eric to them knowingly, for just that reason. And in return I had extracted the maximum price I could hope for. But no way could I stand by if his safety was compromised. I knew I'd have to keep a close eye on things, whatever Roger said, even if for the time being I was barred from having further contact with him.

Meanwhile Eric drove on, in a haze of contentment. If he still felt any doubts about what he was doing they had been swept away when Roger gave him the photos. That had been a masterstroke, even if I had thought of it first.

Which, to his credit, he hadn't forgotten.

'Thank you for getting those photos,' he said after a while.

'You're welcome. I'm sorry they couldn't do much about your father's family yet, but we can ask them again when this is all over. I'm sure they'll come up with something.'

I didn't tell him about the passports. It was too early for that.

'Do you think I could join them later on?'

I smiled. I'd been pretty well expecting that question. The combination of spycraft, Sam's smile and his father's memory was irresistible.

'I don't see why not,' I said. 'You'll need to go to university first. Get a degree. And you'd have to become an Australian citizen. But I'm sure that can be arranged.'

'I'd like to do further study. Asian history. And languages. Vietnamese for a start.'

'You couldn't go wrong with those. But what about Britain? Don't you want to go back to Leeds?'

'No. I'd rather stay here. I never liked Leeds much anyway. Especially after Uncle Khiem died.'

'Your aunt told me about that. You must miss him a lot.'

'Yes. He was always very kind to me. She had a hard time after he died.'

I wanted to ask more, about what kind of man Khiem had been, but I didn't know what questions to ask, that would help me visualise him, and I didn't want to give Eric the impression I was spying on her. I thought of George, or whoever that man was, waiting for her. I wondered if she'd tell me about him.

We finished the trip in friendly silence. On the outskirts of Sydney I took over again for the last lap. I drove along the M5 to King George's Road, then up through the tangle of back streets to Marrickville. I pulled up around the corner from the cousins' house.

'Aren't you coming?' he asked, suddenly suspicious.

'In a while. It's safer if we're not seen together. Even by the cousins. How long do you think you'll be?'

'Not long. I don't want to hang round the cousins.'

'Tell her I'll be there in half an hour. Now off you go, before it gets too late. And take care of yourself, alright? Don't do anything stupid. If things start to look dangerous I want you to come away fast. Doesn't matter what Sam or Roger tell you. I don't want you to take unnecessary risks.'

'I'll be OK. Stop worrying.'

'I'll stop worrying when this is all over.'

He took one last look at the photos, then got out of the car. I watched him stride off into the night and silently wished him luck. He and I would both need it over coming days.

Chapter Twenty-three

There was an odd little incident when I picked Hao up at the cousins' house thirty minutes later. Eric had gone and the front door was closed but the porch light was on and she opened as soon as I knocked. She was dressed to go out, in a dress and heels with a coat on top, and her luggage stood in the hallway behind her. She even wore hose and had put her hair up. But she also looked rather harassed. For a second I feared the worst.

'Are you alright?' I asked. 'Don't tell me you've changed your mind, and you're on your way to the airport!'

'No, of course not! I'm coming with you. Oh Paul, I'm so glad to see you!'

She moved forward and stepped into my arms. I hugged her cautiously back.

'I've missed you,' she said. 'I'm sorry I walked out on you like that. I didn't mean to hurt you. But I had to get away, I needed to think –'

'It's alright. I deserved it. I behaved like an idiot.'

'No you didn't.'

We clung to each other for a moment, while I marvelled at the way my luck had changed once again. Then she disengaged.

'Could you come in for a minute? I'm ready now, but I still have to say goodbye, and I – I'd like you to be there.'

'Of course.'

She took my hand and I followed her in. I hadn't been past the front door before. She led me through to the back of the house, where the whole family was gathered around a large kitchen table, making *chả giò*, the small Vietnamese rolls, for the shop no doubt: father, mother, several children ranging from toddlers to young adults, and a grandmother or aged aunt of some sort. They looked up as we came in but no one said anything and when I said hello all I got in reply was a curt nod or two, which I thought odd. Vietnamese are normally very polite to strangers.

'You remember Paul, don't you?' Hao said, still gripping my hand. I could feel the tension in her, like a tremor. '*Anh Chị nhớ Anh Paul không?* I'm going back with him now.'

She let go of my hand and took an envelope from her coat pocket. She spoke to the mother, a grim-faced woman in brown slacks and a grey cardigan, who stared back at us with hard suspicious eyes.

'*Chị,* I must thank you for letting me stay here. I know it hasn't been easy for you. You've been very kind to me. But it's better this way.' She spoke in Vietnamese, in the northern accent, which gave a sharp edge to her words. The family, I remembered, were northerners, like Khiem, and although born and bred in the south Hao could speak pure northern when she wanted, thanks to her father. My own Vietnamese had much improved in recent weeks and I understood most of what she said.

'This is for you. I've already given you money for my room but this should cover any other expenses.'

She held the envelope out, but the mother made no move to take it. Hao put it on the table. The envelope was unsealed and contained a bundle of notes, in hundreds and fifties.

'Please. Take it. It's yours. I would hate to think you've lost money because of Eric or me.'

The woman hesitated, then took the envelope and put it in the pocket of her cardigan.

'*Chắc Ông nay giàu lắm, nên Cô mới có nhiều tiền như thế!*' she said in a cutting tone. She had the kind of grating voice common to many Vietnamese women, which seems made for sarcasm. I translated mentally. This gentleman must be very rich, for you to have so much money. Hao flushed angrily.

'*Anh Paul là người hiền và đạo đức, và toi không phải là gái bán thân! Tiền này là tiền của tôi!*' she retorted. Paul is a kind and decent man, and I'm not a prostitute who sells her body. This is my money! 'But he's been very helpful to me and I'm very happy to be going back with him!'

I couldn't resist.

'*Tôi cũng mừng lắm, vì Cô Hảo la một người bạn quý mến,*' I trotted out in my best Vietnamese. I'm also very glad, because Hao is a dear and precious friend. Everyone stared, Hao included. She was the first to recover. She bent down to the older woman, said a few words of farewell, then turned to me. Vietnamese are invariably respectful to the old, no matter what the circumstances. 'We can go now,' she said in a low voice. There was a sheen of tears in her eyes. She took my hand again, I nodded around one more time, received a few more nods in return, and we left, picking her luggage up on the way.

'What was that all about?' I asked as we drove off. She sat upright in her seat, clutching her coat around her, still visibly upset.

'I didn't know you still spoke such good Vietnamese.'

'I've been revising it. I wanted to give you a surprise.'

She smiled faintly.

'She called me a whore.'

'I thought that's what she said.'

'Not just then. On Friday, after I called you. And yesterday, when I told her I was coming back with you. She said I was behaving like a bar-girl, the way I was chasing after you, I was bringing shame on the family, and on Khiem's name. If only she knew!'

'What a nasty thing to say! Didn't she know why you came to stay in the first place?'

'I don't think she cares. All she could think of was the family name. She said who did I think I was, with my fancy clothes, running after white men, if I wanted you so much why had I come back, you must have got tired of me –'

'You should have told me! I could have come yesterday.'

She shook her head.

'It was my fault. I shouldn't have gone back there. I knew what she was like. And they've only got a small house, and they're a large family – but that's the way with Vietnamese, when you're family you can always make room for one more, and it wasn't as if I didn't do anything, I paid for my board, I helped as much as I could, in the house, in the shop –'

'You certainly paid them enough. That was quite a sum you gave her.'

'I didn't want them to think I was leaving because I owed them money.'

I reached across and put my hand on hers. She gripped it briefly, then released it so that I could concentrate on my driving.

'How was your trip to Canberra?' she asked. 'Did everything go as you wanted?'

'Pretty well. Did Eric tell you about it?'

'He hardly said anything. He said you'd explain. But he was very excited. He kept talking about some photos you'd got him.'

'They're photos of his father. I'll show them to you later. I asked if they had any and they got some from records.' I knew I owed her a detailed explanation, but I didn't want to go into it just then.

'I'll tell you about it tomorrow. Don't worry. Everything went well. They liked him.'

She didn't say anything, and we finished the trip in silence. When we got home we put her luggage in her bedroom, then went to the sitting room. The flat was chilly and I switched on the heater. I asked if she wanted anything to eat but neither of us was hungry. I helped her off with her coat and recognised the brown dress with white spots she'd worn when I had taken her out to dinner, nearly four weeks earlier.

'I love that dress,' I said. 'That's the evening I started to fall in love with you.'

She smiled.

'I bought it specially. I went into town straight after your phone call. I was so happy that you'd met Eric, and you seemed to be getting on.'

She put her arms around me again. I held her close, feeling her supple strength through the thin material. I still couldn't believe my luck.

'You do love me, don't you Paul?' she asked. 'You weren't just saying that?'

'No, I mean it. Why, don't you believe me?'

'I do. But I need to be sure. Sometimes people imagine things.'

'Believe me, I've never been surer of anything. What about you? Do you love me?'

'Yes. I do. Very much.'

'That's alright then. We don't really need that talk after all.'

'Yes we do.'

'Alright. Let me clean up first. I feel rather grotty after that long drive.'

She sat down, and I went off to have a shower. I shaved as well, even put on deodorant. Whatever the evening held in store I wasn't taking any chances. I changed into clean clothes and went back to the sitting room.

Hao was still sitting where I'd left her, staring gloomily at the heater. I sat down next to her.

'Don't let that woman get to you,' I said. 'She's probably just jealous. I'm sure deep down she wishes she could be like you, wearing fine clothes, free to do what you want.'

'Maybe. But she was right you know. I have behaved like a whore.'

'Don't say that.'

'Not with you. Before. I had an affair, Paul. When Khiem was still alive. For the past two years I've been having an affair with one of my bosses. And I behaved pretty badly.'

'It's alright. You don't have to tell me. It's none of my business.'

'No. I want to tell you. You need to know about it, if we're going to be together. I'm just afraid you'll think what a slut I've been.'

'I'll never do that.'

Chapter Twenty-four

His name was Robert, and he was one of the partners at the place where she worked. It was a family firm, his older brother George was the managing director. She worked for them both. He was about forty-nine, married, handsome – she liked him, they got on well together. She was even attracted to him. And she knew he liked her too. But she never expected anything to happen.

'I was going through a bad stage at the time. I'm not saying that to give myself an excuse. But Khiem and I weren't happy together. I'm not sure why, we still loved each other in some ways, but it was as if we'd grown apart, lost touch with each other. Maybe it was the strain after all these years. We both worked hard of course, but apart from Eric we didn't have much to talk about, we seemed to live almost separate lives. We hardly even made love any more. I often felt very lonely.'

'One evening I went to a party, at George's place – a large dinner party, for friends and contacts of the company, nearly two hundred people. They have a big house just outside Leeds. Khiem was supposed to come too but at the last minute he decided to stay home. He said he was tired, he still had work to finish for the following week, and anyway he didn't like large parties like that very much. I was angry. I'd been looking forward to it, we didn't go out very much. I told him he was being selfish, these were the people I worked for, he could make an effort. But he wouldn't budge. You go, he said. You'll enjoy it better without me. So I went alone.'

'Robert was there of course, without his wife, she was visiting their daughter in the US. He asked me why Khiem hadn't come. I told him. I'd told George and his wife that Khiem wasn't feeling well, but I was tired of making excuses and I told Robert the truth. I said we'd had a quarrel, Khiem preferred his work to my company. I even said my marriage wasn't going well. I shouldn't have, it wasn't very loyal, but I was still angry with him.'

'I tried to enjoy the party. I mixed with people, helped to look after the guests. There was a band there, people were dancing, I danced with Robert. He kept me company, when he wasn't busy with guests. But it didn't work very well. I was too depressed. I also drank a bit too much. I don't normally drink very much. At one

stage we went out, to find somewhere quiet. It was towards the end
of the evening, the party was very noisy. He took me to another part
of the house, some kind of guests wing, there was no one about. In
one of the rooms he kissed me, he said he loved me, I kissed him
back…'

'Nothing happened that night. Nothing else I mean. He wanted
me to stay after the party, but I wouldn't. We went back in, and soon
after I went home. But afterwards I kept thinking about it. I didn't
love Robert. I liked him, a lot, but that was all. But when he'd kissed
me – it was as if something had snapped. I'd almost given in. It was
only the thought of Khiem that stopped me. He'd even – I'm sorry,
I shouldn't be telling you this – I was wearing stockings, not tights
as I usually wore, I'd put them on specially that evening, I'd hoped
earlier that Khiem and I might make love when we went home after
the party. He'd pulled my dress up and he was caressing my legs.
That was when I stopped him. I couldn't, not like that. Khiem was
asleep when I got home. I wanted to wake him, to shake him, tell
him what I'd done, what had almost happened, but I didn't. I just
lay there all night, thinking about it. I kept wishing I'd said yes.'

'After that I suppose it was just a matter of time. Two weeks
later Khiem went to London for a maths conference. Eric wanted to
stay over with a friend. I told Robert. His wife was still away, she
wasn't due back for another week. He asked if I was sure this time.
I said I was. He took me out to dinner. Afterwards we went to a
hotel, and I spent the night with him.'

'I'd never done anything like that before. I'd never been with
anyone other than Khiem. Unless you count those men on the boat.
I don't know what I was expecting – something like Khiem I
suppose. But when it happened – it was totally different. It was like
a dam breaking. We made love all night. Literally. We hardly slept.
I'd never felt anything like it. The next morning I didn't even feel
guilty. The first time after the party I'd felt like a criminal. This time
all I felt was a – an enormous sense of liberation. As if it was
something I should have done long ago. When Khiem came home I
just said I'd had a quiet week-end, gone to see a film…'

'And that's how it started. We started meeting after that.
Secretly. I didn't want to hurt Khiem in any way, and even less Eric,
and he didn't want to damage his own marriage either. We went to

hotels at first, but we didn't like that very much, and it was too risky. So after a while Robert rented a flat, a small apartment in town, and we used that, when it was safe. I'd go there after work, once or twice a week, for an hour or two before I went home. I'd tell Khiem I was working late, or going out with friends after work. I didn't like lying to him like that, but there was no way round, and he never questioned it. Sometimes we met on week-ends, but that was harder to arrange.'

'Khiem wasn't sick then,' I interrupted.

'No. That came later. I knew I was behaving very badly, like a trollop, but I didn't care. I enjoyed it too much. It was just sex, Paul. Maybe I did love him for a time. But when we were together all we did was have sex. As if I was trying to catch up, after all this time. I told myself it didn't really matter, I wasn't doing any harm, as long as Khiem didn't find out, it wasn't as if I was taking anything much away from our marriage. I even looked on it as a kind of compensation sometimes, a reward – for all those hard years, the loneliness, the unhappiness – almost a revenge, for what had happened on the boat. I told you I wasn't very nice.'

'Why the boat?' I asked. 'That wasn't Khiem's fault.'

She was silent for a moment.

'No. You're right. But there's something I didn't tell you about that. You remember when I said that some men had resisted, tried to stop the Thais from taking us, and they were beaten up and one man was killed? Well Khiem didn't.'

'You mean he didn't do anything?'

'No. He just stood there. As if paralysed. Even when we were being carried away to the other boat, screaming, calling out to him to do something, to save us, he didn't do anything.'

'What could he have done?'

'Nothing. I know. He would only have been beaten up, and maybe killed. Like the man they stabbed and threw overboard. I know it's unfair, it wouldn't have made any difference. But he didn't even try. And I could never forget that. I still can't.'

I was startled by this revelation, more than by the affair itself. From what she'd said earlier I'd assumed that Khiem had been among those who had resisted, and been beaten up for his pains. The reality it seemed had been very different. I pictured the scene –

the women screaming, being dragged away, the threatening Thais, the men cowering, hanging back, even the rise and fall of the boats on the water. I asked myself what I would have done in his place. Would I have had the courage to resist, to try and stop them, even though I knew it was hopeless, I would only get beaten up or worse? It was easy enough to imagine being heroic, leaping forward, fighting tooth and nail to save the woman I loved, but short of being there myself there was no way to know for certain. It was a frightening thought. And the knowledge of his failure thereafter, whether due to cowardice or simple awareness of the futility of doing anything, must have been almost too much to bear, must have eaten at him like a disease, like the cancer that had finally killed him. No wonder they'd had a poor sex life.

'When Khiem fell sick I started to feel guilty. I didn't stop seeing Robert straightaway. But I felt as if I was somehow responsible for his illness, had helped cause it with my behaviour. Robert said I was being superstitious, but I couldn't help feeling that. When he got worse I told Robert I had to stop. I couldn't go on having sex with him while Khiem was dying of cancer. So we stopped, and I concentrated on looking after Khiem. It was a sad time. It was clear by then that he wouldn't make it. I thought how unfair I'd been. He'd tried his best, he'd accepted Eric as his son, he'd worked hard to give us a decent life in England, and I'd repaid him by having an affair. I didn't regret my affair with Robert. But it seemed so cruel, that he should have to die as well. He was still young, not yet forty-five. He deserved better than that.'

'He never suspected anything?'

'No. We were always very careful. That would have been too cruel.'

'After Khiem's death I went back to Robert. About a month later. I didn't really want to then. We'd been apart nearly five months, and things had changed. I hadn't missed him as much as I'd thought. We still saw each other at work of course. But Robert said he'd missed me too much, he needed me, it was time to move on. He even said if I didn't want to I should think of leaving, find another job. He couldn't go on working with me if he couldn't have me. So I went back to him. I needed my job, especially now, with Khiem gone. And I still liked him, it was no great hardship. But I didn't enjoy it so much any more. Oh the sex was still good, he always made sure of that. But I knew now that I didn't love him. And I missed Khiem too, more than I'd expected. It seemed rather sordid to be meeting like that just for sex. But I told myself it was no more than I deserved, for having had that affair in the first place. So I put up with it. Until I left to come here. And I met you.'

'What did he say when you left? He must have been unhappy.'

'He was. But there was nothing he could do about it. He knew how much I cared about Eric, how worried I was about him. He asked if I'd be coming back. I said I didn't know...'

She turned to me.

'It was Robert who rang the other day. When you thought it was George. He didn't want to use his own name, he thought I might have told you about him. He's rung me several times since I've been here. He keeps asking when I'm coming back...'

'But I'm not going back to him, Paul. It's over. I know he says he loves me, he keeps saying how much he misses me, and I'm not really sorry I had that affair. It was devious and deceitful and not very nice, but if I hadn't I think I would have done something worse, maybe left Khiem altogether, I couldn't go on as I was, I was slowly going crazy. But I don't love Robert. I don't even like him very much any more. Whatever happens between us I'm not going back.'

She sighed.

'So this is me, Paul. This is the woman I am. I lied, I cheated, I had an affair with a man I don't love – do you still want me, after what I've told you?'

'Of course I want you. Do you think I'd stop loving you, because you've had an affair? I've had affairs too you know, and some of them have been pretty steamy. I'll tell you about them sometime if you want. I'm very glad your affair is over. I'm especially glad that you don't love him. If you did I expect you wouldn't be here. But I'm not upset that you had an affair. I'm only sorry you were so unhappy.'

'But I liked it, Paul! Even towards the end, when I didn't really want to be with him I still loved the way he fucked me! I couldn't get enough of it!'

'So what,' I said, mildly shocked by the crudity. It sounded out of place on her mouth. 'I like sex too. There's nothing wrong with that. I can understand why you want to feel guilty towards Khiem. Though if you ask me I think he may have been asking for it a little. But don't blame yourself because you enjoyed having sex with Robert. That's what affairs are about. Stop blaming yourself, Hao. It's not your fault that you were unhappy. It's not your fault these things have happened to you. You have a right to be happy too. You don't have to feel guilty all the time.'

I meant what I said. I wasn't disturbed or even particularly surprised that she'd had an affair. A beautiful woman like her, lonely, trapped in an unhappy marriage, something like that was almost bound to happen. I wasn't so sure about Robert. Maybe he did love her, as he claimed, but I couldn't help feeling he'd taken advantage of her. I've never approved of married men who sleep with their assistant, especially when she herself is a vulnerable married woman. It sounds too much like abuse of power. If anything it was Khiem I felt sympathy for. Whatever his failings as a husband, he too must have suffered over the years. But the fact that she'd enjoyed having sex with Robert didn't bother me. On the contrary, it was reassuring. I'd begun to fear she might be frigid.

'There's just one thing,' I said. 'I love you, Hao. I love you more than any woman I've ever known. Except for Rachel, and that's different of course. I'd love you as much if you'd had a dozen affairs. But you need to be sure about this. I'm not Robert. If things don't work out between us I won't try to keep you. If you're not happy with me, or you meet someone else you'd rather be with. But I'd rather not go through that. I've already been through one painful divorce, and you've been through worse. So if you have any doubts, about me, us, your feelings for me, now's the time to say so. I don't want to lose you. But I'd rather do it now than go through the pain of watching you leave in six or twelve months' time because you realise too late you've made a mistake.'

I must have spoken more harshly than I meant. She looked at me for a moment, as if assessing my words. Then she stood up. She took her dress off. She did it with the simplicity of a woman undressing in her bedroom, pulling it off over her head and putting it over the back of a chair. Underneath she wore a slip, which she also took off. Then she faced me. She wore stockings this time too, the old-fashioned kind, with a suspender belt and garters, minimalist bra and briefs. The stockings were black, sheer, the bra and pants also black, trimmed with lace and see-through, the nipples and smudge of pubic hair clearly visible. The effect on her slender frame was both graceful and fiercely erotic.

'Tell me you don't want me just for this.'

'Hao, I would do without sex for the rest of my life if that was the only way I could be with you.'

I noticed a scar, partly hidden by her underwear: a long thin runnel of shiny scar tissue that ran like a centipede down the length of her belly, from just below her navel to the top of her pubis, with little pock marks on either side like miniature lizard paws. I reached out to touch it, gently followed its course with my finger.

'My hysterectomy scar,' she said, looking down at herself. 'I have colloidal skin, I scar very badly.'

She looked briefly very sad, remembering no doubt what it signified. Then she seized my hand and held it against her.

'Take me to bed, Paul. Take me to bed and make love to me.'

Chapter Twenty-five

The next two days were some of the happiest that I've ever lived. We had made love during the night, not once but several times, with love, and lust, and tenderness and passion, and an intensity which took our breath away. Facing each other over breakfast the next morning we looked as if we'd been dragged through a hedge. But we were both deliriously happy, or would have been except for the shadow still hanging over us.

'Will you marry me, Hao?'

She was eating a fried egg, Vietnamese style, with chopsticks over a bowl of rice and a bit of soy sauce. She managed to do it without losing any of the yolk. She looked up and smiled.

'Yes,' she said.

I told her about the Agency. I'd reasoned on the way back from Canberra that this was the best way to reassure her, by showing her that Eric was in capable hands, and it was time for her to know anyway. She listened patiently as I went through my little speech, leaving out only the plot to kill Loc, and Eric's role in it. He was right, she would have gone ballistic.

'I knew,' she said when I'd finished.

'How did you know?'

'Hien told me. David had told her, when he asked her to marry him, and she told me after his death. We thought you must be too when you took over his job.'

Lesson number one in the spy-catcher's handbook. How to spot the spooks in an embassy: through the line of succession. Those two would have made a formidable team.

'How long will they want to keep him there?' she asked. 'With the Mad Buffaloes? What a silly name. Like children playing at a game.'

'Quite. Not very long I expect. Until they know a bit more about what that mob are up to. After that they'll pull him out.'

'You'll look after him, won't you? You won't let anything happen to him?'

'Yes. I promise. But don't worry. Nothing's going to happen to him.'

You'd better believe it, I told myself. Or my life wouldn't be worth living.

Vivien was the one who got a surprise, when I brought Hao to the office later that morning. I'd rung first to say I'd be late, but I hadn't warned her what to expect. She almost wept with joy.

'Oh you darling!' she said, as she embraced Hao. 'I've never seen anyone as miserable as that man last week. I thought I'd have to go and bring you back myself.'

She was even happier when I told her Hao was going to join us.

'Starting Wednesday,' I said. 'You'll see, we'll make this place hum.'

That was something we'd agreed on during the night. Hao's funds were running low, but she wouldn't accept any from me, except as an advance. So we had reached a compromise: she would work for me, for a salary, as a prelude to full partnership. She wasn't supposed to, under the rules of her tourist visa, but rules are meant to be bent, and considering what she and Eric were doing in the national interest, it was the least Australia could do in return.

After that, Immigration. Roger was as good as his word, the reference number worked like a magic formula, in half an hour Hao had a new visa, valid for another three months.

After which we went home, via a Chinese takeaway, had an early dinner and went straight to bed – mostly to sleep this time. There's only so much the body can take, past the age of forty.

The next day, Tuesday, was a holiday. Anzac day, 25th of April, 1995, twenty years to the day since we'd flown out of Saigon in that RAAF plane, leaving behind all those we should have taken along. I didn't remind her of that anniversary.

Instead I took her up to the Hunter Valley, to see my sister and my brother–in-law. It was too early yet to expect any report from Eric. We spent the day there. Hao had already met them when they'd come down to visit me after my beating, now was a good time to know each other better. It was moving to see how readily they accepted her in the family. Geoff took us on the obligatory tour of the vineyard (it didn't look its best at that time of year, with the leaves mostly fallen and the pruning not yet begun, canes and suckers straggling in all directions like a mad woman's hair, but that didn't lessen his enthusiasm) and Cathy showed her round the old farmhouse, Hao slim as a boy beside her.

'You'll look after her, won't you,' Cathy said to me before we left. 'Don't let her go, like all the others. I think she needs you.'

'Don't worry. I need her too.'

Chapter Twenty-Six

The next morning we came back to a harsher reality. We had just settled in at the office, at the start of our first working day together, when Jack Lipton rang: the police had released Quang's body, he was being cremated that morning, ten thirty, at Rookwood cemetery crematorium. It was the first time we'd spoken since that fateful morning nine days earlier, when he'd rung to announce Quang's murder, and his voice was still heavy with suspicion.

'I tried to ring you yesterday,' he said. 'What about your lady friend? Hao? I don't know how to contact her.'

'I'll tell her. I'm sure she'll want to come too.'

'Of course I want to come,' Hao said when I told her. 'What about Eric? Do you think we should ring him?'

'Better not. It mightn't be safe if he was seen there with us.'

'I suppose you're right,' she said a little sadly.

'We can take him there later, when this is all over.'

'Yes. I think we should.' I could tell she was disappointed. We still hadn't heard from him. I was beginning to fret.

It was a sad little group that met at the crematorium later that morning. The service had started when we arrived but we gathered outside afterwards, near the rose garden where Quang's ashes would soon come to rest. Jack and Sen were there of course, and so were Nghiem and Ann: I didn't know they knew Quang, until Nghiem explained they'd been at school together. The world of the old Saigon elite was small. There was also a cluster of elderly Vietnamese in ill-fitting suits and *ao dai* that had grown too tight. I wondered if Quang's informant was among them. I recognised Linh, the white-headed doctor who had treated me, and we exchanged a few words. He seemed glad to see me. A bonze in grey robes chanted some prayers. *Nam Mô A Di Đà Phật.*

Jack introduced me to a thin, scholarly-looking Vietnamese woman in her twenties, looking remarkably like her father.

'This is Nga. Quang's daughter. She's just arrived from France. She's staying with us for a few days.'

'I was terribly sad at your father's death,' I said to her formally. 'I didn't know him very well but I admired him a lot. We shall all miss him.'

'Thank you,' she said simply, in strongly accented English. 'I hadn't seen him since many years. But I will miss him also. Thank you for coming.'

'Nga lives with her mother in Paris,' Jack explained while she talked with Hao and Sen. 'They'd been separated for years. Quang had the sense to send them abroad before the end. He was prepared to stay and work for the new regime, but he didn't trust them very far.'

'Why didn't he stay in France too when he came out?'

'He didn't want to live there. He blamed them too for the mess in Vietnam. He said it would never have happened if they hadn't insisted on regaining their colonies in Indochina after World War Two. Same for the Americans. He didn't blame them so much for the war, they'd let themselves get sucked into it, but he couldn't forgive them for the way they had dropped the south in the end. He said at least Australia had a clear conscience, whatever our reasons for going to Vietnam we'd actually tried to help the country, and we'd also paid a heavy price. He liked this place better.'

I'm not jingoistic, but it made me proud for a moment of being Australian. Maybe that was the advantage of being a minor player on the world stage. We were less inclined to exploit others for our own ends.

Another visitor joined us: Detective Sergeant Emerson, dressed in grey this time. He gave me a grey look to go with it.

'I didn't know you two knew each other,' he said, making it sound like an accusation.

'Hello, Peter,' Jack said a little uncomfortably.

'We were together in Saigon,' I explained. 'How are you getting on with your investigation? Any ideas yet?'

'We have some leads' he said non-committally. 'Early days.' He looked at me. 'Are you sure you've told us everything you know?'

'Of course. Why would I want to hide anything? I'm as anxious as you to see his killer brought to justice. More, if anything. Quang was becoming my friend.'

He moved off, giving me another sceptical look. I wondered why he'd come. To pay his respects? Did he expect some dramatic revelation, the killer to appear and be struck down with guilt? Or was it just routine police procedure? I also wondered, irrelevantly, whether Quang had believed in God. I doubted it, for much the same reason that I didn't. Not the kind that allowed a murder like that to take place, or the sort of vileness that Hao and her sister and countless others had been subjected to.

'We're having a small wake at our place,' Jack said. 'If you'd like to come.'

'Sorry. I'd love to, but I have to get back to work. Hao might like to.'

'No. I'd better come back with you, Paul.'

She looked sad. I guessed she too felt this was a poor send-off for someone like him.

Hao was thoughtful on the way back. I put it down to the funeral, and worry about Eric. But there was something else on her mind.

'Would you mind if I went back to Leeds?' she asked suddenly. I felt a little stab of terror.

'I mean now, by myself. To sort things out.'

'I thought we were going together, when this is all over.'

'I don't think I should wait that long. There's such a lot to do. I have to put the house up for sale, and the car, and I need to organise my departure from work…'

'You're not having second thoughts, are you?'

'Of course not! How can you think that!'

'Because I can't quite believe my luck. When you see someone like Quang die so easily, it makes you realise how fragile everything is.'

She put her hand on mine.

'No! It's nothing like that. It's just – I hate the place, Paul! All that unhappiness, the things I did, watching Khiem die...I don't want to go back. But I have to, and the quicker I do it the better. And if you're not there it'll be easier. I don't want you to be contaminated with all that, when I come back I want to start afresh. You understand that, don't you?'

'I suppose so.'

'Besides, it'll be easier for you too. I know you're not telling me everything. I can understand, I expect there are things you can't tell me, but I don't like it, and I don't want that to lie between us, as it's doing now. It'll be better if I'm not here.'

'What will you tell Eric?'

'He'll understand. I'll just tell him I have to go back to sort things out...just promise me you won't let anything happen to him. Whatever happens. Promise me you'll look after him, and make sure he'll come to no harm.'

'I promise. I don't want anything to happen to him either.'

In return I talked her into letting me upgrade her to business class. Flights were heavily booked at that time of year, this way she'd be surer of getting an early seat – and coming back earlier too. I trusted her, but Robert not at all.

'Let me check with Roger about your visa. To make sure you have no problem getting back.'

———

There was a travel agent on the ground floor of our building. I rang Roger while she went down to check on flights.

'I was about to ring you,' he said. 'I'm coming up tomorrow, maybe we could meet.'

'Of course,' I said. 'But first I need your help.'

I explained about Hao's trip, and the visa. He listened with resignation.

'I'll see what I can do,' he said. 'I'll have to ring you back.'

'Thanks. What's happening with Eric? Have you heard from him?'

'He rang Sam last night, they're due to meet tonight. That's why I'm coming up. We should know more after that. I've got a meeting in the morning, but we can have lunch together if you're free.'

'Sure. Is your meeting about Eric?'

He hesitated. 'Yes,' he said.

'Can I be there too?'

'No. I'll fill you in afterwards. It's an inter-agency thing and we'll be discussing matters that don't concern you.'

'Everything to do with Eric concerns me! Who'll be there? A-S Ten?'

He laughed curtly. An old piece of Agency slang, to refer to ASIO if there was fear of being overheard. Read the last two letters as digits. ASIA was A-S 14.

'Of course they'll be there. I told you they'd have to get involved.'

'You also told me they'd want to talk to me. What better time?'

'Look, it's strictly insiders only! You don't have any clearances any more!'

'Then get me cleared!' I cried. 'Come on, Roger. I'm not trying to tell you your job. But I'm involved too. Who knows, I might even be of some use. I'm the one who started this whole thing, remember?'

He was silent for so long I thought he'd hung up.

'I'll try,' he said finally. 'You're pushing your luck.'

Then he did hang up.

He rang back an hour later. Hao had come back and was sitting at her desk. I didn't have to say much.

'On one condition. You don't interfere. You're there simply as an observer. Is that understood?'

'Perfectly.'

'Eleven thirty. Their office. Know where it is?'

'Still in the same place?'

'Yes.'

'Thanks. I'll be there.'

'Your lady friend's visa. Done. Multiple re-entry visa, valid for three months. But she'll have to go to Immigration before she leaves to make sure it's amended on her passport. That do you?'

'Yes. Thanks. I really appreciate that.'

'So you should,' he said. Hao looked up as I put down the phone.

'That was Roger,' I said. 'He's coming up tomorrow, and we're having a meeting. He's going to bring me up to date.'

I told her about the visa. She said she would go to Immigration at once.

'Thank you, Paul. And thank him.'

'It's the least he can do.'

I wasn't looking forward to Hao's departure. But she was right. It would make life much easier for me over the coming days. I was finding it increasingly unpleasant having to lie to her, and I knew it would only get worse as the climax drew nearer. This way, I'd be able to get on with the job unhindered.

The job? As far as I was concerned, all that mattered now was protecting Eric. I kept having second thoughts, and wished I'd listened harder to her. It was too late to back out now, I was stuck with what I had started, all I could do was stay with it and make sure he came out unharmed.

The problem was, I didn't have a clue how to do it.

Chapter twenty-seven

I felt a little rebellious the next morning when I went to attend Roger's meeting at ASIO's regional office. It was in Kurraba Road in Neutral Bay, a short drive from the office, in a large red-brick Federation-era mansion which had been extended at the back. Roger met me at the glassed-in reception area inside the entrance.

'A word of caution,' he said as he signed me in. 'We've got some brass here and they're keen to meet you, but you haven't come here to tell them what to do. Is that clear?'

'Very clear,' I said, determined not to let him bully me. Whatever happened, I was going to make sure I was heard. He led me through to a room at the back, with a conference table and a large picture window overlooking Shell Cove and Cremorne Point. A group of people in office suits and dresses stood looking at the view and drinking coffee. To judge by the papers on the table the meeting had already started.

One of the group detached himself and came over. This was Bob Maynard, the ASIO Regional Director, a slender pleasant man about my own age. I'd met him years earlier when he and I had worked together on a joint operation, and I remembered him as a quiet achiever.

'Paul, how are you! It's good to see you.'

We shook hands, and he introduced me to the rest. Most of them were from Canberra, and I recognised other faces from the past: Tanya Throsby, from Foreign Affairs, Edwin Truscott, from PM&C – the Department of Prime Minister and Cabinet, also formerly from Foreign. Two or three senior police officers in civvies, from New South Wales Police and the AFP – the Australian Federal Police – and another heavy, Tony Scarferi from the NSW Premier's office. I wondered briefly at this concentration of bureaucratic artillery, then remembered that we were dealing with an attempt to assassinate a foreign leader on Australian soil. It stood to reason that government at both federal and state level would want to monitor this with great care. Maynard's deputy was also there and Roger had brought Keith along, but there was no sign of Samantha.

'Grab yourself some coffee,' Maynard said. He motioned me to a place near him as the others resumed their seats. As host he chaired the meeting, even though he was outranked by several of the participants.

'Paul Quinn has been kind enough to attend this meeting,' he started. 'As you've gathered he's now a private citizen.' He ran briefly through my background, then asked Roger to bring me up to date. Roger looked at me with a bland expression, giving no hint of his earlier displeasure.

'Very quickly, Paul, everyone here has been briefed about this case, which is codenamed *Dragon*, so I won't go over the basics again. I've told the meeting what we know about the Mad Buffaloes, how you came to us with what you'd found out, and the role your young man is playing. He's also got a code name by the way, *Jason*, and his case officer is *Medea*.' That was Samantha of course. Some classical wag in Security.

'She met him last night, and we now know a little more about the Mad Buffaloes' plans. It seems clear they'll try and mount their attack here in Sydney and not in Canberra. Canberra's too open, too easy to protect, it would be too difficult for them there. They're organising some noisy demonstrations both there and in Sydney, but that's mainly atmospherics. The attack is likely to be much more stealthy. That's all we know so far, Jason still can't tell us exactly where or when, or how.'

'One point I should make. Both the PM and the Premier are watching this case with great attention. And this is now very much a police operation, together with ASIO – New South Wales police here in Sydney, AFP in Canberra. We'll continue to run Jason ourselves, but apart from that we're here as observers. This case now belongs to Commander Considine –' he nodded towards one of the police officers – 'and to Bob's crowd. Just so we're clear.'

'Of course.' It made sense. The Agency had no business providing VIP security, that was a police job, and the intelligence side was now essentially an ASIO matter. But this raised questions, not least about Eric's role. I kept quiet.

'One other thing. Security. Everyone here knows you used to be with us, and you've behaved throughout with the discretion one would expect from a former ASIA officer. But you're an outsider now, and you no longer have any clearances. Strictly speaking you shouldn't be here. Just so you know, this operation is Top Secret, and strictly limited. No leaks, no words to the press, or to anyone outside this room. Under pain of death. Is that clear?'

'Crystal,' I said drily, starting to get irritated. Then I understood. His words were really meant for the others. Not all public servants had the same sense of discretion as spies. That went for the police as well, and particularly for political appointees. Scarferi had all the hallmarks of a party apparatchik.

'Good.' He passed me back to Maynard, who smiled at me as if to make up for Roger's asperity, and thanked me again for having brought the case to them. Then he threw the debate open for questions.

The first was from Kathy Whitmont, a sharp-faced woman from the Attorney-General's Department in Canberra.

'Could you tell us how you came to be involved in this business.'

I nodded. That was the logical place to start.

'Certainly. It was by coincidence, really. I was approached by a relative of the young man in question. Jason.' I'd have to remember to call him that.

'Is that his aunt?'

'Yes.' I explained the background, and the steps which had led me to Quang.

'That's the man who was murdered, correct?'

This from Truscott. A jowly, heavy man with a pompous manner, who'd been ambassador in a couple of B-grade missions before moving closer to the centre of power. Not to be underestimated for all that. PM&C didn't go in for deadwood.

'Yes.'

'What makes you think his death was connected to this?'

'Gut feeling. Nothing I could prove. But he was inquiring into the Mad Buffaloes, he was getting deeper into them, his last comments to me before he was killed suggested he was on the verge of finding out something pretty sensitive. There was that. And I already knew they were capable of violence. I'd been beaten up by them myself only two weeks earlier. It made sense.'

'You didn't go to the police with that.'

'No.' The Whitmont woman again, with the look of an examiner putting a candidate through his paces. I didn't mind. I'd have my turn later.

She looked at me, waiting for me to elaborate. Another one observing me was Commander Brian Considine, head of the State Protection Group in the NSW Police. He was a powerful, muscular man with the head of a bull, tough and uncompromising, topped by a cap of tight black curls beginning to go grey, about Roger's age. He had the hard flat stare of a cop, but there was an intelligent gleam in his eyes and I had the feeling that he didn't miss much.

'A couple of reasons,' I said. 'First, I couldn't prove anything. All I had were suspicions. Strong suspicions, but nothing that would stand up in court. And I knew enough about Vietnamese to know that if the police started to question them they would simply clam up. So I decided instead to go to Roger. My old employer. I thought in the circumstances they would know best what to do. If Quang was right, and if my gut feeling was right, this murder and everything connected with it was part of a deeper plot, which was to do something nasty to Loc. And that was something Canberra needed to know about.'

I paused. They waited, still watching me. I went on.

'My second reason was Jason. Especially after my beating. He'd been very defensive towards me at first, very suspicious. I knew that if I reported it to the police they would come down pretty hard on that gang, including him. But I was starting to know him better, and I was pretty sure he wasn't involved in my beating. So I took a decision. I wouldn't tell the police, but I'd use it on him. I'd use that incident to gain his trust. And it worked. From that moment on he began to trust me. He was shocked by what had happened. He felt responsible, because he'd told his friends I was harassing him, and that was what had led to the beating. But he hadn't expected it to happen, and he was genuinely dismayed by it. He still felt a strong loyalty to that group. But it began to shake him. And when Quang was killed he was really shaken. That's when I put the hard word on him. And when he agreed to help me.'

'What made you so sure he wasn't part of it all? That he hadn't himself taken part in the beating? Or wanted it to happen?'

'I could tell. He's an emotional lad, with a great capacity for commitment. But he's not violent. Not in that sense. He dislikes injustice more than anything else. I could see his reactions were genuine. And after Quang's death he himself contacted us –

contacted me, and there was no hesitation then about working for me.'

'When you say working for you, you mean you used him as a source?'

'Yes.'

There was a pause, while people thought of their next questions. I was still aware of Considine studying me. Maynard filled the hiatus.

'Can you tell us something about the Vietnamese community, Paul. It's not an area I've had much to do with. Apart from Brian here I doubt any of us know much about it.'

'I don't know much either,' said Considine, speaking for the first time. He had a deep, rather pleasant baritone voice. 'I've never dealt with them myself. And I don't want to ask our area command in Cabramatta. We're also playing this close to the chest.' A dig back at Roger. His face remained bland.

'I'm not sure they'd be much use to you anyway, Commander,' I said. 'I don't think the Mad Buffaloes are very involved in crime. Sorry. It's years since I had anything to do with the Vietnamese in Sydney, my knowledge is way out of date. But here's what I know, for what it's worth.'

I gave them a quick thumbnail sketch. I talked of a hard-working community, with its various components, the regional variations, the religious affiliations, their wariness of outsiders, which made them secretive at first, but the way they opened up to those who took the trouble to know them, their generosity, their combination of hard work, intelligence, and sometimes fractious individualism. I talked rather more than I intended, but my audience didn't seem to mind. And after that came more questions. About the Mad Buffaloes, Quang. And about Eric/Jason.

'Do you think Quang was genuine?'

'Absolutely. I'd stake my life on it.'

'What about the Mad Buffaloes: are they capable of carrying out this threat?'

'I think so. I don't know much about them apart from what Jason has told me. Some of them are probably not much better than thugs. But others are very committed, they're fiercely anti-communist, and there's some brains there as well. Their leader, the man I suspect is their real leader, Bach, is very clever. Vo Khanh, the ex-Marine major, is just a fighting man, courageous but not very smart. But Bach is very sharp. If he's behind it all, and if Jason weren't working for us, I think there's a good chance they'd succeed.'

'Hmm.' Truscott again. 'You think Jason would be up to it? If he weren't working for us, as you say?'

'Yes. He's very courageous too. As I told you he's the kind of idealistic young man who would be very committed, once he espoused a cause. That's why I know you can rely on him for this job. If he were really working for them, I have no doubt he'd try just as hard.'

'Do you think they're using him as a decoy? Knowing that we may be on to him, because of his association with you?'

That came from Considine, and it was a shrewd question. I considered it.

'No, I don't. I think I know why they've picked him.'

'Why's that?' Ms Whitmont, making her mark again.

'Several reasons. First, because of what I said. He's good. He's intelligent, resourceful, quick, and from their point of view totally committed. He's both available and expendable. But there's another reason, which I think is even more important. He doesn't look Vietnamese.'

Considine nodded.

'He doesn't even look Eurasian. And he speaks perfect English, without a trace of an accent. If anyone is going to get close to Loc he's much more likely to succeed than someone who looks as if they've just come off a refugee boat.'

Tony Scarferi spoke up from the other end of the table. He was a plump, dark-chinned man with suspicious eyes and a flat grating voice.

'What makes you so sure he'll stick with us? He's already switched sides once. What's to stop him from switching sides again? If he hates the communists so much.'

There spoke the true party man, I thought. He'd know all about switching sides. But I nodded, to show I took his question seriously.

'Two reasons, mainly. He hates murder, and injustice. He was genuinely distressed by Quang's murder. He'd begun to waver before that, but that was the last straw. And he owes me. I'm the one who gave him his father. I didn't betray him, after I was beaten up, by going to the cops as I could have, I did that to protect him, and he knows that. And I told him about his father, I helped him get photos of him, thanks to Roger. He now knows his father worked for the Agency. He's not going to betray that.'

Scarferi nodded dubiously. It probably took more than that in his game to ensure your full loyalty.

'What about his aunt?' asked Truscott. 'Can she be trusted too?'

'Yes. She's fine. She's on side. She knows nothing about the assassination plot, by the way. And she's about to fly back to Britain for a few days. On personal business. I can vouch for her.'

'Where is she now?'

'Staying with me.'

He shot me a look from under his beetling eyebrows. No one said anything, though there was a stir of interest. Maybe they noticed the shadows under my eyes. Maynard spoke up.

'Good. Well, that's all been very useful. Thanks again, Paul. If nobody else has any further questions?'

I put my hand up.

'I've got a few.'

They all looked at me again. The examinee who asked questions back. Roger gave me a look of warning but I ignored him. Maynard nodded.

'Of course. Go ahead.'

'First, what's to stop you stepping in right now and putting an end to it? Why can't you just go and arrest them?'

There was a general shuffle around the table. Roger looked at Maynard, who looked back at him. Whitmont looked at her hands. Commander Considine rubbed his chin and looked at me. Truscott glowered and sat back in his chair. Roger finally spoke up.

'Because we can't,' he said flatly. 'We don't have enough information to charge any of them. We could step in right now but all that would achieve would be to warn them we're on to them and probably drive them underground.'

'But that would stop the assassination attempt, wouldn't it?'

'Not necessarily. We don't know what else they have up their sleeve. Commander Considine may be right. Maybe Jason is only meant as a decoy. In any case we have nothing that would stand up in court. We need to know more.'

'How much more do you need before you can pull Jason out?'

He looked round again, at Maynard and Truscott.

'We need at the very least to know what their plan is. How they propose to kill Loc. When we know that we'll be able to decide what to do.'

'Meanwhile he may be risking his neck.'

'We're taking every care, Paul,' he said sharply. 'We're not taking any chances on that. You've met his handler, Medea. She's one of our best. There's no reason why he should come to grief. Stop worrying. He volunteered, remember!'

Yes, I thought. And he's just a boy. But I let it ride. Considine was watching me closely. I went on.

'Do you have any idea at this stage what that plan may be? How they can get close enough to Loc to take a shot at him?'

'Not yet.' Roger looked at Considine.

'We're looking at all the options,' Considine said. 'But until we hear more from him we don't really know.'

'Where's Loc staying, do you know?'

He looked at Maynard, who looked at Roger, then back at me.

'Southern Aurora Apartments. In Clarence Street, in the city, between Erskine and King. Upmarket serviced apartments.'

'Not a hotel.'

'No. Apparently he likes quiet places, and it's quieter than a hotel. Also cheaper. They've taken a couple of suites there.'

'Just for the one night?'

'Yes. Wednesday the 3rd. Arriving after lunch from Canberra, leaving mid-morning the next day for New Zealand.' He looked at his notes, checked himself. 'Actually no. He's only staying one night, but one or two of his party will be staying there the night before as well, instead of going on to Canberra.'

'And who's that?'

'Not sure yet. There's several people coming with him, Tanya has details.'

Maynard looked at Tanya Throsby.

'He's got a personal assistant,' she said. 'Plus a senior official from their Ministry of Trade, another one from their Foreign Ministry, and one security man. Five altogether.'

'We suspect the Foreign Ministry man is really from their Ministry of Interior, probably from the Department of Public Security,' added Roger. 'A minder, to make sure he says the right things. That's all we know. His name is Truong Dzu, but we have no traces on him.'

'Thanks. I assume he'll have a full programme when he's here.'

'Pretty well,' said Maynard. 'Meeting at the airport, taken to the consulate while some of the party go to the apartments, a call on the Premier, then he'll go to his apartment too, late afternoon meeting with some business leaders, including some from the Vietnamese community, evening reception hosted by the Deputy Premier. Early night, back to the apartments about ten, ten thirty, I should think. In the morning, straight to the airport and off to New Zealand.'

'Thanks.' I looked at Considine.

'Commander, may I ask what measures you're taking for Loc's protection?'

'Paul!' Roger cut in sharply, but I put my hand up.

'I know. Strictly speaking that's none of my business. But I'm concerned about the young man. Commander, I don't want to see Loc assassinated any more than you do. From all I hear he's a good man. But it's Jason I'm worried about. I brought him into this, I'm the one who asked him to stick his neck out. Precisely to make sure that this assassination attempt doesn't succeed and those responsible are caught. What assurances can you give me that he himself won't get killed in the process?'

Considine nodded.

'Fair enough,' he said in his deep baritone. 'Until we know more about what they're planning our precautions can only be general. But they'll be thorough. Loc will be escorted at all times by a team of plain clothes officers. All visitors and guests will be screened. All his public appearances are indoors, he won't be seen out in the open, except briefly at the airport, and that'll also be secured. Access to the apartments will be strictly controlled.'

'Where do you think the attack is likely to take place?' I asked.

He shook his head.

'Too early to say.'

'Have you thought of switching the venues at the last minute?'

'We can't do that for his public meetings. Too difficult to manage, and the guests wouldn't put up with it.'

'What about his accommodation? What's to stop you moving him to a hotel instead at the last minute? Who chose it in the first place?'

'His consulate I expect. Don't worry, we're looking at that too. Rest assured, Paul, we'll be doing everything we can. And that includes protecting your young man. No one's going to get killed on my beat.'

'Thank you.' I looked around. No one stirred for a moment. Then Maynard spoke.

'Fine. I think that's it for today. Thank you everyone. I'll keep you posted about our next meeting. And thank you again for coming, Paul. You've been a great help. Can we call on you if we need your assistance again?'

'Of course.' He stood up, the rest followed, milling about for a moment. Roger came up to me. He wasn't amused. 'I told you to let the grown-ups do the talking!'

'Come on, you didn't expect me to sit still and say nothing, did you? What's happening with Bach, by the way?'

'What about him?'

'You were going to get something from the Americans. Has anything come through yet?'

He shook his head. Behind him Considine loomed. He was strangely built, almost top-heavy, with his massive chest on top of slim hips and long spindly legs.

'What's this about Bach?' he asked.

'Nothing much,' Roger said. 'We've asked the Americans if they have anything on him but they haven't responded yet.'

'I'll be interested when they do,' Considine said. 'There's something I don't like about that man.'

'Me either,' I said. 'Roger? Still on for lunch?'

'Sorry. Cancelled. I have to rush back to Canberra.'

'Hey –'

'Bob will escort you out. I've got to go. I'll give you a ring when anything comes up.' He made off before I could say anything, with

Keith in tow. Considine looked after him thoughtfully. Then back at me.

'Can I have your phone number, Paul? In case I need to get in touch with you myself.'

'Of course.' I gave him my business card, and wrote my home number and address on the back. He gave me his own card in return, with the NSW Police crest, and his rank and name and a phone number.

'In case you need to get in touch with me. That's a direct line. If someone else answers just say the codeword Dragon. That'll bring either me or Barnes.' Barnes was his deputy, also at the meeting.

'Thank you Commander.'

'Call me Brian. That was interesting, what you told us. You've done some good work there.'

Then he too was gone. Maynard escorted me to the front door.

'If I don't see you again over this,' he said, 'give me a ring sometime, we'll have lunch together.'

Hao was out when I came back to the office. The agent had called, to say that he'd put her on a flight the next day, and she had gone home to pack. I took the opportunity to talk to Vivien. I'd done some hard thinking on the way back, and a plan was beginning to form in my mind. A rather crazy plan, but there were several things I didn't like out of that meeting, and it was better to be prepared.

It pays to have a suspicious mind.

PART III

A reckoning

Chapter Twenty-Eight

I didn't much enjoy taking Hao to the airport on the Friday evening. We had made love again the night before, long and tenderly, as if we sensed that it might be our last chance for some time. I was filled with an uneasy foreboding. We spent a few last minutes together before she went through Immigration. Eric was there too, looking sombre. She'd rung him the day before and he'd said he'd try to make it. I nodded at him and he nodded coolly back but otherwise kept his distance.

'Why aren't you two talking?' she asked in alarm.

'It's alright,' I said. 'He's just sticking to his cover. We're not supposed to be friendly. You can talk to him. Tell him I said hello.'

She went and spoke with him for a moment. His face lit up, and he gave me a quick glance. He said something back to her and she smiled and hugged him. Then he resumed his stern look.

'What did you say to him?' I asked.

'I told him we're going to get married. He's so happy. He was afraid we'd had another quarrel. He says he hopes you don't mind, but he's not going to call you Daddy.'

'Thank God for that.'

'He also said not to worry, everything's going well. You will look after him, Paul? You promised.'

'I will. I'll guard him with my life if need be.'

We clung to each other briefly. Passionate in private, reserved in public, like all well-bred Asian women.

'I'll ring you Sunday morning.'

Then she was gone. When I turned round Eric had also disappeared.

The week-end went as lonely week-ends do, too slowly for comfort. When I got home I rang Vivien to check how things were going, and she told me everything was well in hand. On Saturday I went to work for a few hours, but that was more to kill time than to achieve anything. I tried to contact Roger but he wasn't at home or in his office, and the Agency in those days didn't allow mobile phones. On Sunday I made the first of several purchases. Then at five I drove to Vivien's flat in Greenwich, to pick her up and start implementing the first part of my plan. And that night Hao rang as promised.

'How was the trip?' I asked. 'Not too tiring?'

'A bit, but much more comfortable than on the way out. They certainly look after you better in business. Thank you for that.'

She was home, having come up by train the day before from London. It was eight pm in Sydney, ten that morning in Leeds. She was still jet-lagged and we didn't talk long.

'The bed's very empty without you,' I said.

'I know. I couldn't get to sleep last night. I kept thinking of you. I love you.'

'I love you too. When are you coming back?'

She said she was going into work the next day, to start her termination process, then she'd see an agent about selling the house. That shouldn't take more than a few days. She wanted to ring me during the week, but I said it would be easier for me to ring her, in case I wasn't home when she called.

'Are you going somewhere?'

'In case I have to go to Canberra or whatever.'

We told each other again how much we loved each other, and that was that. I felt almost more lonely afterwards than before.

A few minutes later I was about to try Roger again when I had another phone call: from Considine this time, the New South Wales copper I'd met at the ASIO meeting. He asked if he could come to see me.

'I know it's a bit late, but I have to go to Canberra tomorrow, and there's a couple of things I'd like to check with you first. Should only take a few minutes.'

'Of course, Commander. Glad to help.'

'Brian, please. I'll be there shortly.'

He was there in minutes. If I hadn't had his features firmly in mind I mightn't have recognised him. He wore jeans and a black leather jacket this time, and looked more like a hard man out to settle a few scores than the senior officer of an elite police unit. But his intentions were peaceful enough. I settled him into an armchair deep enough to accommodate him and offered him a whisky.

'Just a small one,' he said. 'I can't afford to do any serious drinking until this is over.'

I poured him a dose of single-malt scotch, a smaller one for myself, and sat down facing him. He took a sip and looked at his glass approvingly.

'Thanks. I needed that.'

'Been busy?'

He nodded. 'Nothing but meetings the past few days. The Commissioner, the Minister, even the Premier. You'd think we had a royal visit on our hands.'

He stretched his long legs, looked around, then fixed me with his dark eyes. He seemed in no hurry to go now. But I was glad of his company.

'Nice place you have here. Been here long?'

'About three years.'

'On your own?'

'Most of the time, yes.'

He grinned quickly, pulling his lips back over even white teeth. I remembered the way he'd sat at that conference table, staring at me like a brooding Minotaur. But there was genuine warmth in the grin. This guy could be a charmer.

'Sorry. Cop's habit, asking questions. You've had the young man's aunt staying here, you said. Is she still here?'

'No. She left for the UK a couple of days ago. She should be back in a week or so.'

He nodded.

'What about you?' I asked. 'Are you married?'

'Wife, two daughters, that I don't see enough of. The usual thing. So far they've put up with it with good grace.'

'It must be a pretty demanding job, protecting VIPs. Have you heard from Jason?'

'Yes. Not directly, through Bob Maynard's office. He had another meeting with his handler, on Friday night. Medea. A good session apparently. But he didn't add much to what we already know. He still doesn't know where or how he's supposed to make the hit, or even when. He also said he was going to the hills for a couple of days, he'd contact her when he got back, but she hasn't heard from him since.'

'That would be at their training camp presumably.'

'Sounds like it. He said they were pumping him up non-stop.'

My heart went out to him, alone, bravely coping with a job a grown man might have quailed at.

'I still don't know why you can't arrest the lot of them right now. Surely you'd have enough evidence, with his testimony, to crack down on them and make sure nothing happens.'

He shook his head.

'Canberra won't hear of it. They keep saying it's too early, they need to know more, they need to know exactly what's being planned, and who else is involved. In case this is just a decoy and they're preparing something else as well. I'm not sure they're right, but I keep getting over-ruled. You'd better keep that to yourself, by the way.'

'Of course.'

'I'm not sure I should be telling you all this. I got the impression Roger Bentinck didn't really want you at that meeting.'

I said nothing to that. He gave me a half smile. I had the feeling that what Roger wanted didn't count all that much with him.

'Personally I thought you did a good job. Even that fat prick Truscott was impressed.'

'Thanks. Do you know how long they plan to keep Jason there?'

He made a non-committal face.

'Probably until close to the end. If he's the one who's meant to do it, they won't want to pull him out and find that someone else has been put in his place. Which is really why I'm here. I want to ask if there's anything else you can tell me about that group. Especially their leader, that man Bach Ho.'

'Not much more than I told you at the meeting. I've only met him once.'

'True, but that's more than anyone else has done. And you've talked to Jason about him, and that man Quang, who was killed. You know more about him than the rest of us put together.'

I went over once more what I had said at the meeting

'I can't prove anything. I told you. The clear impression I have is that he's at the centre of things, but that's all it is, just an impression. What I can say is that he struck me as a very tough person, very self-possessed. Very clever and very much in control of himself. If he is running things, then you can expect they'll be well run.'

'What about that other man? Vo Khanh? From what you said they're very different types.'

'Yes. Vo Khanh is a very physical man. He's impulsive and hot tempered and no doubt courageous, but I don't think he's very bright. My guess is he's overawed by Bach's intelligence. And it's possible Bach's got a financial hold over him too. Quang thought he'd probably financed Vo Khanh's restaurant.'

Considine nodded.

'You were talking to Bentinck about him. Something about asking the Americans.'

'Yes. When Roger and I were discussing him earlier, it emerged he hadn't been interviewed by any of our people on the ground, at the time. In the refugee camp, I mean. Other than Immigration interviews, which didn't go very deep. I thought he might have been vetted by the Americans and Roger said he'd check it out. But when I asked him on Thursday he said he hadn't received anything back from them yet.'

'How long does it normally take to get a response?'

'Depends I guess. What they've got in their data base. We had this discussion on Tuesday last week. So it would have been about a week.'

'Should be long enough to get something back. Maybe I'll know more tomorrow. I can't help feeling he's the key to all this. Call it an old cop's instinct.'

He finished his drink, stood up, declined a second.

'My shout next time. What was it? Laphroaig?'

'Yes.'

I accompanied him to the door. I had more questions.

'How was Jason on Friday? Did he say anything else?'

'I don't know the details. I only got a summary. But it seems he was in good shape, holding up well. Sounds a good lad, from all I hear.'

'He is. And he really wasn't able to tell them anything else? About how it's supposed to happen?'

'No. All he said was he was going off for a couple of days, and he'd try to ring her when he came back.'

'Do you have any idea yourself where it's likely to take place?' I asked.

'A couple. But it's hard to be sure. I've been over every inch of that route, and I can't see that there are many ways they can get at him, unless they try a suicide bid – and that doesn't seem likely, that's not the way Jason's talking. He says they expect him to make a clean getaway, they'll help him. Where would you do it, if you had to plan a hit like that?'

'I don't know. It's not something I've ever had to do. Maybe I'd go for a rifle shot, you know, with a marksman. But if I couldn't get a good shot at him…Maybe try the apartments. Get access there under some pretext.'

He looked at me.

'I'm going to have the place covered. Everyone searched on entry. There's no way he could bring a gun in with him.'

'What if they've already stashed one in there?'

'I've had my team go over every inch of that place, and we'll be doing that every day until the big day. There's no way they could hide anything there. Not for quick retrieval, anyway.'

He hesitated.

'Something else you should know. I probably shouldn't be telling you this either. But you've been straight with us and I feel we owe you. That meeting, on Friday. Jason was followed.'

'How do you know?' I asked, suddenly alarmed.

'Maynard told me. He had the meeting covered. Don't worry, it was very professional. They met in a pub in Bondi, apparently, near the safe flat where she's staying, had a couple of drinks and then she took him back to the flat. Roger wanted to be there but Maynard wouldn't allow it. Let's play it straight, he said, she'll tell us about it afterwards, if she's in doubt she can ring. He was there for nearly two hours. When he left she came down with him. They were seen to embrace passionately, I'm told. Lucky young man. They say she's quite a looker. So I wouldn't worry too much about him. I have a feeling he'll be alright. But that's why everything has to be done right.'

'Of course,' I said. 'Thanks for telling me that.'

'Don't go doing anything stupid like trying to contact him. It might well be the worst thing you could do right now.'

'I know.'

After Considine left I washed the glasses, put the bottle away, resisting the temptation to have another drink. Like him, I needed a clear head for the days to come. I sat down and went over our talk. I could see where his thoughts were heading, alright. Mine had already gone in that direction. For all his cop's instincts, I suspected I had a more devious mind. I thanked my lucky stars I'd had the wits to act in time.

Chapter Twenty-Nine

It had been by instinct, more than rational thought, and it was more of a precaution as yet than a fully-formed plan. But it was the only thing I could come up with, and I couldn't afford to neglect it.

Basically it was very simple. What I wanted was somewhere to stay, a base of my own in that block of serviced apartments, where I could hole up and be ready to act if things went sour for Eric. I'd felt clearly enough at that meeting that I was an outsider, as far as they were concerned I had fulfilled my role, apart from Considine no one seemed to need me any more. If I was to do anything to help Eric I would have to do it alone.

And so when I returned to the office on the Thursday after the ASIO meeting I'd had a long talk with Viv. I needed to act quickly, before my options were closed off. Viv had an older sister, Maisie, who lived on the far south coast and occasionally came up to Sydney to visit her. My plan was to have Maisie book one of the apartments in her name, covering the period when Loc would be there, and spend a few days there with Viv. I would play the part of Maisie's fictitious son Jonathan, also visiting from the country, and join them at the appropriate time. That would give me the base I needed. The rest would be up to me.

Viv had agreed without too much fuss, but Maisie had taken longer to convince. Fortunately I got on well with her too. I'd told her that I needed to get away from the gang that had bashed me up, and I needed somewhere safe to help Eric, and this was the only way I could do it. I assured her it was not illegal. And I promised her the best week on the town she'd ever had. Whether it was that or the thrill of helping out on something so far out of the ordinary, she finally agreed.

Within half an hour she rang back. She had rung the Southern Aurora Apartments and booked a two-bedroom serviced apartment, for a week, from Sunday through to the following week-end. She paid the deposit over the phone with her credit card. I told her I would transfer money at once into her bank account, and explain everything in more detail when she arrived.

On Sunday afternoon I went with Viv to meet her at the coach terminal at Central Station. I drove them both to the apartments, adding to their luggage the small case I had brought along. I left them to register by themselves, and an hour later went in to see them. They'd had no problem booking in, under Maisie's identity. I told them what I had in mind, and swore them both to secrecy. As keen fans of thrillers and whodunits they were thrilled at being caught up in a real-life version. Then I went home to wait for Hao's call.

It was too late after Considine had left to go back to the apartments that night. I needed to keep a low profile, keep my comings and goings to daylight hours, when I was less likely to be noticed. I rang the two women, checked they were comfortable, stayed home, did some more thinking.

On Monday I went to work as usual. So did Vivien, coming in from the apartment via her flat in Greenwich. I found it hard to concentrate, managed to conduct a couple of interviews without afterwards remembering anything of the applicants. I went out, made more purchases, tried to ring Roger, finally got him at work late that afternoon. He told me he was coming up to Sydney again the next day, for another meeting, but quickly pre-empted any attempt to get myself invited.

'Sorry Paul, this one you can't attend. It's just a working meeting. But I can see you straight after, if you're free. I can come to your office about eleven thirty or twelve.'

'Have you heard from Eric?' I asked.

'We'll talk about that tomorrow.'

He hung up before I could say anything else.

That night I debated whether to stay home, in case Considine rang again. But it was time to start acting my part. I checked with Vivien, went home, packed another case, put on the kind of conservative clothes Maisie's rural offspring might wear, and went to the apartments. Maisie met me downstairs, playing her role like a trooper.

'Jonathan. Come up. You're just in time for dinner.'

The apartment was on the seventh floor. I moved into the second bedroom, unpacked. We ordered take away, watched television. I discreetly explored the building. There was more reconnoitring to be done, but it would have to wait until Tuesday afternoon, when the first VIPs arrived, and I would have to rely on Maisie and Viv for that. That night I slept badly, thinking of Hao. I wondered how she was getting on in Leeds.

———————

On Tuesday I was up before six. The two sisters were still asleep. I wanted to ring Hao, but didn't want to do it from the apartment. I left them a note and went out for a walk, found a phone booth in Martin Place. It should be seven thirty pm in Leeds. Her phone didn't answer. I caught a taxi, went home, changed into my normal clothes, had breakfast, rang again at seven, and again at eight. That would be ten pm there. She must have gone out with friends. I went to the office, tried a fourth time at nine, still no answer. Give it up, I told myself, you're getting obsessive.

Vivien came in at ten, looking relaxed.

'You were up early,' she commented. 'Everything alright? You look tired.'

'I never sleep well in strange beds.'

I spent the morning waiting for Roger's visit. At twelve thirty he rang, to say he couldn't make it. The meeting had dragged on, he had to rush back to Canberra.

'I have to see you, Roger!' I said. 'We need to talk about what's happening.'

'You'd better come to the airport then. We can talk there before my flight.'

He gave me his flight number and time. I took a taxi, rushed to the departure lobbies in the Qantas domestic terminal, caught up with him as he waited for his flight to be called. Barely time for a quick conversation. We moved out of hearing of the other passengers. He looked harassed, and if I hadn't been so keyed up myself I might have felt sorry for him.

'Have you heard from Eric?' I asked.

'Not since Friday. I gather Considine told you about that meeting.'

'He mentioned it. He said Eric was supposed to ring in as soon as he came back from the hills. He hasn't rung in at all?'

'I wish he'd stick to his job!' he said irritably. 'No, we're still waiting to hear. But that doesn't mean anything. He's probably still up there.'

'What about the restaurant? Is anyone monitoring it to see if he's back?'

'Bob Maynard's covering that. There's been no sign of him there either.'

'I hope they know what they're doing.'

'Of course they do! What do you think, that we're a bunch of amateurs? All it means is that he hasn't come back to town yet. They're probably keeping him on ice until the last moment. He'll be back tonight or tomorrow morning. Stop worrying! He'll turn up.'

'Yes, but that may be too late. Too late even to get in touch. What happens if you don't hear from him in time? What do you do then?'

'If that happens we'll play it by ear. We'll have everything covered, there's no way he can get in close without our knowing it. If we don't hear from him first, we'll wait until we see him and then we'll simply move in and grab him and take it from there.'

'And hope no one gets shot in the process! That's hardly good enough, is it!'

'What else do you want us to do?'

'You could have stepped in earlier! When he reported on Friday! You could have stopped the whole thing there and then! Why didn't you? Why are you waiting until the last minute?'

He shook his head.

'And why are you stopping Considine from doing his job properly? What are you up to, Roger?'

'Christ! He has been talking, hasn't he!'

'I'm glad someone has! It seems to me he's got a point!' I was fuming, with frustration and anger. 'I hope to God nothing's happened to Eric. What if they've got wind of something and simply got rid of him? Have you thought about that possibility?'

'Of course we have!' he snapped. 'What do you think? We're not stupid either! But they won't have done that. You were right at that meeting. They need him, that's what they need him for, because of what he looks like. So stop worrying! He knows what he's doing. He was fine on Friday. He'll come through!'

His flight was announced. Passengers stood up and started to mill towards the gate. He picked up his briefcase.

'What about Bach?' I said urgently. 'Have you heard back from them yet?'

He hesitated. I sensed he was holding something back, but even in his predicament he was reluctant to lie outright.

'Come on Roger! I was the one who suggested you try them!'

'Yes, we got something back. Not much.'

'What did they say?'

'Not much, I told you. They did look at him, you were right, he did apply to go to the States. But they knocked him back. That's all they could tell us. They had to dig through all their records to get that far. That's why it took them so long. No big deal. Nothing there to help us. Sorry, I've got to go.'

'But why did they knock him back? They must have had a reason!'

'They didn't say.' He looked straight at me as he said that, and I knew then that he was lying. Professional liars look you in the eye when they're telling you a fib. 'Who knows anyway? They didn't take everyone, you know. Maybe they thought he was already accepted here. You know what a bugger's muddle those refugee camps were like, agencies falling over themselves in all directions, it's a wonder anyone got through sometimes.'

He started to move off but I called after him.

'I think I should ring him.'

He turned round and came back to me. He looked furious.

'Don't even think of it!' he hissed. 'That's the worst thing you could possibly do! Stay right out of it, Paul. You've done your bit, everyone's grateful to you for it, but now you're fast becoming a pain in the arse! So stay away, go home, do nothing. Let us handle it. We've done more delicate things before and you know it. Otherwise you'll give us no choice but to have you arrested. For his safety and yours.'

He nodded curtly and strode off. I looked after him, aghast, and close to fury myself. I knew very well what I had to do, and it wasn't going to be to stay home.

I took a train back to North Sydney. This exercise was starting to cost. I sat in the office that afternoon, my mind in a whirl, wishing I could talk to someone, someone who could help me think rationally instead of worrying myself sick. But there was no one, I couldn't talk to Viv or Maisie, that would only frighten them out of their wits. I thought of ringing Considine, to check if he'd heard anything, but decided to wait until morning. More and more I knew I'd been right to make the preparations I had.

Viv left, and at five I packed up and went to the apartments, getting in without attracting attention. The two women were in the sitting room comparing notes. They'd done their job well: Viv had explored the building, on the pretext of getting off on the wrong floor, and Maisie had sat in the lobby from mid-afternoon, reading a book while ostensibly waiting for her sister to arrive. When a group of Asian men in suits arrived instead she put her book away and made her way slowly to the lift, as if to go up too. The lift was too crowded and she waited patiently for it to come back down, noting that it had stopped at the third floor. The day manager had accompanied the party, and another Australian who looked like a security man. Viv confirmed this: she had wandered from floor to floor, looking vaguely dotty, and noted activity there, people moving in and out of a suite of rooms, Asians with luggage, who she said didn't look or sound Japanese (she and Maisie had once holidayed in Kyoto). I surmised this was the advance party, with an escort from their consulate. Loc himself and his chief companions weren't due until the next day.

That evening I took them out to dinner, and we came back to the flat and played poker for an hour or so before going to bed. We played for fun, with small change, which was just as well as otherwise they would have skinned me. I did my best to be calm. I suggested that the next evening they should go off together, see a show – the Phantom of the Opera was on – stay out late, even spend the night at Viv's place in Greenwich.

'Don't you think we should stay here?' Maisie said. 'In case you need someone to keep watch?'

'No, it's best if you stay away. If anything happens I don't want you to be involved. If you're not here you can always say you knew nothing about it.'

That night as I lay in bed vainly chasing sleep I thought again about Roger's advice. In a way he was right. The worst thing I could do was stick my oar in at the wrong moment. If they were watching Eric – and the fact that they'd had his meeting with Samantha under surveillance showed they had their doubts – then I might well be attracting more suspicion towards him by trying to ring him. On the other hand I was the man who was going to marry his aunt, I had every reason to want to keep in touch, especially if I had a message to pass on from her. I thought I'd better try again to ring her in the morning.

I thought too about what he'd said about Bach, and the response from the States. If anything that was even more worrying. Roger was right, the refugee camps had been in a mess at times, it was perfectly plausible for records to be lost, or be very sparse. Refugees had come through in their thousands, tens of thousands, processing had sometimes been haphazard. I remembered Pulau Bidong, the island camp off Malaysia's east coast, where we had done most of our interviewing, the long queues forming up as new boats arrived and disgorged their human cargo, squatting in the open for hours while waiting to be processed, the difficulty of keeping track of people as agencies and selection teams from different countries worked around each other, sometimes overlapping, sometimes leaving gaps. It would be easy for someone to fall through.

But I also remembered how thorough the vetting process had been, when we came upon individuals who looked as if they might have some intelligence value. And even more if we thought that person might be a plant, an agent of the Vietnamese intelligence services, trying to infiltrate the refugee flow. The destination of choice for people like that was always the US, and the Americans had been particularly watchful.

So if someone of Bach's background had been knocked back by them, you had to ask yourself why. What was it that had made the American selectors suspicious? Was it as Roger had suggested, that they'd just passed him by in the lottery of selection? Or was there a more sinister reason? I didn't know. But all my instincts told me something wasn't right. I remembered what Quang had said. That he had been on the verge of uncovering something about Bach. And my conclusion, that that was quite possibly why he'd been killed. If that was the case, then the situation was even more dangerous than I had imagined.

But there was no point in trying to discuss this with Roger. Even if he agreed he wouldn't say so. Bob Maynard? Maybe. Something told me Considine would be the best bet. With his cop's instinct and his desire to do his job well I sensed he would be the better ally.

Chapter Thirty

By Wednesday morning I was starting to feel rather jaded. But I was too keyed up to rest. Just a few more hours, I told myself. Like that refrain from *My Fair Lady*. *A few more hours*. By five I was up, and at six I was back at the phone booth in Martin Place. It was too early to bother Considine, but I had to talk to Hao. If all went well we'd be rejoicing that night, congratulating ourselves on a job well done. If my fears were correct and the worst came to pass, it might be the last time she'd ever speak to me.

She was home this time.

'Paul?' she cried as soon as she heard my voice. 'I've been trying to ring you since Sunday! Where have you been?'

'Here and there,' I said. 'Why? What's happened?'

'I have to go to the US, to San Diego. My mother's had a stroke. She's in hospital. I have to go and see her, Paul.'

'Of course! Oh, I'm sorry to hear that. How bad is she?'

She had rung her brother, who had told her. They'd been trying to contact her, and didn't know she was back in Leeds. Her mother's condition was serious: she was conscious, but her speech was impaired, and they feared she might have another stroke. Hao had booked a flight to the US, for the next day (it was still Tuesday evening in Leeds). She didn't know how long she'd be there.

'I'm sorry Paul, I won't be able to get back as soon as I hoped.'

'Don't worry about that. Stay as long as you want. Do you need more money?'

'No, I'm fine, they've given me all my severance pay at work, I've got more than enough. I'll even be able to pay you back what I borrowed.'

'Don't be silly!'

'Can you tell Eric, please? How is he?'

'He's fine,' I said, lying in my teeth. 'Everything's going well. We should be through in a couple of hours. I'll give him a ring as soon as I get to work.'

'Are you alright, Paul? I'm worried about you.'

'Yes, I'm fine too. Don't worry about me.'

'You're not going round seeing all your old girl-friends while I'm away?'

'What do you think!'

'Where did you go? On Monday and Tuesday?'

'Oh...I just had to go out a few times. Don't worry, I'll explain it all later.'

'You sound so mysterious. Are you sure everything's alright?'

'Yes, don't worry, everything's fine. You just worry about your mother.' There was no way I could tell her the truth. Especially not at that moment. 'Anyway, I'm not asking where *you* spend your evenings. I tried to ring you on Monday night, but you weren't home.'

'I went out to dinner.'

'I thought as much.'

She paused. Maybe she too was having trouble deciding how much to tell me. She chose to tell the truth.

'I went out with Robert.'

'Ah.'

'He asked me out. I thought I owed him that.'

'How did it go? If it's any of my business.'

'Of course it is! I told him about us. He was pretty unhappy. He said he was going to ask me to marry him. He wants to leave his wife. I told him he was too late. He should have thought of that a year ago. And even then I would have said no. He asked me if I knew what I was doing. He said he could give me everything I wanted.'

'Pretty tempting offer. All that money, plus sex on demand.'

'Are you serious? You're the only man I want, Paul! I told you. Stop talking nonsense. And stop being jealous too. There's no need. I told you it's over.'

'You're right. I'm contrite.'

'But I'm glad you are,' she added.

I asked about her house. She said she'd found a good agent, who'd put it up for sale, she could expect over three hundred thousand pounds. More than twice that in dollars. And he'd sell the furniture for her as well. Meanwhile she'd sold her car to a friend at work.

'You'll be rich.'

I suggested she put the money in a trust, for herself and Eric. She gave me her brother's number in San Diego. I said I'd ring her on the Thursday evening, local time. That would give her time to get there.

'I'd like that. Listen, about Eric, I'll wait until I get there, but I think I'd like him to come. To San Diego. To see his grandmother.'

'Of course.'

'She hasn't seen him for over five years. Do you think you could help him, the way you helped me? With his visa and things? I'm sorry to be such a nuisance.'

'Don't be so silly. Of course I will.'

'What about you, Paul? Would you like to come? We could all fly back to Sydney together.'

'Do you want me to?'

'Of course I do! I want you to meet her.'

'I'd like that too. Let me work on it. We'll talk about it again on Thursday.'

'You won't forget to call him, will you?'

'I won't.'

'When you ring me on Thursday, can you ask him to be there too? I'd like to talk to him.'

'I will.'

'I miss you.'

'I miss you too. I hope it's not too serious about your mother. People recover from strokes, you know.'

'I know. But I'm very worried.'

'I love you.'

'I love you too. I really do. I can't wait to be back with you.'

We hung up on a tender note, that brief moment of tension pushed aside. I felt guilty about my deception of her. But I had no choice. And something else had come out of that phone call: she had given me the perfect excuse to call Eric. It was too early to ring him, assuming he was back in town, and I thought I'd better talk to someone else first, to make sure I didn't cross any wires. Considine would be best. I'd ring him as soon as I got to the office.

I went back to the apartment. Vivien was up now. I gave her Hao's news, asked if she could be in the office before nine.

'I have to ring Eric, and I may need your help.'

'Of course. Oh, poor thing. She must be so worried!'

I had a quick breakfast, went home, changed, went to the office. At eight I rang Considine, at the operational number he'd given me. He wasn't there but I said it was urgent and gave the codeword, *Dragon*. Within seconds his deputy was on the line.

'Ric Barnes. Anything I can help with?'

'Thanks, Ric, but it's something I have to discuss with Brian direct. It follows on something we talked about on Sunday. It's pretty urgent.'

'He should be here soon. I'll get him to contact you as soon as he comes in.'

I sat back and fretted. At eight-twenty Viv came in, and soon after Considine rang.

'I tried to ring you last night,' he said.

'I had to go out for a couple of hours. Why? What's up?'

'Nothing. That's the trouble. We still haven't heard from Jason, and there's a bit of a flap. We'd like to know what's going on.'

'You and me both. Look. I'm going to try and ring him. I've just spoken with his aunt in Britain.' I gave him a quick rundown of my talk with Hao. 'I have every reason to want to speak to him now.'

'Do you think you should clear it first with Bentinck?'

'No. You can tell him if you want, but this is something I have to do. In fact I'll ring as soon as we've finished speaking. But I thought you ought to know first.'

'Thanks. If it's any help I agree with you. Will you let us know what happens?'

'Of course.' A thought struck me. 'Listen, did he and Medea have any arrangement, for when he rang? Some kind of code, in case he couldn't speak freely?'

'Let me check. Maynard may know. If not I'll have to wait until Bentinck gets here. I can't get in touch with her myself. He should be in in about an hour.'

'I don't think I should wait. By all means check up, but I'll ring him anyway. I'll just keep my ears open. I'll ring you back after.'

'Good luck.'

I asked Viv to make the initial call. If anyone other than Eric answered it would sound less suspicious, and she could explain why she needed to get in touch with him. I listened in on my extension as she dialled.

A Vietnamese voice answered, a young man by the sound of it, in the rough approximate English I was getting used to.

'Hello, may I speak with Eric Tran please?' Viv said in her most civilised tone.

'What you want him for?'

'I have a message for him from his aunt. His adoptive mother, Mrs Tran.'

'He sleep.' At least he was there, I thought with relief. 'What message?' It sounded like 'messit'.

'I'm sorry. I have to speak with him myself,' she said more firmly. 'She's asked me specially to ring him. It's very important. It's about his grandmother.'

'I tell him.'

'No, I need to speak to him directly!' She could sound like a prim headmistress when she chose. 'Please ask him to ring me as soon as he wakes up! It's most important, and very urgent! Are you sure he's not awake? Tell him it's Mrs Berridge calling.'

Something in her tone must have got through. There was a brief silence, then a grudging:

'I go and see.'

We waited. I heard muffled sounds, voices in the background, footsteps, breathing, then Eric's voice on the phone.

'Hello,' he said drowsily.

'Eric? Is that you?'

'Yes. Who's that?'

'It's Viv, Eric. Paul's assistant.'

'Oh, right.'

'I have a message for you, from your aunt. Actually Paul has it, he spoke with her earlier. I'll put him on.' She switched me through without waiting for his answer.

'Hello, Eric,' I said quickly. 'How are you?'

'Oh, fine. And you?'

'Fine too. Listen, I'm sorry to ring you like this, but I spoke with your aunt earlier this morning, and she asked me to give you a message. It's about your grandmother.'

I told him briefly what Hao had told me, and asked me to pass on.

'I'll be speaking again with her tomorrow, after she gets to San Diego. She said she'd like to speak to you too then if that's possible.'

'Oh...I'm not sure if I'll be free then...'

'She said she'd like you to come to San Diego as soon as you can. She's very worried about her mother. They're afraid she might have another stroke.'

'Right. Thanks. I understand.'

'Are you alright? You sound a bit funny.'

'Yes, I'm okay. I think I got a bit of a chill.'

'Nothing serious I hope.'

'No, I'm fine. I'll live.'

I was listening hard. No sign of a code there.

'When do you think you'd be able to go?'

'Oh...I have to think – sorry, I'm a bit tired, I didn't sleep too well...I'll be right after today...'

'About going to see her. Would you like me to help? I can get the ticket for you if you like. Be glad to. She asked me to help.'

'Thanks.'

'When do you think you can go?' I insisted. 'In case she rings back, I'd like to be able to tell her.'

'Well...not today, obviously...' I could almost feel him getting his brain into gear. 'I guess it would take time to get seats – not tomorrow or Friday, I think...'

'Saturday then? I can make a booking for you.'

'I don't have enough money –'

'Don't worry about it. You can pay me back later.'

'Thank you.'

He sounded stilted. I guessed others were listening.

'Saturday would be fine, I think. Not too early. Got something on Friday night, don't want to miss that...Saturday evening, is there a flight Saturday evening? Or maybe Sunday?'

'I'll have to check. Can I ring you back?'

'No, it's okay, I'll ring you later...thanks. Saturday evening would be okay, or Sunday...'

I scribbled his words as he spoke, trying to read some meaning into them, some hidden message. Maybe there was something in his insistence on the days, Saturday, Sunday. I tried another tack.

'I can come and pick you up, take you to the airport. Do you need any luggage? I can lend you some.'

'No, it's alright, I won't have much luggage – I like travelling light...'

'Alright. Let me know if you need anything.'

'Thanks. Don't worry . I'll be okay. How is she?'

'Your aunt? She's fine. She's keen to get back here. But she's very worried about her mother. That's why she wants you to go and see her too.'

'Yeah, she's nice...I like my nan...'

'Anything else I can do for you, Eric? In the meantime?'

'No, thanks, I'll be alright...I'll give you a ring later on...maybe tomorrow...'

'Okay. Look after yourself then.'

'Thanks.'

'Ring me if you need anything.'

'Yeah, thanks. Bye.'

I hung up, and rang Considine at once. He answered straightaway.

'Roger's here,' he said. 'He wants to speak to you.'

'I don't –'

Too late. Roger's voice came on the line, sounding grim.

'Paul? I told you shouldn't –'

'Fuck off Roger. I want to talk to Brian.'

'Paul –'

'Put Brian back on. Or else I hang up.'

He obeyed, with much gnashing of teeth no doubt. Considine came back on.

'Paul?'

'Sorry Brian, but you're the one I need to talk to. You're the one who has to run things here.'

I told him what Eric had told me, as accurately as I could from my notes. He listened in silence.

'Hold on,' he said. I waited as he conferred with the others.

'You're right. It fits. Most of it anyway. They did have a code.'

'What was it?'

'Based on time slots and days of the week. If he rang her they were going to talk about the next time they could get together.

Today was out of the question. Tomorrow – Thursday – meant this afternoon, before six. Friday meant between six and eight. Saturday meant eight to ten. Sunday meant after ten.'

'Sounds as if it's planned for tonight then, probably late-ish.'

'Sounds like it.'

'What about the rest? The luggage bit?'

'Probably means a handgun. They had a second code, using heavy for a rifle, light for a handgun. He said he would be travelling light?'

'Yes. That's what he said.'

'Sounds as if that's what he meant.'

'What about the chill bit? I've caught a bit of a chill?'

'Not sure. Not part of the code. Maybe it's for real. Or maybe it was meant as a warning. I'm being watched, or something like that. You're sure that's all he said?'

'Yes. You've got it, word for word.'

'Thanks. That's great. At least now we know he's back in town and we have some idea of what's likely to happen. Thanks Paul, you've done a great job.'

I thought.

'You know what, Brian? I think I know what they're going to do.'

'Good for you. Wish I did!'

'Can I come and see you? I need to talk to you about it.'

'Can't you tell me now?'

'No. It's too complicated to discuss over the phone. Can we meet somewhere? Just you and me. I'd like to discuss this just with you first.'

'You're sure?'

'Yes. This is only a guess, but if I'm right this is something you need to know, and I need to tell you, without anybody else there.'

'Alright. How soon can you get here?'

'Forty minutes?'

We made an appointment for ten o'clock, in Hyde Park, near the Anzac memorial, a stone's throw from Police Headquarters across the road on College Street.

He was there, in a dark suit, the better to blend in with the crowd. We found an empty bench and sat down.

'This is what I think,' I said. I outlined what I'd surmised. He listened in silence.

'I can't prove any of it,' I said. 'But it fits. And I think Roger knows it too. That's why I wanted to talk to you alone, Brian. I know you both don't want Loc to get killed, Bentinck possibly even less than you. But he's working to a different agenda from yours, and I think he's prepared to sacrifice Jason if need be. I'm not, and I don't think you are either.'

'No. I don't want anyone to get killed.'

'I don't care how noble the cause is. And frankly I don't think it's all that noble.'

He nodded.

'We talked it over after you rang,' he said. 'It makes sense. I've had a funny feeling about this. That cop's instinct I was telling you about. There's something smelly about it.'

'What are you going to do to stop it?'

'Well, what I was going to do all along. Only better now you've told me all this. The Vietnamese don't want any police presence on their floor, but we've booked rooms on the floor below, without telling them. There's a quick way up by way of the stairs. And we'll have two uniformed police in the lobby and some in the street outside, in case the demonstrators try to get close to the building. Though they probably won't try that at night.'

'How do you think he's going to try to get in?'

'No idea. What do you think?'

'Remember what I said? That I thought I knew why they wanted to use him? Because he didn't look Asian? I think he's going to come in the front door, under some pretext, looking very innocent and non-threatening. Maybe to visit one of the residents.'

'We've checked all the residents, there's no one there who fits the bill.'

Thank you Maisie, I thought.

'Will your guys be able to spot him?'

'Yes. They've all got a photo of him.'

'Presumably you'll search everyone who comes in.'

'Of course. All hand luggage. Anything they bring in with them. And we'll run a metal detector over them too.'

'You'll be doing that in the lobby, I take it.'

'Yes. As soon as they get in. Just inside the door.'

'Can I make a suggestion? Go one further. Take a room on the ground floor, near the lobby, and take everyone there. Especially if they're carrying something. That allows you to do more thorough searches if you want. Then when Jason gets in, take him there too. Search him too of course. Go through all the motions. But put body armour on him.'

He looked at me, his dark eyes steady.

'You really think they're going to try to kill him, don't you.'

'I would, if I were them.'

————————————

There was little else to discuss. For form's sake I asked if I could be included in his operation, but he refused, as I expected, politely but firmly.

'I can't, Paul. This is a police job. I can't have any civilians. Too risky. Besides, Bentinck's right, you know. You're too close to this, you're too emotionally involved. Sorry. I know you mean well, but this has to be totally professional. That's the only way I can be sure we'll do everything right.'

I nodded, and looked resigned.

'Go home, Paul. Get some sleep. You look exhausted. Don't worry. We won't let anything happen to him.'

'I know. Thanks, Brian.'

I walked back to the city, caught a train at Town Hall station, heading for North Sydney. If anyone was following that's where I wanted them to think I was going. I got off at Wynyard instead, the next stop along. I bought some take-away food, checked again I wasn't followed – my street skills were rusty, but I was fairly sure I wasn't – then walked up to Kent Street and the apartment building. No one paid attention as I went in. I went up to the apartment, and settled down to wait.

Chapter Thirty-One

Waiting. I did a lot of waiting that day. It's not something I enjoy. But I was used to it from my old profession, and there was a reason. Security would only get tighter as the day progressed, if I left it too late to get into position I might be challenged or even recognised as I came into the building, and that wasn't a risk I could take. So I made the best of it, read the papers, used the time to catch up on badly needed sleep.

Around two I got up, ate my cold take-away food, then watched the news on TV, looking for coverage of the demonstrations in Canberra. They had been particularly vocal the evening before, flags and banners waving, people shouting and surging against the barriers, occasionally throwing things, police moving in to make a few arrests. I was more interested in Loc, and there was coverage of him too, being greeted at the airport, shaking hands with the Deputy Prime Minister, arriving at Parliament House, meeting the PM. A thin, spare man, taller than the average Vietnamese, with iron-grey hair and a large bony head, almost simian with its protruding shelf above the eyes. When he turned to the cameras to make a brief speech in slow but serviceable English there was a flash of intelligence deep in his eyes and a self-deprecating curl of the lip. We are a small country but we have some large problems and we have come to ask for your help. When asked for his comments on the demonstrations he smiled politely. He didn't look the kind to be upset by a few flags and some noise. When he turned to go into the building he walked with a pronounced limp.

At five-thirty I took a shower, turning it to cold to sharpen my wits. I pulled out the suitcase which Maisie had brought in for me on the first day, and put on the kit it contained: old jeans loose enough not to cramp my movements, a sturdy canvas jacket over an old windcheater, a scarf to protect my neck. Rubber-soled boots, old leather gloves with the tips cut off, a balaclava to go over my head. I even had a pair of industrial goggles on a strap, in case I had to smash my way through a window. In one of the loops of my belt I hooked a small jemmy, tied with a piece of string. The rest of the gear I put on the floor near the door. Then at six I pulled my chair nearer the window and started to watch.

It was a long vigil. I sat in the gathering dark, with the lights off, looking down at the street. A few people moved about, sometimes a car drove past, but mostly it was quiet. Considine's instructions to his men, as he'd explained them to me, were to let people go by, only stepping in if someone did something visibly wrong. Only people entering the building would be searched. Within reach on a small table I had put more provisions, coffee and a drink and some snacks, even a plastic bottle to pee in if need be. No radio. I wanted nothing to distract my attention. It was still some hours before I expected much action, but I needed to be ready well in advance, in case Eric arrived earlier, for whatever reason, perhaps to lie in wait until the time came. I just hoped I hadn't made a monstrous cock-up and it wasn't all going to happen somewhere else.

While waiting I thought of Hao. This was the day she was flying to the States, catching an early flight out of Leeds, she'd told me, connecting at Heathrow with a British Airways flight to New York, then another flight to San Diego via Los Angeles, arriving there in mid-afternoon. Over sixteen hours. She should be at London airport by now, about to board her transatlantic flight. She wouldn't be at her brother's house until ten the next morning, Sydney time. I wished I could be with her, and if I could have rung her I would have. But I was glad she wasn't in Sydney just then. She would have been beside herself with anguish. I promised myself I'd ring her the next day, when if all worked out as I hoped I'd have Eric with me. I was also glad she was no longer in Leeds. I trusted her, and yet I couldn't help feeling a tremor of neanderthal angst at the thought of her in the same city as Robert. When all this was over, I thought, we would need time to build a normal life.

Seven o'clock, eight o'clock passed. At nine thirty there was a brief flurry of movement, three or four cars drove up and parked near the front of the building, people emerged and walked towards the entrance, out of sight around the corner. That would be the official party returning from their last engagement. I looked up and down the street but saw no sign of Eric, or anyone else. Whatever their plan, they were being very cautious. The hubbub died down, the cars drove off. I imagined the visitors being cleared into their apartment, settling down for a discussion of the day's events before going to bed, careful not to speak too freely. With their background

216

they would expect their rooms to be bugged. For all I knew, they probably were.

It was another hour before anything happened. I was leaning with my forehead against the glass, numb with boredom, hypnotically staring at the same spot in the street below, when I saw movement on the other side of the street. A short stumpy figure, foreshortened from above, wearing a baseball cap and a bright shirt and carrying some kind of box. He was walking along the footpath on the other side and I wasn't sure at first that it was him. Then he turned to cross the street and glanced up at the building and I recognised his face, pale and expressionless in the lamplight. When he reached the near side I briefly lost sight of him, before he reappeared, walking towards the corner and the front entrance.

I moved. This was the moment I'd been waiting for, and from now on there'd be no time for second thoughts. I checked my equipment one last time, went to the door, picked up the coils of rope which lay there, with a grappling hook at one end, and gently opened the door. No one about. Holding the hook securely to make sure I didn't impale myself on one of its prongs I walked quickly to the window at the end of the corridor. It was a single pane window with a metal frame which swung outwards, as I knew from my earlier recce. I pushed the handle down and out. It was stiff in its frame but it opened without making a noise. A gust of cold air hit me but I ignored it. I looked out, saw no one below. I placed the hook inside the window opening, near the bottom right-hand corner, one prong either side, pushed it hard against the wall and threw the rope out, keeping it clear of the wall. I watched it snake its way down, coming to an end a few feet off the ground. I jammed the hook tighter, tugged with my left hand to test it, looked out again, then took a deep breath.

I've never liked heights. I like them even less than waiting at night for something nasty to happen. Ever since I was a child I've been afraid of standing near the edge of cliffs or on the top of tall buildings. But there are times in life when you have to overcome your fears, and I knew what I had to do: act, not think. I put one leg over the sill, swung myself out, seized the rope with both hands. When I was clear of the window I reached up with my right hand and pushed it back towards the opening. Then I started to go down.

It wasn't a long climb, even by my modest standards. As a further precaution I'd tied a series of knots along the rope, one metre apart, to make it easier to hang on and help me judge the distance. We were on the seventh floor, they were on the third, sixteen to eighteen metres overall. I made my way down hand over hand, holding myself off the wall with my feet and counting the knots as I went, careful not to think of the void beneath. I passed the next floor down, then the next, then a third. One more to go. I was breathing hard, with nervous tension as much as with effort. I gripped the rope more tightly, went down another three knots, until I was level with the third-floor window. I wrapped my leg around the rope for extra purchase and rested against the wall for a moment, catching my breath. My arms were beginning to tremble with the strain.

I knew it wouldn't be long now. Eric would be held up in the lobby while they went through the motions of checking him through, took him into a separate room, made him take his shirt off to put his bullet-proof vest on. I pictured Considine sizing him up, quickly questioning him, giving him last-minute instructions. Would Roger be there too, and Keith or Bob Maynard? Four, five minutes at most. They wouldn't want to risk alerting anyone by keeping him too long. I wouldn't have been the only one watching out for him. I peered cautiously around the edge.

The corridor was empty. I was looking in from the left hand side of the window and I had a good view of the opposite wall, all the way to the other end. I identified the lift door, halfway down, next to it the door to the emergency stairs. Down the left hand side I thought I saw a door open a fraction, but I couldn't be certain and I didn't dare stick my head out too far. The light in the panel next to the lift moved, then stopped. The lift door opened, Eric came out, still holding his box. I saw now that it was four large pizza boxes, stacked on top of each other. Was he supposed to smuggle his weapon inside a pizza? I wondered. Surely not, it would have been discovered at once. He glanced up and down the corridor, moved to his left, put the boxes down and opened a panel in the wall. There was a similar panel on our floor, marked Fire Hose and Reel. He rummaged inside, pulled out a long flat package at the end of a string. The package appeared to be wrapped in cloth. He pulled off the wrapping and took out its contents. There was no mistaking the shape, even at that distance: a long narrow pistol, with a thick cylinder at the end of the barrel. He looked at it for a moment, as if puzzled by it, then turned it over to look at the grip.

Meanwhile other things were starting to happen. The door which I'd noticed earlier now opened fully, and two men came out, both Asians. One was tall, the other short but solidly built. I wondered which one might be Truong Dzu, Loc's security man. The taller one seemed to have more authority. They wore suits and gloves and the tall one carried two lengths of wood. They moved quickly. By the time Eric noticed them it was too late: as he turned to face them the shorter one slipped behind him, clamped a hand over his mouth, with his other hand put a knife to his throat and pulled him back hard on his heels. The tall man smiled and put a finger to his lips.

I watched, horrified, as the drama began to unfold. The tall man immobilised the lift with one of the pieces of wood, jamming it in the open door, then used the second to secure the door to the emergency stairs, tying it crossways to the handle so it couldn't be pulled open from the stairs. Eric meanwhile stood still, unable to move, his back arched against the shorter man's chest, his mouth hidden by his captor's gloved hand. The tall man turned back to him, fished a flat object out of his pocket, took the pistol out of Eric's hand and inserted the object into the butt. A magazine, obviously, the pistol must have been placed unloaded in its hiding place, that was why Eric had been puzzled by it. He held the pistol up, cocked it, looked at Eric again for a second longer. With his left hand he took another gun from his pocket, a shorter, stubbier weapon, without a silencer this time. He held it down by his side. Then he turned on his heel and began to walk towards the far end of the corridor.

I knew at once what was about to happen. There was no time to lose. But as I watched I saw the tall man pause, look over his shoulder as if to listen. He looked back towards Eric, as if uncertain what to do next. I heard muffled thumps and shouts, coming it seemed from the other side of the stairwell door.

The tall man now moved with greater urgency. He hurried to the end of the corridor, faced the last door on his right, and knocked. The door stayed shut. He knocked again, tried the handle, to no avail. He put his shoulder to the door and shoved, then stepped back and kicked at the lock with his heel. Still it stayed closed. I could almost sense his panic. He raised his pistol, seemed for a second about to shoot the lock out, then turned back towards Eric. He said something and gestured violently at the other man, who seemed confused at first – then, realising what was expected of him, released Eric and stepped aside. Eric stumbled, tried to regain his balance, as the tall man ran back towards him, raising his gun.

'No!' I shouted. I let go of the rope with my right hand, began to hit at the window. 'No! Don't do that you bastard! Don't shoot him!' I struck again. The window didn't budge, but he looked in my direction. Eric also looked round, then started to move, to get away from him. No time for the jemmy at my belt. I seized the rope with both hands, kicked out against the wall and swung back with my feet towards the window. The pane cracked but didn't break. I swung back harder, kicked again. This time the pane gave way, I plunged feet first, elbows up, no time for the safety glasses. The jemmy snagged against the window frame, the string snapped, a sharp sting as my right sleeve caught on something, then I was through, stumbling on my feet, somehow managing to stay upright. There was a shot, loud as a thunderclap in that confined space. Eric cried out, clutching his right arm.

'No!' I shouted again. ' No! Shoot me instead you vile piece of shit!'

I hurled myself forward, desperate to get at him before he could shoot again. Too late. He fired a second shot, I saw Eric stagger and fall. The man turned towards me. He was still a good five metres away, I had no hope of getting to him in time, but I kept charging, screaming at the top of my lungs. I seemed to see his face for the first time, hard, full of hate, his eyes like burning black holes. He levelled his gun at me, fired two more shots. I felt a hard punch to the shoulder which half spun me round, then a tremendous kick to the chest. Dimly as I fell I heard the crash of metal, shouting, more shooting, before all became black.

Chapter Thirty-Two

Coming back to life was almost worse than trying to leave it.

When I regained consciousness I was in Royal North Shore Hospital at St Leonard's, a short drive up the Pacific Highway from my office in North Sydney and less than ten minutes over the Bridge by high speed ambulance from the scene of the shooting. Considine had had a medical team on standby, and they had wasted no time. That, and the skill of the surgeons, were what saved me.

I was badly wounded: a bullet through the right shoulder – relatively minor – a deep cut on the upper arm, another shot to the chest. It was the second shot which had done the damage. The bullet had missed my heart but perforated my left lung front and back, causing it to collapse, with massive internal bleeding, and then had careened in a downward spiral, fortunately missing any other major organs but ending up against my spine, in my lower back. Between the second and third lumbar vertebrae, to be exact. The spinal cord wasn't severed but the bullet was too firmly wedged to be removed without a further operation, which was dicey. For the present I was forced to lie still, wrapped like a mummy from my waist to my neck, unable to move my arms, or even my legs very much.

Worse than my wounds was my anguish. I was convinced that Eric was dead. I had seen him fall, seconds before I was shot myself. What had gone wrong? Had Considine forgotten to put a protective vest on him? Had a bullet got through somehow, had he been shot in the head? When I tried to find out all I could manage was a groan. Don't try to speak, someone said. You've been badly wounded and we've just operated. You're going to be alright. But right now you must rest.

I remained in that state for over twenty-four hours, alternately sleeping and staring at the ceiling, not sure when I was awake or hallucinating. When I slept I dreamt of falling, of being pursued by demons through monstrous landscapes, like a painting by

Hieronymus Bosch, of being branded on the chest with red-hot irons.

When I woke I thought of Eric, and how I had failed him.

Then, on the morning of the second day, two police officers came to see me. They were from Internal Affairs, and they were investigating the circumstances of the shooting at the Southern Cross Apartments, during which a foreign official had been killed. I was still in intensive care and wore an oxygen mask but I was able to communicate by then and the doctor reluctantly allowed them in. They said it was urgent.

I answered their questions as best I could, by sign language where possible, pushing my oxygen mask aside when I had to talk. They seemed satisfied with most of my answers, but the question they kept coming to was what I had seen when Truong Dzu was shot.

'Who?' I asked.

'Truong Dzu. The man who shot you. The tall Vietnamese. Did you see what happened when he was shot? What he was doing?'

'No,' I said. By then I was flat on the floor, trying hard not to scream my head off. I thought I had heard shouting, and another shot, but I couldn't remember even that part clearly before I blacked out.

'Who shot him?' I asked, but they wouldn't tell me.

'That's still under investigation.'

They were about to leave when I pushed the mask aside again.

'Why are you so concerned about how he was killed?' I rasped out. 'That man Truong Dzu. Why don't you ask about the young man he killed?'

They stared.

'You mean Eric Tran? He's not dead. We interviewed him last night. He's got a flesh wound in his arm and some bad bruising but otherwise he's fine. Sorry, we thought you knew.'

After they left I went back to sleep. This time there were no more dreams.

———————————

After that the visitors came.

The first was Eric, closely followed by Brian Considine. Eric was being released from hospital and the Considines were taking him in, until something more permanent could be arranged. We spent an emotional moment together. He wore his arm in a sling and had dark rings under his eyes, but otherwise looked unharmed.

'I thought you were going to die,' he said, a glint of tears in his eyes. 'I wanted to come in the ambulance with you but they wouldn't let me.'

'I didn't look after you very well, did I.'

'Commander Considine says you saved my life. He said if you hadn't come in when you did I'd almost certainly have been killed.'

He hadn't heard from his aunt, and didn't know how to reach her in San Diego. I told him Viv had the number, and suggested he get the key to the flat from her as well, so he could move in whenever he wanted.

'Just one thing,' I said. 'When you speak to her, don't tell her I've been badly wounded. Just say I'm OK, I'm recovering well.'

I wanted to ask what was happening in Cabramatta, but I was too tired, and it was Considine who brought me up to date, on his next visit. He was in uniform this time, complete with shoulder tabs and that broken down cap of theirs, which makes them all look a bit thuggish. He sat down next to the bed and took his cap off.

'Was it you who shot Truong Dzu?' I asked. He grunted.

'Bastard gave me no choice. When I came through that door I told him to put down his weapon but he refused. Twice. I thought he was about to shoot you again, or one of my men. So I shot him.'

He shook his head ruefully.

'First time I've ever killed a man, would you believe? Over thirty years in the force. I know the bugger deserved it, but I can't say I enjoyed it very much.'

He ran his hand through his wiry hair. He looked tired too, and not very happy.

'Now of course there's all hell to pay. It's standard procedure to have an inquiry when there's been a fatality during a police operation, but when a foreigner's involved, with diplomatic status...That's what the fuss is all about. That's why they wanted to interview you so soon. Fortunately Eric was able to tell them quite a lot.'

'But what happened?' I asked. 'What took you so long to get there?'

'Oh, it's a long and sorry tale,' he said wearily. 'As the senior man I should never have let things get to that stage. But there was nothing I could do! I wanted to put someone on that floor, take a room and stick a couple of my men in it, but Roger wouldn't allow it. Mustn't do anything which might tip them off, he kept saying, otherwise they'll abort and the whole exercise will have been in vain. We've got to catch them red-handed. Even went over my head. Special request from Canberra, straight to the Minister and the Commissioner. Highly sensitive political case, let our man on the ground have the final say. Fortunately Bob Maynard was more reasonable. His men had installed a concealed camera in one of the ventilation vents, thanks to him we were able to get video coverage. Otherwise we would have been blind.'

He filled in the details. How Eric had turned up, carrying his pizza boxes. Considine had commandeered a room on the ground floor, as I'd suggested, and his men had taken Eric there, ostensibly to search him. Considine was there too and together they'd gone over the next stage. Considine told him they'd be watching him on CCTV, and they'd jump in at the first sign of trouble. They didn't talk long. Considine made him put on a flak jacket under his shirt – luckily it was a large size and the jacket didn't show. Then they sent him on his way.

'Cool as ice, he was,' Considine said. 'I could see he was tense, but there was no way he was going to back out. Don't worry about me, he said. I'll be alright. Of course what none of us had foreseen was that they'd pounce on him so quickly and block access to the floor.'

They had tracked his progress on a screen on the floor below. As soon as they saw the two men, Truong Dzu and his associate, move up and grab Eric they knew they had to act fast. They raced up the stairs, only to find the door locked and barred against them. By the time they broke the door down it was almost too late: I had burst in through the window, Eric and I had both been shot, Truong Dzu stood sneering at the big policeman. He had thrown the silenced twenty-two pistol at Eric's feet but kept hold of his own weapon, even raised it when Considine shouted at him to drop it, as if to challenge him – whereupon Considine had quite properly shot him.

'We had it all on tape. Didn't see you coming in, the camera was pointing the other way, but everything else, when we played it back it was all there: how Truong Dzu took the pistol from Eric, loaded it, started down the corridor, turned round, started to panic...right up to the moment I shot him. But you know what? The tape's gone! Roger took it! Wanted in Canberra, he said, Top Secret Sensitive, the Minister needs to see it, can't leave it lying around, might fall into the wrong hands. I couldn't even use it in my defence when I was challenged to prove I had acted correctly. That's why Internal Affairs had to interview you, as well as Eric and the other cops with me. Fortunately it was all fairly straightforward.'

'What about the man with the knife?' I asked.

'Oh, he dropped it quickly enough! I arrested him and we took him into custody. But he refused to answer any questions and we had to release him less than an hour later. Diplomatic immunity again. Seems you can do anything when you have a diplomatic passport and not be held to account. The best we could do was kick him out of the country. PNG'd, as Roger put it. Persona non gratis.'

'*Non grata.*'

'What?'

'*Persona non grata.* It means he's no longer welcome.'

'Bloody right he wasn't! That was the one thing that gave me pleasure. Putting him on the next plane to Hanoi without letting him go home to change. His consulate kicked up a fuss but there was no way we were going to show him any favours! Almost made me wish I'd shot him as well.'

'Where was Loc during all this?'

'In his room, at the other end of the corridor. Where Truong Dzu was heading when you broke in so rudely. Locked in his bathroom. Seems someone in Roger's mob had got word to him earlier, said they thought there'd be an attempt against him that evening, asked him how he wanted to play it. Go ahead, he said, let them go ahead with their plan, if you think you can stop them in time – I want them caught too. Another one with ice in his veins. When it was over he came out, not a drop of sweat on him. Called his embassy, and his government too I think, told them what had happened, helped us sort out the mess. Postponed his departure for New Zealand by a day to do it. A tough one, no doubt about that. I wouldn't want to be in his enemies' shoes when he gets back to Hanoi.'

It had gone pretty well as I had expected, give or take a few details.

'One thing I don't understand,' I said, 'is how they managed to fix that pizza delivery. They were taking a big chance, weren't they?'

He laughed curtly.

'They'd worked that out as well. Seems Loc has a craving for pizzas. Well known in his entourage, it seems. Whenever he travels abroad he has to have one. Can't get the real stuff at home apparently. Odd, isn't it. What some of these people need to keep 'em happy. At least he didn't ask for a woman, the way some of them do. That would have complicated matters.'

As we reconstructed it, someone in Loc's group, perhaps Truong Dzu himself, had rung a local pizza shop to place an order that evening, about an hour after they came home from the reception. Asked for it to be delivered to the apartments. Then soon after someone else had rung – the pizza shop thought it was the same man, but they couldn't be sure, more likely it was someone working with Bach, maybe Bach himself – said forget the delivery, they'd send someone to pick it up. An Asian man had come in, the pizza shop staff said, well-dressed in a dark suit, had paid for the order in cash, and taken the boxes. They didn't think they could recognise him. Eric was waiting in a car nearby, already dressed for his role in a red and white shirt and a cap, complete with the shop's logo – they'd even thought of that. The man had handed the pizzas to him and he had gone on his way.

'They must have been planning it for months. God knows what would have happened if you hadn't put a spoke in their wheels. They might have got away with it.'

I thought about that too, then and later. Something I never really discussed with Eric. Would he have gone through with it, if the plot had been left to take its course without interference from me? I remembered how hard I'd had to work to turn him round, convince him that he was not on the side of the angels. But I also thought of him, as I had got to know him. He had never been meant to pull the trigger, of course – that was Truong Dzu's job, all that was required of Eric by then was to let himself be conveniently killed. Even so, had it come to the crunch I couldn't see him willing to shoot down a defenceless man. If he'd really been required to do it, instead of merely playing a deadly role of make-believe, I was sure, I believed deep inside me that he would have balked, found a way out, refused to become a cold-blooded killer.

At least I very much hoped so.

'And the others involved? Bach Ho? Vo Khanh and the Mad Buffaloes? What's going to happen to them?'

'We've rounded up most of them. The small fry anyway. Raided that farm up in the hills, took the owner in as well. We'll have to let most of them go, with a caution. They didn't have much of a clue, all they did was take part in the demonstrations in Canberra. But as for the top guys...we caught Vo Khanh too, as he was about to leave. But with Bach Ho I'm afraid we were too late. Him and his offsider, that young man Binh, who you think committed the earlier murder – they've disappeared. They won't get far. We'll catch them eventually. But right now no one knows where they are. They must have prepared their escape in advance.'

'All this is strictly between us,' he went on, still sounding bitter. 'Canberra wants to put a lid on it! I'm not sure if it's Roger's idea or comes from higher up. But they want to put it out that it was just an amateurish assassination attempt by a group of lunatic extremists among the Vietnamese community, that Truong Dzu and his friend were only doing their job defending their leader, and you and Eric were innocent bystanders who got caught in the cross-fire. Perpetrator or perpetrators unknown, apparently broke in through a window at the end of a rope, tried to shoot their way through, failed but escaped the same way, whereabouts currently unknown...We know it's bullshit, Roger says, and they know that we know it's bullshit, but this is the best way to help them save face, let them wash their dirty linen in private...'

He stood up, screwed his cap down on his head, tilted it at a rakish angle.

'Nasty business, politics. Makes police work look like kindergarten stuff. Now I'd better go. Got to face another hearing. When's that woman of yours coming back?'

'I'll tell you when I know,' I said.

'Nice homecoming she'll be having. At least you're still alive. The both of you.'

He leaned over, gripped my right hand in his, in a brief, oddly touching gesture. Then he left.

By now I had most of the puzzle worked out. That was one advantage of lying flat on my back – the only one. I had time to think. It had been an inside job alright, as I'd begun to suspect earlier. That was what I'd told Considine when I'd met him in Hyde Park on the last morning, and he hadn't needed much convincing. Truong Dzu's actions had been the final proof.

What was interesting was the care and the time they had taken over it. They must have been working on it for months, perhaps ever since Eric had first appeared on the scene and planning had started for Loc's visit to Australia. Who were they working for? We'd never know for sure, but my guess was some hard-line faction in Hanoi, wanting to get rid of a troublesome liberal, and make it look like the work of anti-communist fanatics among expatriate Vietnamese in Sydney. Neat! That meant Bach Ho and at least one other must have been working for them. Not that fat oaf Vo Khanh, all muscle and no brains. As an ex-Marines officer he probably hated the communists more than anything on earth. Most probably Binh, whom I suspected of having murdered Quang.

What would have happened if they'd succeeded? With Eric killed, shot dead by Truong Dzu as the latter (apparently) tried to protect Loc (too late) against an unknown assassin, there would have been no witnesses, nothing that could incriminate Bach or even Vo Khanh. Whatever the police or ASIO or anyone suspected, they would have been unable to prove it. It was only Eric's testimony, and what I had seen myself, which could bring them undone. And that they couldn't foresee.

I had to admire the evil ingenuity of it all, even if we'd never know all the details.

But there were other questions which bothered me, and to which I wanted answers. And when Roger came I pulled no punches. He was among the last of my visitors, as he'd had to return at once to Canberra, no doubt to explain himself to his masters, only reappearing a few days later.

'You bastard!' I said. 'You knew! You knew all along they were planning to kill Loc, and they were going to pin it on Eric! What was it? A power struggle inside the Vietnamese Politburo? The hardliners trying to get rid of a rival, and blame it on anti-communist extremists? Was that it?'

He didn't say anything.

'And when did you find out, that's what I want to know! Was it when you got the traces on Bach, from the Americans? Was that it? When you told Considine and me they had nothing on him, you were lying! They did! I bet they knew all about him! They had to! Otherwise why would they have refused to accept him into the US? Come on, Roger! Tell me the truth! I've got a right to know, surely!'

'Nothing would have happened to you if you'd done what you were told. But you always were an insubordinate sod!'

'Thank Christ I was! Why, do you think it would have ended happily if I hadn't been there? You saw what happened, Roger! You saw what those bastards tried to do to Eric! They would have killed him, and might have killed Loc too. There was no way Considine could have got through that door in time! But you don't care, do you! You were quite prepared to sacrifice him if need be, to push your little scheme through!'

He made to say something but I ploughed on.

'You were in this with the Yanks, weren't you! To make sure that Loc came out on top and his enemies were unmasked. Loc's their golden boy, isn't he! They want him to get the top job. And so do you. And you were prepared to do anything to make sure he gets it. Foiling an assassination attempt wasn't enough! Identifying the inside men wasn't enough! You had to make sure they got caught red-handed, so that the hard men in Hanoi would know, so that Loc's faction would get the upper hand, take the fight back to them...I bet you've even sent them a copy of the tape, to make sure it's all there on record. What's going to happen now, Roger? A few demotions among the hard men on the left? A few hardliners pushed aside for a time, so that the golden boy can have a smooth ride to the top? What is he, Roger? Is he working for you? For the Americans? Is that it? Their top man in Hanoi?'

That stung him.

'Don't be stupid, Paul! Do you think a man of that calibre would work for another country? He's a nationalist, for Christ's sake! You said it yourself! He loves his country!'

'So why did you do it Roger? To uphold democratic values?'

'Don't sneer, Paul. Is that so wrong? Loc's one of the key men in that government. He'll be prime minister one day. And he's one of the few who's got any understanding of the outside world, who's ready to open his country to the west instead of trying to push it back to some Stalinist paradise! Of course he was worth defending! That's our job, remember? That's what we're in the business of doing, when we get the chance! So what's your beef all about?'

'Nothing! Except that you very nearly got Eric killed! And now you're trying to pin the blame on anybody except the real culprits. Make it look as if it was all the work of some loonies in the Vietnamese community! Isn't that a little self-defeating? Playing Hanoi's game for them?'

'It's the price we have to pay! We can't afford to rub their face into it publicly. This is the only way we can be sure the information will be used properly. Otherwise it'll have the opposite effect and strengthen the hand of the hardliners in Hanoi. Besides, that's the way Loc wanted it played. He asked us himself to handle it like this. Of course it's nasty. Whoever said it wasn't? Don't be so naïve, Paul.'

We glared at each other.

'What about the Vietnamese community here? Don't you care that their reputation will suffer? They already get a bad enough press as it is!'

He shook his head.

'It won't last long. People will soon see it was just a lunatic fringe. If necessary we can push that line with the press, feed it through some tame journalist. Besides, don't forget that some members of that community were only too happy to take part. Even if it was hatched by Bach Ho. Vo Khanh, for one. And those others who volunteered for it. Eric himself probably, if you hadn't turned him!'

I was silent. His cynicism floored me.

'I'm sorry to see you laid up like this, Paul,' he went on. 'I really am. If it's any help, I got approval from Bill for the office to cover all your medical bills, and we'll pay you something, a consultancy fee of some sort, to cover all your expenses and lost time. But please don't play the innocent with us. You knew we would have to take this all the way, or you should have known. Don't forget, he volunteered, Paul. And you brought him to us. Did you think we were just going to sit on our hands? Come on! And think what would have happened if you hadn't brought him to us. If you hadn't turned him and he'd genuinely tried to do the job for them. He would surely have been killed then! So don't play the injured party, Paul. It won't wash.'

He paused, seemed to pull himself back, conscious that he was going too far.

'Besides, you got what you wanted,' he went on more calmly. He pulled an envelope out from his coat pocket, took out two passports. He held them out for me to see. But when I reached for them he pulled his hand back.

'Sorry, can't let you have them just yet. When she comes back from her trip. She and Eric will have to go to Immigration in person, and be sworn in like everyone else. You can be there as witness. No need to look so grateful. Did you think I was going to renege on the deal? But there's one condition, Paul.'

'What's that?'

'Not a word, to anyone! I mean it! Stick to the approved version. You can say if you must that you got wind through Eric of some attempt to attack Loc and you tried to step in and got shot for your pains, but nothing else, not a word about Truong Dzu or inside help. I need your word, Paul! Otherwise they don't get these.'

He held the passports up, then put them back in the envelope. I nodded reluctantly.

'You have it.'

'Good. That's settled. I'd better be going. I have a plane to catch. I'll come back and see you in a couple of days. Meanwhile Bill and the mob send their love. He thinks you did well, by the way.'

'Thanks. But I still have one request.'

He sighed in exasperation.

'Not another one, surely! Don't you ever stop?'

'Not for me. For Quang. He had a daughter. She came to the funeral last week. Lives in Paris with her mother. From what I saw she's not too well off. I think some compensation would be a nice gesture. Anonymously, of course. Some investment of Quang's that paid off? A hundred thousand dollars? That shouldn't be too much for the Service's coffers, should it? After all, it's not as if this operation cost you much. Others did most of the work. You can use my fee if you're skint.'

He sighed again, but nodded.

'I'll put it to Bill. You're right. I'm sure we can work something out. And you'll still get your fee.'

I looked after him as he went. Roger had tried to be decent at the end, and had lived up to his promise about the passports. I had to give him that. But I couldn't forgive him for the way he'd been prepared to sacrifice Eric. I knew that nothing would ever be the same between us from now on.

———————————

More visitors. Vivien of course, almost every day. Maisie was back on the south coast, but I'd instinctively played it Roger's way with them, telling them how Eric and I had helped foil an attempted assassination, but were now under strict orders not to reveal any further details, for fear others might learn from them. They were both thrilled to the core, beneath their concern for me.

With Jack Lipton I was much more frank, when he and Sen came to see me. I didn't see why I should lie to him, when it was through him that I had first met Quang, and because of it that Quang had been killed. So I told him the bare bones of the truth: that Bach had been at the centre of a plot to kill Loc, working through a group of crazy extremists, but that he himself was in fact an agent of Hanoi, working for some unholy elements there; I also told him I was pretty sure that was why Quang had been killed, because he was getting too close to the truth, and that it was probably Binh, Bach's offsider, who had done the killing. I said it for a reason: both Bach and Binh had disappeared; but Jack had many contacts in the Vietnamese community. If he discreetly spread it about that they were in the pay of Hanoi, it would make it that much harder for them to escape. He said little, but took it all in. I knew he'd put the information to good use.

As for the man himself, Dang van Loc, that was another surprise. He showed not the slightest distress at what had happened, as if it was all part of the job. He'd been through worse in his life. But on the way back from New Zealand he made an unexpected stop, breaking his journey in Sydney to come and see me in hospital. We had been forewarned, Eric was there, with Brian Considine. He didn't stay long, an hour between two flights, but he shook my hand warmly, and Eric's and Brian's, and praised our courage for what we had done, and expressed his regret at the way I'd been hurt. He was startled when I spoke to him in Vietnamese: a couple of stilted phrases I'd rehearsed beforehand, to which he replied in his own stilted English.

'Where did you learn Vietnamese?' he asked. 'Were you a soldier?'

'*Thư'a, không,*' I said mischievously, keeping to Vietnamese, using an old-fashioned term of respect. 'No. I worked in the embassy, in Saigon.' I deliberately used the old pre-communist name. 'April 1975. I was there at the end.'

He nodded and smiled.

'We call it the new beginning,' he said.

I smiled back and we savoured each other's wit.

'I recently met an old friend of yours,' I went on more seriously, in English. 'Le Minh Quang. I believe he worked for you for a while on the Ho Chi Minh City People's Committee.'

'That's right. An old friend, as you say.'

'He was killed two weeks ago. Murdered by one of the men who plotted to kill you.'

He nodded gravely.

'It was largely due to him that we found out about the plot. He was very anxious that you should be protected.'

'Thank you for telling me. I had heard he was dead, but I wasn't sure how. I am very sorry.'

We exchanged a few more comments. He shook hands again with Brian and Eric, and thanked them both too, and all who had helped foil the plot.

'My life is not important. But what those people tried to do is bad for Vietnam, and such people must not be allowed to succeed. Thank you for that.'

He turned back to me. His large head was all skin and sinew and bone, alive with an intense energy. His black eyes bored into me.

'I will not forget my friend Quang. Or you either, Mr Quinn. Good-bye.'

His eyes swept over the others in the room, rested gently on Eric for a second. When he limped out, with his assistant in tow, who hadn't uttered a word, the air felt a little less charged.

My wounds were healing nicely, and I was now able to sit up. My legs were the worry. Physio didn't seem to be doing much good, I had hardly any sensation in them, and the neurologist who took x-rays was still reluctant to operate.

'The bullet is deeply embedded. The spinal cord itself doesn't appear to have been directly damaged but there's a good deal of pressure on it and we may do more harm than good if we try and remove it. Let's try more physio first. If it doesn't work then we can think again. I think tomorrow you can start using the walking machine.'

Anything was better than staring at the ceiling.

'I talked to my aunt.' Eric had finally contacted Hao. He'd moved into the flat, and reached her at her brother's house. She had caught the bare facts of the assassination attempt on the news and she was in a high state of alarm.

'I had to tell her you were still in hospital. She's going to ring you tonight.'

I waited anxiously for her call. It was now ten days since her departure, and so much had happened since that it felt as if she'd been gone much longer. When I heard her voice I almost couldn't speak at first.

'Paul? Can you hear me?'

'Yes.' I cleared my throat. 'How are you? How's your mother?'

'Better. She's back home now. She still can't talk or move very well but the doctor thinks she'll recover most of that in due course...How are you? Viv told me you were shot! Are you badly hurt?'

'Not too badly. Recovering satisfactorily, as they say. I'll be okay.'

I didn't tell her about my legs. I didn't want to tug at her pity.

'What happened? Paul? Why didn't you call me earlier? Eric said he also got shot...'

'It's a long story. I'll tell you when you get back. But don't worry about him. He's fine, it was just a small wound...'

'He said you saved his life.'

I didn't say anything.

'Paul? Is that true? He said you were wounded when you tried to stop someone from shooting him...'

'It's okay,' I tried to say. 'He's being dramatic. It was my fault. You were right. I should never have let things get to that stage.'

I sighed.

'I'll tell you all about it later,' I said again, lamely. 'When are you coming back? Is everything alright with you?'

'Yes. No. How can it be?'

'What do you mean?'

'Here I am worried to death, and missing you dreadfully, and you're lying in a hospital bed...I've been trying to book a seat to Sydney but all the flights are booked up for a week – I'm on stand-by for Wednesday evening. I should never have left you!'

'Yes you should. You had to.'

'Do you still want to marry me?'

'What a stupid question! Have you changed your mind?'

'Of course not! When I was in Leeds, I kept thinking of you, and how much my life has changed since I met you...and...'

She paused. I waited. I could hear her breathing.

'When I saw Robert I told him all about you,' she said. 'I told him you were sweet, and loveable, and you would never have forced me to have an affair with you. I also told him – I told him – you make love even better than him. Except I used a cruder word.'

Laughing hurt too much.

Only one more hurdle to clear: how would she face having to live with a cripple?

I was at physio when she came. Straining on the walking machine, sweat pouring down my face, trying to put one foot in front of the other and avoid putting too much stress on my chest. I wasn't aware of her at first, it wasn't until the physiotherapist looked towards the door that I turned and saw her. For a moment I stood there, gripping the bars and trying to stay upright. Then I levered myself into my wheelchair and she came forward.

'Oh Paul! What did they do to you!' she cried, and ran towards me. She knelt and put her arms around me. We wet each other's shirt with our tears.

Epilogue

We were married four weeks later, one Saturday in June, on the back veranda of Geoff and Cathy's house, overlooking the vineyard. A bright sunny winter's day, with the Brokenback mountains standing clear and sharp on the western horizon and the rows of pruned vines stark against the short winter grass.

Also present were most of the usual suspects, who had taken the trouble to drive up from Sydney: Jack and Sen Lipton, and Ann and Nghiem, Liz and her husband, a scattering of old friends. Rachel of course, who had flown up the day before from Melbourne and driven up with Vivien: there was no room in the flat and she was staying with Viv for the week-end.

Not present were any of the cousins, although Hao had made a point of inviting them. They had sent a short reply regretting that they couldn't take time away from the shop. More likely, I thought, they couldn't bear to fork out the traditional Vietnamese wedding gift of money.

Nor Roger or his wife. I liked Nancy, she'd been a good friend to Sandy in the old days, and I would have liked her to meet Hao as well, but a shadow had fallen over our friendship and I had no wish to see him again soon. But Brian Considine was there, with his spouse Barbara, resplendent in pink. In losing an old friend I had gained a new one.

And also the pretty Samantha, invited at Eric's request. I'm not quite sure why: he'd brought Hong along, the girl from the restaurant, Vo Khanh's niece, which was a nice thing to do. She'd been cut adrift by recent events and her uncle's arrest, and he and Hao had taken her under their wing. As far as Samantha was concerned I couldn't see much future in the relationship. There was too much of an age gap, and she was due for another posting. But there was a secretive, amused look in her eye when she looked at him, and I couldn't help wondering how close they'd become during their short time together, how far they'd taken those debriefing sessions in the safe flat in Bondi. He'd been very quiet on the subject.

On Hao's side, apart from Eric, her brother Nhan, who had also arrived the day before, from LA, and was staying with us. He'd come alone: they probably couldn't afford more than one fare, and someone had to stay home to look after her mother. She was recovering but in no shape to undertake long-distance travel. An early trip to the States was on the program.

Before the ceremony they came to talk to me, bending down to my level in my wheelchair. I hadn't made much progress with physio, and could barely walk across a room unaided, even with sticks. But a few days before I'd reached a decision. I was going to have the operation, with all its risks. Better that than remain a cripple. I wanted to have it done before the wedding, in case it failed, to give Hao the chance to reconsider. But she would have none of it. She wanted us to be married, whatever happened. And she was very insistent.

Liz, looking wistful and moist about the eyes, gave me a chaste kiss on the cheek, her husband Frank standing beside her with a glass of bubbly in hand. 'She's beautiful, Paul!' she whispered into my ear. 'I can see why you were so besotted. You will get well again soon, won't you my love? If only for her sake?'

Jack, who clutched a cold beer instead, waited until there was no one within earshot.

'About our friends,' he said. 'You may be interested. A rumour I heard.'

'You mean Bach?'

'Yes. And his offsider Binh, the one you think killed Quang.'

'What have you heard?'

'Seems they made it up to Queensland. Among Vietnamese fishermen there. There's quite a few who've resettled there, running deep-sea fishing boats. They were trying to arrange a passage to Vanuatu.'

'Did they get there?'

'They got part of the way. They went out alright, and when the boat came back they weren't on it.'

He paused.

'You're sure of this?' I asked.

'My source seemed to be. I have a couple of contacts up there. Ex Vietnamese Special Forces. I passed the word along, as you suggested…Seems they put some burley out first, to attract the sharks. He said they weren't at all happy as they went over the side.'

We stayed silent for a while, with him standing next to my chair, thinking about it. It was a chilling picture, but a fitting end, I thought grimly, and only wished it could have been made public.

'You haven't heard any of this.'

'Of course. But thanks...and thanks for telling me.'

'Anything for a friend.'

I didn't tell Considine. Or Hao or Eric either, much as I would have liked to. I couldn't run the risk of incriminating Jack or his friends. Brian had quit the police, taking early retirement after a gruelling inquiry which had left him with little option and dashed any chance he might have had of running security for the Sydney Olympics, as he had once hoped. Once a cop, I thought, always on the side of the law, and he might not have condoned such rough justice, however well-deserved. He had taken his fate philosophically and looked much happier than when I'd last seen him.

'It was that or an office job for the rest of my days,' he said. 'They offered me Human Resources, would you believe? I took the package. Human Resources indeed!'

'Nothing wrong with Human Resources,' I said mildly.

He snorted. 'For you maybe. Interviewing young women all day. I didn't fancy redrafting leave application forms for the rest of my life. Rather become a civilian.'

'What are you going to do?'

'Take a holiday, first. I'm taking Barbara and the girls overseas for a couple of months. God knows they deserve it, after putting up with me and my job for so long.'

'Where are you going?'

'Ireland, UK, France, Germany...stopping over in Vietnam on the way. See what the fuss was all about.' He paused. 'When we get back I'd like to start my own security service. Would you be interested?'

I half laughed.

'Are you offering me a job? In my condition?'

'I was thinking more of a partnership, actually. Why not? I could use someone with a brain. You could look after the Human Resources side. Seriously. Why don't you think about it?'

'Thanks. I will. But not right now.'

'We won't be back until September.' He looked at Hao, who turned at that moment to smile at me. There was a querying concern in her eye. I smiled back and shook my head gently. She wore a red *áo dài* she'd had specially made, over white trousers, with a flat red turban framing her head like a tiara. She looked ravishingly beautiful, like an exotic butterfly.

'I can see why you made such a fuss,' he remarked.

The ceremony was short and simple. The celebrant was a woman, a retired judge and a friend of Geoff's. We stuck in the main to traditional wording, with a few amendments. No mention of obeying, but much of cherishing. And until death do us part stayed in. When it came to the operative part I reached up and seized Eric's shoulder.

'I need your strength,' I muttered.

With his help I stood up between him and Hao, with Nhan on her left. Nhan *in loco parentis*, but Eric very much *in loco filii*, standing in for the young son she'd never had, lavishing her maternal love on him instead. I thought that they stood for others as well, who in an ideal world would also have been there, and perhaps were in a sense, hovering somewhere at the back: her father, and Hien, David, the father he'd never known. Even Khiem perhaps was also there, giving his ghostly assent to our union. I hoped so. I wished him no harm, wherever he was.

My back was on fire, but I kept my face still. I'd learnt a number of things over the past weeks. I'd learnt a new kind of love, passionate, demanding, but also generous, rich and complex and fulfilling, and endlessly exciting. I'd found someone I'd be proud to claim as a son. I'd lost one friend but found another, and possibly would have found one in Quang too if he'd been allowed to live.

I'd also learnt something valuable about myself. I didn't think I was especially brave. What I had done in that corridor had been an act of desperation rather than courage. But now I knew that if I'd been on that boat I wouldn't have stood back. I would have tried to defend her and Hien, whatever the cost, even if it had killed me. I hadn't told her that, but I felt she knew it too. And that, I thought, was worth all the pain in my back.

I stood beside Hao, holding her hand and leaning on Eric, listening to the words of the retired judge.

'Do you, Paul, accept this woman as your lawful wedded wife?'
'Do you, Hao...'

Do you, Hao Tran, *née Hòang thị Minh-Hảo* in the Year of the Horse, accept me, Paul Quinn, somewhat bedraggled Tiger, as your awful wedded husband?

I do. I do.

As we exchanged vows I made another promise, silently, to her and to myself. I will walk again, I said to myself. I will. I will!

Appendix

A brief note on Vietnam and the Vietnam War

Vietnam, which lies just below China, facing the South China Sea (see map at front), has a long history, stretching back over two thousand years when a distinct Vietnamese people first emerged in the Red River delta around present-day Hanoi. For most of its early history Vietnam was ruled directly by China, from which it inherited much of its culture, but from the start the Vietnamese possessed a strong sense of their identity, and Chinese rule was marked by numerous revolts.

After finally shaking off Chinese domination in 938 AD, Vietnam expanded southward along the narrow coastal strip in what is now central Vietnam (present-day Hue and Danang) and then into the fertile Mekong delta, which was then part of the Khmer empire of Angkor. Saigon, later renamed Ho Chi Minh City by the communists, was founded in 1698.

French interest in the region developed slowly at first, but culminated from the 1850s onward with the colonial conquest of the three regions of Vietnam – Tonkin in the north, Annam in the centre, and Cochin-China in the south. These, together with Laos and Cambodia, became known as French Indochina.

French rule ended with World War II. After the war France attempted to reassert its rule but was confronted by a communist-dominated independence movement, the *Vietminh*, led by Ho Chi Minh. An eight-year war followed, ending with the French defeat at Dien Bien Phu in 1954 and the partition of Vietnam into communist North and non-communist South.

Partition was meant to be followed by general elections, leading to reunification, but the South, with US support, rejected these, fearing that they would be dominated by the more populous North. Communist subversion in the south resumed in the late 1950s, and by the mid-sixties had evolved into full-scale warfare, with the southern communist guerrillas, the *Viet Cong*, increasingly supplemented by North Vietnamese troops, which later on came to dominate the fighting. US military involvement had started with advisers, but from 1965 included growing numbers of combat troops, reaching over 500,000 by 1969. Australia and other US allies also sent troops. The Australian Task Force at its peak numbered over 7500. Following the withdrawal of US and allied forces after 1972 the South continued to resist alone, until Saigon fell to North Vietnamese forces in April 1975.

———————————

Over one and a half million people fled from Vietnam by boat in the years following the communist victory. Of these, it is estimated that between 200,000 and 400,000 died at sea. Some 137,000 were resettled in Australia.

Acknowledgements

I wish to thank Margaret Renaud, without whose advice and encouragement this book could not have been written; Dr Jack Dempsey, American writer and historian, whose professional editing and dialogue helped so much to make it readable; the late writers Dennis Miller and Paul Stirling for their insights and contributions; Graham Rendoth and Ingrid Urh of Reno Design for their professionalism and patient understanding; Simon Hart for his enthusiastic and expert contribution in designing the author's original website. And most of all my wife Kieu, whose unflagging support over the years made this book possible. Its strengths are largely due to them. Its flaws are entirely my own.